# THE REVOLT
## OF THE
## COCKROACH
## PEOPLE

Introduction by

**HUNTER S. THOMPSON**


Afterword by

**MARCO ACOSTA**

**VINTAGE BOOKS**
A Division of Random House, Inc.
New York

# THE REVOLT OF THE COCKROACH PEOPLE

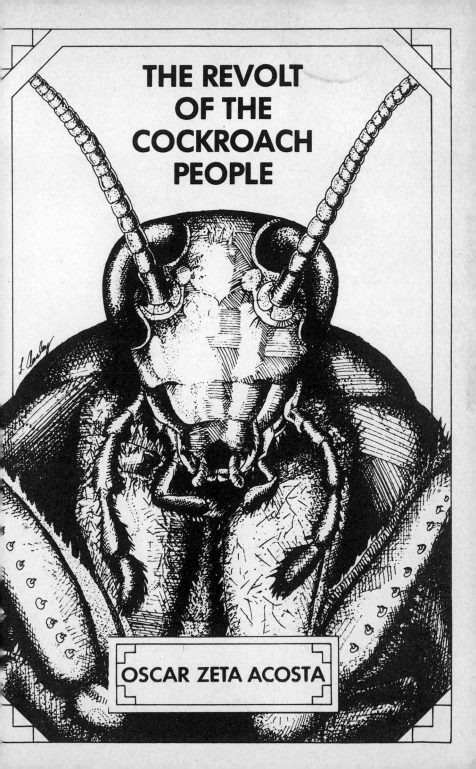

OSCAR ZETA ACOSTA

First Vintage Books Edition, July 1989

Library of Congress Cataloging-in-Publication Data
Acosta, Oscar Zeta.
  Revolt of the cockroach people / by Oscar Zeta Acosta.–1st
Vintage Books ed.
        p.        cm.
  Reprint. Originally published: San Francisco: Straight Arrow
Books, 1973.
  ISBN 0-679-72212-2 : $7.95
  1. Acosta, Oscar Zeta.   2. Mexican Americans–California–
Los Angeles–Biography.   3. Mexican Americans–California–
Los Angeles–Ethnic identity.   4. Mexican Americans–
California–Los Angeles–Political Activity.   5. Los Angeles
(Calif.)–Biography.
I. Title.
[CT275.A186A3    1989b]
979.4'9405'–dc19                                    88-40355
[B]                                                          CIP

Manufactured in the United States of America
3579C864

This book is for Leila Thigpen,
Laurel Gonsalves and Joan Baez.

I am indebted to Alan Rinzler, my publisher, editor and friend, for his patience and understanding of my own personal struggle as well as that of my people.

I also wish to express my appreciation to all the staff at Straight Arrow, particularly Jon Goodchild, and my social secretary, Miss Judy-Blue.

Oscar Z. Acosta
Chicano lawyer

Hotel Royan
The Mission's Finest
Frisco Bay
July, 1973

# INTRODUCTION

Oscar was a wild boy. He stomped on any terra he wandered into, and many people feared him....His birthday is not noted on any calendar, and his death was barely noticed....But the hole that he left was a big one, and nobody even tried to sew it up. He was a player. He was Big. And when he roared into your driveway at night, you knew he was bringing music, whether you wanted it or not.

I have never liked writing about him, because it makes me think too much, and I can never find the right words to explain the terrible joy that he brought with him wherever he went.... You had to be there, I guess, and you had to understand that the man was never comfortable unless he was in the company of people who were crazier than he was.

When he died, I wrote an epitaph, and I don't feel like doing it again, so here is what it felt like at the time...Res Ipsa Loquitor.

Oscar Zeta Acosta–despite any claims to the contrary–was a dangerous thug who lived every day of his life as a stalking monument to the notion that a man with a greed for the Truth should expect no mercy and give none....

When the great scorer comes to write against Oscar's name, one of the first few lines in the Ledger will note that he usually lacked the courage of his consistently monstrous convictions. There was more mercy, madness, dignity, and generosity in that overweight, overworked and always overindulged brown cannonball of a body than most of us will meet in any human package even three times Oscar's size for the rest of our lives–which are all running noticeably leaner on the high side, since that rotten fat spic disappeared.

By the time I first met him, in the summer of 1967, he was long past what he called his "puppy love trip with The Law." It had gone the same way as his earlier missionary zeal, and after the one year of casework at an East Oakland "poverty law center," he was ready to dump Holmes and Brandeis for Huey Newton and a Black Panther style of dealing with the laws and courts of America.

When he came booming into a bar called Daisy Duck in Aspen and announced that he was the trouble we'd all been waiting for, he was definitely into the politics of confrontation–and on all fronts: in the bars or the courts or even the streets, if necessary.

Oscar was not into serious street-fighting, but he was hell on wheels in a bar brawl. Any combination of a 250-pound Mexican and LSD-25 is a potentially terminal menace for anything it can reach–but when the alleged Mexican is in fact a profoundly angry Chicano lawyer with no fear at all of anything that walks on less than three legs and a de facto suicidal conviction that he *will* die at the age of thirty-three–just like Jesus Christ–you have a serious piece of work on your hands. Specially if the bastard is *already* thirty-three and a half years old with a head full of Sandoz acid, a loaded .357 Magnum in his belt, a hatchet-wielding Chicano bodyguard on his elbow at all times, and a disconcerting habit of projectile-vomiting geysers of pure red blood off the front porch every thirty or forty minutes, or whenever his malignant ulcer can't handle any more raw tequila.

This was the Brown Buffalo in the full crazed flower of his prime–a man, indeed, for all seasons. And it was somewhere in the middle of his thirty-third year, in fact, when he came out to Colorado–with his faithful bodyguard Frank–to rest for a while after his grueling campaign for sheriff of Los Angeles County, which he lost by a million or so votes. But in defeat, Oscar managed to create an instant political base for himself in the vast Chicano barrio of East Los Angeles–where even the most conservative of the old-line "Mexican-Americans" were suddenly calling themselves "Chicanos" and getting their first taste of tear gas at "La Raza" demonstrations, which Oscar was quickly learning to use as a fire and brimstone forum to feature himself as the main spokesman for a mushrooming "Brown Power" movement that the LAPD called more dangerous than the Black Panthers.

The weird grapevine will not wither for the lack of bulletins, warnings, and other twisted rumors of the latest Brown Buffalo sightings. He will be seen at least once in Calcutta, buying nine-year-old girls out of cages on the White Slave Market…and also in Houston, tending bar at a roadhouse on South Main that was once the Blue Fox…or perhaps once again on the midnight run to Bimini: standing tall on his own hind legs in the cockpit of a fifty-foot black cigarette boat with a silver Uzi in one hand and a magnum of smack in the other, always running ninety miles an hour with no lights and howling Old Testament gibberish at the top of his bleeding lungs.…

It might even come to pass that he will suddenly appear on my porch in Woody Creek on some moonless night when the peacocks are screeching with lust.…Maybe so, and that is one ghost who will always be welcome in this house, even with a head full of acid and a chain of bull maggots around his neck.

Yeah, that's him, folks–my boy, my brother, my partner in too many crimes. Oscar Zeta Acosta. Stand back. He is gone now, but even his memory stirs up winds that will blow heavy cars off the road. He was a monster, a true child of the century–faster than Bo Jackson and crazier than Neal Cassady.…When the Brown Buffalo disappeared, we all lost one of those high notes that we will never hear again. Oscar was one of God's own prototypes–a high-powered mutant of some kind who was never even considered for mass production. He was too weird to live and too rare to die.…

Hunter S. Thompson
*March 1989*

# THE REVOLT
# OF THE
# COCKROACH
# PEOPLE

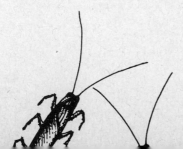

# 1

It is Christmas Eve in the year of Huitzilopochtli, 1969. Three hundred Chicanos have gathered in front of St. Basil's Roman Catholic Church. Three hundred brown-eyed children of the sun have come to drive the money-changers out of the richest temple in Los Angeles. It is a dark moonless night and ice-cold wind meets us at the doorstep. We carry little white candles as weapons. In pairs on the sidewalk, we trickle and bump and sing with the candles in our hands, like a bunch of cockroaches gone crazy. I am walking around giving orders like a drill sergeant.

From the mansions of Beverly Hills, the Faithful have come in black shawls, in dead fur of beasts out of foreign jungles. Calling us savages, they have already gone into the church, pearls in hand, diamonds in their Colgate teeth. Now they and Cardinal James Francis McIntyre sit patiently on wooden benches inside, crossing themselves and waiting for the bell to strike twelve, while out in the night three hundred greasers from across town march and sing tribal songs in an ancient language.

St. Basil's is McIntyre's personal monstrosity. He recently built it for five million bucks: a harsh structure for puritanical worship, a simple solid excess of concrete, white marble and black steel. It is a tall building with a golden cross and jagged cuts of purple stained glass thirty feet in the air, where bleeding Christ bears down on the

11

people of America below. Inside, the fantastic organ pumps out a spooky religious hymn to this Christ Child of Golden Locks and Blue Eyes overlooking the richest drag in town.

All around us, insurance companies with patriotic names are housed in gigantic towers of white plaster. Here prestigious law firms perform their business for rich people who live next to jaded movie stars. The Bank of America, Coast Federal Savings, and all those other money institutions that sit in judgment over our lives, keep the vaults across the street behind solid locks. But the personalized checkbooks now sit on the pews of St. Basil's, under seige by a gang of cockroaches from east of the Los Angeles River, from a "Mexican-American" barrio there called Tooner Flats.

It is dark out on the sidewalks. Cars pass along Wilshire Boulevard and slow down when they see us. Most of our crowd are kids. Most of them have never attacked a church before. One way or another, I've been doing it for years. And for this and other reasons, I have been designated *Vato Número Uno*, Number One Man for this gig.

The young wear clothes for battle, the old in thick woolen ponchos, gavans and serapes. College-age kids in long hair and combat garb: khaki pants, olive-drab field jackets and paratrooper boots spit-shined like those of the old *veteranos* who once went to war against America's enemies. Girls with long mascara-eyes, long black hair done up *chola* style, with tight asses and full blouses bursting out with song.

Three priests in black and brown shirts pass out the tortillas. Three hundred Chicanos and other forms of Cockroaches munch on the buttered body of Huitzilopochtli, on the land-baked pancake of corn, lime, lard and salt. Teetering over our heads are five gigantic papier-maché figures with blank faces, front-lipped beaks, stonehead bishop dunce caps. A guitar gently plucks and sways *Las Posadas* to the memory of the White and Blue Hummingbird, the god of our fathers. We chew the tortillas softly. It is a night of miracles: never before have the sons of the conquered *Aztecas* worshipped their dead gods on the doorstep of the living Christ. While the priests offer red wine and the poor people up-tilt earthen pottery to their brown cold lips, there are tears here, quiet tears of history.

When the singing has ended and the prayers for the dead and the living are complete, I step forward and announce that we have been permitted to enter St. Basil's. A Chicano sergeant from Judd Davis' SOC Squad just told me we could enter if we left our "demonstration" outside.

"Do we need special passes?" I had baited him.

"This is a *church*, Brown. Just tell them to hold it down when they go in. It's being *televised*."

I knew that, of course. We were at the home base of the holy man who encouraged presidents to drop fire on poor Cockroaches in far-off villages in Vietnam. From behind these stained glass windows, this man in the red frock and beanie, with the big blue ring on his knuckle, begs his god to give victory to the flames.

"Viva La Raza!" the crowd shouts at my announcement.

We turn and start walking up the cement steps. But at the top, the fifteen-foot doors of glass are shut in our faces. And when we try them, they are locked. Left out, once again; tricked into thinking we are welcome. An usher with a dark blue suit and red hair flaps his lips against the thick soundproof glass: *No More Room.*

There is a stirring. Pushing towards the front. What do they mean? No more room. Locked out. Period. Just like Jesus.

The wind is still cold. Everyone huddles together on the steps. Our leaders regroup in one corner. It's up to us. This is the nut, our test of strength. Are we men? Do we want freedom? Will we get laid tonight if we cop out now? And what would our children say?

"Fuck it, *ese*. Let's get in there!" Gilbert shouts at the student intellectuals who want to organize outside.

"Yeah, fuck these *putos*," Pelon puts in. Both are regular *vatos locos*, crazymen.

"But what will happen?"

"Oh, fuck that, *ese*. Let's go on in.'

A dozen men and women trudge through the questioning crowd. We are going in to find out what's going on, we say. Wait for us. And with that we run around the side of the monster with steeples pointing to a star that no longer shines.

But whoops! Wait! What is this in the parking lot? Black and white and mostly blue. The SOC Squad desperados standing in formation. Clubs and pistols with dumdum bullets. Solid helmets with plastic visors from the moon of Mars. Ugly ants with transistor radios, walkie-talkies and tear gas canisters dangling from their hips. There are fifty pigs waiting for us to make the wrong move. But do they see us?

"Come on," our lawyer exhorts. I, strange fate, am this lawyer.

In the darkness we find a door leading to the basement. We are smiles again. Hah! We have a crack!

Yet caution: I peek into the basement. No mops. No brooms. It is a chapel, filled with the overflow of the Faithful. They are on their knees, clasping fingers and hands in front of their faces. Beads are being kissed, little black crosses dangled about in a cloud of incense. I see no room for us. Beside me is a stairway. We scramble up fast.

We enter a blue room, the vestibule inside the main entrance. There sits holy water in bowls beside the four huge doors. And through the glass we see the Cockroaches outside: faces in a sea of molasses. Teeth and bright colored clothes. The Chicanos are a beautiful people. Brown soft skin, purple lips and zoftig chests. Their fists are raised in victory, though all we may hear is the most reactionary voice in America sing "Joy to the World."

"Hey, what are you doing in here?" Again, the carrottop usher with the dark blue suit. He looms before us out of nowhere.

"We are here to worship, sir," Risco, the cubano says.

"No more room, boys. You'll have to leave."

"How about up in the choir loft?" I say.

"Nope. We don't let nobody up there."

Outside, we see white teeth and feel fists banging on

the doors. But we hear nothing. The glass is four inches thick. Mouths are moving and bodies are agitated. Things are tense.

"Hey, man. Why can't we just *stand* here?" Gilbert asks.

"In here? This isn't, uh . . . Sorry, boys. All the room is taken up. You'll just have to leave."

We all crowd around the usher. He is big but nervous; he keeps looking to his side. The vestibule is dark. The floors, walls and ceiling are all deep blue velvet. A soft room for worship. The light is dim and nearly yellow. Some of the women cross themselves. Some also dip their fingers in holy water and bless themselves.

Then Black Eagle says, "Hey, man. Why don't you just open up that door and we'll listen to the service from here?"

The usher looks up and down at Black Eagle's immense black beard and militant gear. I know he wants to say how that isn't dress for civilized worship.

"No, I just can't do that. All of you will have to leave right now. Or I'll be forced to call the police."

"Well, fuck it, *ese!*" Gilbert shouts at the man.

"Hey, come on, Gilbert," one of our law students reprimands.

"You'd better leave, boy!" The usher is now obviously worked up.

Gilbert reaches for the horizontal panic bar to one of the outside doors.

"Stop!" The usher screams but makes no move.

Gilbert stops. "You *said* to get out." But the door is somehow open a bit.

"Not that way! You'll have to leave the same way you got in." The man is sweating now. He is looking at the crowd of Chicanos banging away on the glass. With the door cracked open we can hear what they have been chanting all along:

LET THE POOR PEOPLE IN! LET THE POOR PEQPLE IN!

Just about then, the choir and the congregation begin

15

to sing. The choir and the organ are in a loft right above the door leading to the main church. This loft overlooks the vestibule and, occasionally, the choir director, waving his baton madly, peers at us over the low wall.

"You leave right now!" he shouts.

So naturally, Gilbert and Black Eagle again reach for the panic bars. Out of desperation the usher grabs Gilbert by the back of his coat and swings him against the bucket of holy water. Black Eagle stops and turns. We all move into a circle with the usher in the middle.

"Touch me again, you *puto*, and I'll let you have it!" Gilbert shouts. Glroosh-flut! The usher has struck Gilbert, the black frog, in the kisser. We stare and wait for the fog to clear. We are in a church, remember.

Gilbert reaches for the door once again. Flluutt!! The usher has struck Gilbert Rodriguez, the poet laureate of East LA, right in the eye.

For two seconds no one moves. How in the fuck are you going to strike an usher? A *Catholic* usher. What would Gilbert's grandmother say? For two seconds time is suspended. And then it comes upon us in a wave: it isn't an usher. The police have tricked us again!

Boom! A solid uppercut to the pig's jaw. Then a scream. He hollers, "Sergeant Armas! Sergeant Armas!" Black Eagle finally opens the front door. Gilbert takes one in the stomach. *Vato Número Uno*, Warrior Number One, does not move. The lawyer stands and watches.

A wall curtain jumps and Sergeant Armas, the *real* boss of the SOC Squad, bowls in with twenty men. The vestibule explodes as men in blue run in formation swinging two feet of solid mahogany. Five other "ushers" run out of nowhere pulling out badges from inside their coats and pinning them on their breast pockets. Then they pull out little canisters and systematically squirt stuff into the faces of Chicanos who are entering now, pushing in through the front doors. And there is swinging and screaming and shouting and we are into a full-scale riot in the blue vestibule of the richest church in town. But I am standing stock still. All around me bodies are falling. Terrified women and children are wailing while the choir sings above my head:

> O come all ye faithful, joyful and triumphant,
> O come ye, O come ye, to Bethlehem . . .

I see Gilbert, the fat Corsican pirate, grappling with a burly cop. Wearing his Humphrey Bogart raincoat, he's on the pig's back. His small brown hands are stuck in the eyes of the monster with the club. They pass me by.

Black Eagle has squared off with two ushers. One squirts Mace in his face while the other kicks him in the balls. Down and down he goes, crashing to the velvet floor. I watch it all serenely while the choir and congregation entertain. I wear a suit and tie. No one lays a hand on me. I take out my pipe and wade through the debris. Crashcrattle and krootle! A thirty-six-inch cement ash-tray flies through the plate glass door. Sticks to hold up posters fly over the crowd. Candles for the gods become missiles in the air. A religious war, a holy riot in full gear. Then, sirens screaming outside, the rest of the SOC squad bursts in to join its brothers. The choir never misses a beat:

> Come and behold Him, born the king of angels . . .

I watch a red-haired girl with glasses and a mini-skirt rush through the door to the main church, which has opened momentarily. It is Duana Doherty, the street nun who once worshipped wearing black robes while her head was bald. Then she joined up with the Chicanos and became a Cockroach herself. I take a few steps to see what she is up to.

Inside another usher, a real one, sees us. I have on my pin-striped blue Edwardian and I've put my pipe back in my pocket. Duana has creamy peach skin. She has the face of an angel. The usher has no hair. The three of us make one of a kind.

"I think there's a seat up front," he says.

Duana doesn't stop for an answer. She runs down the length of the aisle. The Faithful in furs, in diamonds and hats of lace, are staring straight ahead at the altar where seven priests perform for TV.

"Just keep on, my children. Pay no attention to the rabble-rousers out there," Monsignor Hawkes is exhorting them, his red hands cupping the mike.

The usher can't keep up with Duana. She makes it to the front, turns and addresses the congregation: "People of St. Basil's, please, come and help us. They're killing the poor people out in the lobby! Please. Come and help!"

Two ushers finally grab her around the belly and carry her out. I stand aside and watch them pass. And almost at the same moment I see another woman running at full boat. It is Gloria Chavez, the fiery black-haired Chicano Militant. She charges down the aisle in a black satin dancing dress that shows her beautiful knockers and she carries a golf club in her pretty hands. I am aghast! The Faithful are petrified. No one makes a move for her. Her big zoftig ass shakes as she rushes up to the altar, turns to the pie-eyed man in the red cape, and shouts:

## ¡QUÉ VIVA LA RAZA!

Swoosh, swoosh, swoosh! With three deft strokes Gloria clears off the Holy of Holies from the altar of red and gold. The little white house with its cross falls. The little white wafers which stick to the roof of your mouth just before you swallow, the Body of Christ is on the red carpet.

It is too astounding a thing to believe. No one lifts a finger to stop this mad woman with her golf club as she hotfoots it down the aisle toward the vestibule. The ushers, the worshippers and myself simply stand and stare. The congregation has long since stopped singing. It is just the choir:

*O come let us adore Him, O come let us adore Him . . .*

The golden chalice, the cruets for the wine and water are scattered on the floor before the bleeding Christ and the Madonna with child in arm.

"CHICANO POWER!" Gloria shouts as she vanishes inside the battle zone.

I follow her. I stop in the doorway and see Gloria being

taken by three huge pigs. The pigs have already backed the scum out into the streets.

"Just a minute, Officer . . . You don't have to hit her," I say.

"Get out of the way, Mr. Brown," Sergeant Armas says to me.

Gloria is kicking and cussing and slapping away. Her legs are shooting up at the three men who are hustling her to the floor.

"*¡Pinches, cabrones, hijos de la chingada!*" she screams.

I move. I grab the arm of one of the cops. He turns to slug me with his baton, but Armas stops him.

"Leave Brown alone! He's their lawyer," Armas tells the man.

When they have carried her away, I stand and scan the battlefield. The floor is covered with debris. Sand from the ash-trays, broken glass from the doors, papers listing our demands, a shoe, an umbrella, eyeglasses with gold frames, banners with *La Virgen de Guadalupe* drawn in color. Garbage galore litters the holy blue vestibule.

I walk carefully outside. It is the same on the steps. The street is lined with police vans, red lights glaring, sirens howling in the night. And on the other side, hundreds of Chicanos standing or walking around aimlessly.

I see Gilbert and Black Eagle being whacked over the head with batons as they are hauled into a car. I run down the steps, toward the street. Cops hold me back. I struggle, I shove, I kick away. For God's sake, I *want* to be arrested! "Don't touch the lawyer," they say to one another.

I run back toward St. Basil's which now has helmeted pigs standing in a skirmish line at the bottom of the steps. They are tense, their hands gnarled around the batons held before them at parade rest. Fear is in the eyes of black and Chicano cops. So I say to them, "Why don't you guys relax? You ought to see yourselves, you'd be ashamed." I see murder in their eyes. They *have* to take this shit. Armas, their tough Chicano sergeant, has told them to keep their bloody hands off me.

The St. Basil's side of Wilshire is filthy with cops and Wilshire itself is still clogged with police wagons. Beyond them the Chicanos are waiting for a call to regroup. I cup my hands to my mouth and shout, "Hey, *Raza* . . . Go home now. Go home and rest up. Tomorrow, during Christmas Mass, let's meet here again."

I walk up and down the street on the sidewalk. Nobody touches me as I shout at them to go home, shower up and regroup here tomorrow for another battle. To go home, bandage the wounded and heal the sick.

When it is done, the big pig, Sergeant Armas, comes up to thank me. "You're OK, Brown. Things got out of control here tonight. Thanks a lot."

"Ah, fuck you, you asshole!"


I returned alone to my office in downtown LA in the darkness of the first hours of Christmas . For more than a year now I have issued my orders, written my statements to the press and prepared for my daily work out of the tenth floor of a tall building in the middle of skid row.

At this moment, all my friends are bleeding in their cells, heads battered, arms hanging limp from the clubs of the pigs. And even now, as I sip my hot cup of coffee and prepare my newest statements to the press, to the reporters that I know will break down my door before the day is over, even now I sit and stare and ponder the havoc that has been unleashed. What to do?

I dial the phone and listen to the buzz and ring of Stonewall's telephone in Colorado where the snow must be quietly falling upon massive aspen trees, upon green leaves and white trunks.

"Jesus, what the fuck?" a familiar groggy voice wants to know.

For nearly two years now I've called and written this bald-headed journalist who once told me during a volleyball game: "If you ever find a big story in your travels, call me. I'll put you in touch with the right man."

"Uh, sorry to wake you. But I've got us a big one."

"Brown? Jesus, Brown, it's Christmas! It's three o'clock in the morning. Are you loaded?"

"No, man. I just got back from . . . I just witnessed the first religious war in America. A full-blown riot inside a church."

"Just like I thought, you bastard! You're fucked up!"

I begin to explain the events of the past twelve hours. He mumbles and coughs his way through the first half of the story and I have to keep asking, "You still there?" Until I got to the part about the red-headed nun in a mini-skirt and Gloria with her golf club demolishing the tabernacle.

"Hold it! You said a *golf* club?"

"Yeah, a number seven wood, I think."

"You don't mind if I turn on my tape recorder, do you?"

"Jesus, I've been asking you to do that!"

I finish it out on tape. For fifteen minutes I dictate blood and songs and papier-mâché dolls.

"And, uh . . . they didn't arrest you?" he says finally.

"Shit, they didn't *touch* me."

Silence. A long pause. Does he believe it?

"And you were right there? You were inside?"

"Standing in the center of it all."

More silence. Another long pause. Could he afford not to believe it?

"And you want me to come out and write about this?"

"Well . . . either that or get someone of your caliber to do it."

"And you were one of the leaders?"

"In all modesty, yeah."

I can hear wheels grinding in his brain.

"Are you *serious*? Do you see what you've *done*?"

"Yeah, sure. I've upped the ante."

"You mean you've dumped it on your buddies," he says softly.

I don't remember hanging up the phone. When my mind finally thaws, I find myself alone in my tiny legal office on the tenth floor, high above the Cockroaches on the streets of spit and sin and foul air in downtown LA.

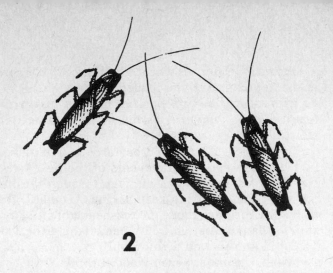

# 2

When I first arrived in Los Angeles in January, '68, I had no intention of practicing law or of pitting myself against anything. I was only anxious to find "THE STORY" and write "THE BOOK" so that I could split to the lands of peace and quiet where people played volleyball, sucked smoke and chased after cool blondes.

For the first time in thirteen years I was no longer fat. Gone were the blubber and the belly, the shanks and jowls. In fact, I was tough and hard; tough from a winter on skis, hard from lifting hundred-pound railroad ties covered with tar. I had worked that winter in the mountains of Mofo, Georgia, slugging it out as a gandy dancer, a man who pounds twelve-inch spikes with a fifteen-pound sledge. For months now, I had been without booze and dope. No whiskey, no wine, no beer. No more acid or grass or hash. My body became like a rock and more importantly, my head had cleared. I could see again. I could find my story, then get fat again and live like a king. It's all a crazy circle, but here I am.

I've been in town six hours and now lie naked on my bed with the window of my sleazy downtown hotel room open to the sounds of the city. I have nothing to do until I see my sister in the morning. After checking into the Belmont at Third and Hill, I walked the streets until dark to shake the cramping bus ride from my bones. But already my bones have told me that I have come to the most detestable city on earth. They have carried me through the filthy air of a broken city filled with battered losers. Winos in tennies, skinny fags in tight pants and whores in purple skirts all ignore the world beyond the local bar, care about nothing except where the booze comes cheapest or the latest score on the radio. Where I am, the buildings are crumbling to pieces. The paint is cracked and falling to the streets covered with green and brown phlegm, with eyeless souls who scuttle between tall buildings hoping to find a bed, a bottle, a joint, a broad or even a loaf of bread. Streets filled with dark people, hunchbacked hobos, bums out of work, garbage of yesterday and tomorrow; with black men and women in bright garish clothes, brown men with mustaches to boost themselves up a notch, coffee-drinking people, wine-sipping sods who haven't had more than five bucks at a time since the last war. And then back to the hotel:

"You crazy sonofabitch! Hit me again and I'll call. . . ." Crash! Boom! Bang! The couple below me are at it again.

"You dumb whore! You drank it all! . . ."

Silence comes hard and heavy. My light is off and I curl my arm under my head, figuring at last to get some sleep. All of a sudden I feel a tingle on my right thigh. I'd seen enough James Bond flicks to know better than to strike or jump. Tense and gritting my teeth, I shut my eyes hard waiting for the beast to move again. It is about three inches from my balls, but either my sex doesn't appeal to him or he just isn't hungry. The next thing I know it has crawled over my bulging muscular ass and disappeared into the bed and the night. I laugh and sing to myself:

> La cucaracha, la cucaracha,
> ya no puede caminar.
> Porque le falta,
> porque le falta,
> marijuana pa' fumar.

The old revolutionary song is just about the only Spanish I know. It puts me to sleep.

The next morning I get up early. Twenty-five each of bends, squats, backbends and pushups. I am still in training. I must hunt my story with all the brains and muscle thirty-three years of dissolute living have left me. I shave at the porcelain sink which is an open grave of cockroaches. Because I haven't seen my sister in over five years, I put on the only decent thing I have to wear, the blue suit my father gave me when I graduated from law school two years ago. I had only gotten the degree and my license to prove that even a fat brown Chicano like me could do it. But my father thought it was worth a new suit as well. I even wore it for nine months while I practiced at sounding like a lawyer in a Legal Aid Office in the slums of East Oakland. Now, of course, it is much too big on me, but it's the only thing left from those days, before the mad cross-country scampering with Stonewall and his crazy hippie friends, looking for the right questions and answers in a life of dope and easy living. Which somehow has tossed me up broke and still hunting in the City of Angels.

She picks me up in front of the hotel. I haven't seen Teresa since she was in the Army. She joined the WACs straight out of Oakdale High while I was still overseas with the fighting 573rd Air Force Band. Now she is twenty-five and filled out. Her long black hair is still the same but her fingernails are violet, I guess because she has come to own half a beauty joint. She is so seriously beautiful beside me in her car that I can't get over it. Just looking at her, I can tell she doesn't bow down to anything or anyone. I haven't thought of her as a sexual object since the age of twelve when I tried to French kiss her. She was only four at the time. But now, my parents tell me, she has married a Marine who quit the service to work as a contract administrator for the aerospace industry.

"Your name is *Hurley*?" I say to her as we buzz down the freeway toward Canoga Park, a San Fernando Valley suburb of LA.

"What's wrong with that?" Such is our total conversation on the road.

We arrive at the Hurley homestead, a huge breadbox

with a white picket fence, a kidney in the back yard for swimming, and a two-car garage. Kids on mini-bikes are criss-crossing in front of every mown lawn on the block, so I know it isn't going to work out even before Dave Hurley gets home. Inside, the thick carpets, the Keane paintings of big-eyed children, the rubber elephant ears and velvet throne in the corner to remind me of the life I left behind when I escaped Law and Oakland. In the space of five martinis, it becomes clear she considers me a renegade. I drink water as I explain that my story must be something *I* believe in. Both of us know I have always been a fanatic. I don't write from a detached point of view. Finally, after she downs another three big ones, she asks me out of the blue: "What about politics?"

I laugh hard. I can just see a dope addict, a bum like me with all my vices, with my love of wild women and song, ex-Baptist missionary in Panama, ex-clarinet player, ex-peach picker-football tackle-parking lot attendant-lawyer, ex-everything, I can just see me running for public office.

"Not as a politician," she says. "I mean like, you know, the civil rights thing."

"I've been there."

"Yeah, but that was with niggers." She refilled her glass again, reminding me of me back when. "Have you ever heard of the Chicano Militants?" Then she begins to explain about some greasers, "sort of like the Black Panthers," who are kicking up dust in East LA. They even have a small newspaper but, before she can get any deeper, her old man comes in.

Dave Hurley has fat lips, blue eyes below blond hair stuck in a plain white envelope. From the first second I see him, I know he is no match for my tough sister. He kisses her dutifully, shakes hands with me, and then disappears to make us breakfast.

"So you got a Sancho to do your work for you, eh?" I say with a smile. She grins back.

Over bacon and eggs, Hurley explains to me the projects he is working on to benefit the US Army against the Viet Cong. I don't even bother to punch him in the mouth.

Then the two of them are off to some art show so they drop me back at the Belmont. Teresa gives me a big goodbye hug before she drives off. She promises to come visit me and hopes I find my story. But all the time I see how she's trapped, chained by herself to that blue-eyed fag and his promise of more make-up and martinis. Only after they have vanished into the smog do I realize that I forgot to hit her for a loan. It's Sunday; I couldn't even hustle a job if I felt like it. So I go back up to my room to ponder my fate.

But before I have the door unlocked an idea hits me: my cousin Manuel whom I haven't seen in over ten years. Almost a year ago, I'd sent him a telegram at his mother's house. It said simply, "Send $150 or I go to jail . . . Oscar." Two days later the money arrived without a word or signature. I spent all of it on two whores in Juarez before I sobered up.

The next thing I know is that I have blown my last few bucks on a cab and found him at his bar, Manny's Fish Bowl. We are sitting at the counter, digging into some burritos his mother made for the occasion.

Manuel stands six-foot five-inches tall. They used to call him Spider when he high-jumped for the University of Southern California in the early fifties. He was one of the first men in the country to clear the bar at 6' 8". After he failed to qualify for the 1952 Olympics he lost interest and faith in himself. He married while still in school, had children and took his Masters, ending up as a coach for a small junior college in South-Central Los Angeles. Now he owned Manny's Fish Bowl in East LA where all his old college chums and high school buddies come and reminisce over cold Coors. He starts on the booze five minutes after I walk in.

"Hey, man. How come you never made it beyond 6'8"?"

This is just part of our small talk but Manuel goes into instant depression. He bows his heavy jowls, plays with the glass of scotch and sighs deeply.

"You don't jump beyond that without help."

26                                    *The Revolt of the Cockroach People*

"But you were jumping better than anyone else your sophomore year . . . Was it booze, a broad, or what?"

"I told you, I didn't know how. You can only go so far on your own, then you need someone to show you the rest."

"You guys had the best coach in the business."

He gives me a dirty look, as if angry for my even mentioning the subject. He downs his glass and spits out, "That sonofabitch. He spent all his time with the other guys." And then a monologue, more therapy than information. His coach, George Mudd, had deliberately not taught him how to jump higher. Mudd never liked him, he said. From the beginning, he was on his own. When the year came around for the Olympics, the coach simply turned his back on him.

"Because you're Chicano?"

Manuel stares at me a long time before he answers. "I haven't been able to come up with any other reason for the past ten years."

We quietly eat re-fried beans. I ask him if he's heard of the Chicano Militants. He laughs and tells me they are just a bunch of young punk communists who don't know their ass from a hole in the ground. "They blame all their troubles on everybody but themselves."

I laugh at the irony. I ask if he isn't doing the same thing with his failure to qualify for the Olympics.

So he screams at me: "That's different! I worked my ass off! I made it on my own. No one gave me a thing. You don't see me going around crying, asking the government for a handout."

We get into heavy arguments. He refuses to acknowledge that his sports scholarship to USC was a handout just like any other handout. I find myself defending a group I don't even know. Before the day is over, Manuel is convinced that I am some sort of Communist agent sent into LA to recruit members for the Party.

We eat more and continue to argue before we finally get into stories about Riverbank. His family lived in a tent in our back yard for two years before they had enough to make it on their own. Manuel picked peaches and fought

27

with Okies down at the canal before he became a city slicker. I laugh at him when he tries to come on like a smooth sophisticated cat. He is as much a greaser and small-town kid as I am.

When he finally drives me back to the Belmont, I have a hundred in my pocket. Immediately I throw down fifty for a month's rent, leaving the rest to carry me until I can round up some kind of gig. Even an artist must eat.

Manuel has mentioned a friend of his who knows the Chicano Militants. As I trot up the ten flights to my room, my mind begins to whirl. My own arguments to Manuel have impressed me. If I didn't give a shit, why was I bothering to argue? My first few hours in Los Angeles seem to point me in a certain direction. Yet I am a stone peacenik, albeit with violent tendencies. If someone attacked me physically, there'd be hell to pay. But no one ever bothers me, not physically. I haven't had a fight since I was a senior at Oakdale. Politically I believe in absolutely nothing. I wouldn't lift a finger to fight anyone. In a way I agree with Manuel: the best way to accomplish what you want is simply to *work* for it, on an individual level.

I open my room and an army of cockroaches disperses into the cracks and darkness. My evening set of calisthenics is full of "and yets . . ." Didn't I argue! Didn't I feel like smashing Hurley into a pulp? What about all those books that got me through the long Mofo nights?

I've been thinking about these things. I'd read a book, *On Agression*, by the German biologist, Konrad Lorenz. It impressed me as much as the Bible had some twelve years earlier during my missionary phase in Panama. And later, after reading Ardrey's *The Territorial Imperative*, I agreed, on a purely intellectual level, that man's hostility was a natural thing, not a factor to be ignored, avoided or feared. But I had never really thought about hostility and groups.

Now as I lie in the creaky bed, I begin to realize that a bit of my life is catching up with me. I haven't thought of myself as a member of a group since I was with the Baptists in 1956. A dozen years have come and gone. I realize

I've hardly even spoken to anyone in Spanish since I left Panama. All through schools, jobs and bumming, I haven't even held the hand of a Mexican woman, excepting whores who are all the same anyhow.

I am sweating, and the smog of the City of Angels burns through the filthy screens in my little green room. How the fuck did this happen? All at once, I remember what my mother said one June so many years ago.

It was the rehearsal for graduation of Riverbank Grammar School. Mr. Green, my eighth-grade teacher, lined us up against the walls of the auditorium according to height. Boys on the left, girls on the right. Now walk toward each other. With ginger steps, I go to meet my partner, Gretchen, the German girl whose tits I squeezed in the seventh grade. We stare at one another. I smile. Wilkie, the principal, saunters in to talk with the teachers in charge of us. We rattle and tattle and tum happily. We've made it. Soon we'll all be in high school.

Wilkie leaves and the teachers get moving again.

"Uh, let's see now . . . We want to get the partners matched as close as possible," Green, the hefty ex-boxer explains, straining his eyes over the crowd. "Uh, yes . . . Alfonso, you're a little tall for Peggy Ann . . . You trade with Floyd. You're closer to Rita."

Al, the best pitcher in school, stands next to Rita Mata, the girl who lives across the street from me.

"And, let's see . . . Juan, you're closer to Anita's size. Burt is better for Suzan."

Juan Perez used to pick peaches with me. He is Anita's second cousin.

"Oscar, why don't you and Senaida pair up? Tom's too short for her."

Senaida Moreno has bigger tits than any girl in school. But that isn't enough. *I see what is happening!*

After all the Chicanos have been paired with their countrymen, we are excused until the afternoon. I gather my seven friends from the wrong side of the tracks.

"You see what he did?" I say.

"What? . . . Come on, let's go eat," Juan says.

"You go, but I'm not. Don't you guys see how old man Wilkie wants us to march?"

"What's wrong with that?" Al says.

"Nothing. . . . But I'm not going to do it. It isn't fair. I almost ended up with Gretchen."

They laugh at me. But I rail on. I tell them they are chickenshits. We almost get into a fight, but finally they agree we've been fucked.

"So what are we going to do about it?" Ben asks.

"I'm just not going to march, that's all," I pout.

"Shit, your ma will beat you up," Juan says.

"I know my dad will kill me if I don't graduate. He didn't want me in school to begin with," Ben says.

But I hold fast. I convince them to go with me to Mr. Wilkie. Reluctantly they agree. We march into his office and I tell him what I suspect. I tell him what I have decided. My heart is pounding furiously.

"And the rest of you? You're going along with Oscar?" Wilkie says.

They all nod shyly.

After a moment of drumming fingers on his desk, Wilkie comes clean: "I'll be honest with you boys . . . It's true. I told the teachers not to let you fellows march with, uh, the partners you had . . . But you see, it's not my fault. The school board told me, instructed me not to let Mexicans march with Americans. . . . I'm sorry boys. But them's my orders."

We leave his office, but stick fast, playing baseball instead of going to rehearsals. When I get home at three-thirty my mother is in tears. Mr. Wilkie has been to see her. Later that evening, I explain it to my father. He agrees that it's wrong.

"But look at it this way," my horsetrader father says. "How do you think Senaida will feel if you refuse to march with her?"

My old ma sees the opening and says, "What will the parents of all the girls say? They're going to say you're stuck-up, that you guys are ashamed to march with a Mexican."

The initial revolt of the Riverbank Chicanos sputtered out that night. Wilkie told all the parents that if we didn't march, we didn't graduate. The Mexican girls never spoke to me again. Even when I became the solo clarinetist in the dance band, when I won my three stripes for varsity football, when I was elected class president, they never forgave me my rejection. I learned how to French kiss when Madeline, a little Dutch girl, stuck her tongue down my throat. And it was Carol, an Italian living in an orange grove, who taught me about brassieres. My first and last trueloves were both pig-tailed belles, and the pattern stuck with me. So what is it? Had my old mother hit it on the head? *Am* I ashamed of my race?

I cannot lie still on my bed any longer, can barely breathe. Who has brought me to this detestable place and robbed me of my sleep and beer-belly? What a bunch of horseshit! It is those faggoty intellectuals who've never gotten it up themselves, social workers, pussy-ass do-gooders, bleeding shrinks with their Jewishness gone awry; it is Germanic blood, the East Coast school of books and snow, the Pilgrims and Baptists; it is the Pope with his lust for Mary, FDR and his quaint limp, Hitler and his ovens, the beastiality of fertility rites, the slaughter of the buffalo, the death of the Incas and Aztecs, the coming of the white barbarians; it is the condition of the human race, the Klan, the Triumph Ceremony of the Geese; it is my entire life! It is everything and then some.

That night I get no sleep. My brain goes off like explosives and by dawn I have made innumerable resolutions. I will change my name. I will learn Spanish. I will write the greatest books ever written. I will become the best criminal lawyer in the history of the world. I will save the world. I will show the world what is what and who the fuck is who. Me in particular.

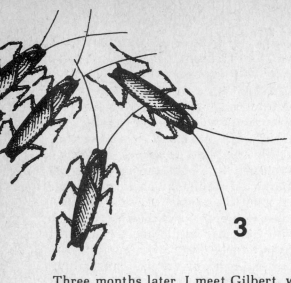

# 3

Three months later, I meet Gilbert, who looks like a cross between a fat black frog and a Corsican pirate. He wears a black frock, a priest's outfit, and he is leaning his chair back against a wall with a gallon of Red Mountain stuck on his finger. He watches me suspiciously as I talk with Risco, a curly-haired *cubano* with a slick tongue and very white teeth. Ruth, Risco's woman, sits behind him at the desk. Her hefty legs are crossed and her flat white face studies me. I have just told them I am searching for material to write an article for the New York *Times* and nobody is impressed.

I look around the room, a large basement office. The thin blockhouse windows open onto the sidewalk. The gutter is visible from where I stand uncomfortably. All around me are homemade plywood tables. Stacks of manuscripts and leaflets are piled on these tables and on the floor, and cockroaches are piled thick and swarming on the manuscripts. A huge banner hangs from the ceiling: BLOW OUT. Picket signs lean up against the wall next to Gilbert:

EDUCATION NOT ERADICATION
FENCES ARE FOR CRIMINALS AND ANIMALS
PUT CHICANOS IN OUR HISTORY BOOKS
CHICANO POWER TODAY AND FOREVER
YANKEES OUT OF AZTLAN

I see a poster of Cesar Chavez, guru-father of Chicanos; a poster of Reis Tijerina, who shot up a Tierra Amarilla courthouse the previous year; a poster of Rodolfo Corky Gonzales, the Denver militant organizer. Their faces overlook an incredible mess of bumper stickers, buttons and cheap paper.

A buddy of Manuel's has taken me here, made the introductions and then left. We are in the basement of an Episcopalian church, a run-down, rattle-bum, paint-cracking slum-box in the heart of Tooner Flats. Father Light, the rector, provides space for the Chicano Militants' propoganda sheet, a four-page underground newspaper published in the Church of the Revelations. The paper is called *La Voz de Huitzilopochtli,* after the principle ancient diety of the Chicanos. Risco is the editor. Only when I accidentally mention that I am a lawyer does anyone seem to thaw.

"Hey, Gilbert," Risco calls to the priest. "Brown Buffalo here is a Chicano lawyer." Since there are maybe a hundred in the state and most of these work for the government, they drink me in. I am wearing cowboy boots, levi's and a blue turtle-neck sweater. I don't look like I work for the government, which is exactly true: the Public Defender's Office fired me three days before.

Gilbert lifts his skirts and feet to the table and leans further back. "Put her there, partner," he says.

I walk over, reaching for his stubby hand. But instead, he locks his thumb in mine, flips to the palm, then back to the thumb. "Jesus," I say. "It feels like the sign of the cross."

"You ain't never seen the power shake, *ese?*" Gilbert says. He is amazed. I feel like an ignorant turd. He looks me up and down again doubtfully. "You got an office?"

"Sort of . . . I work out of the Belmont Hotel."

"Hey, that's where Rose Chernin's office is," Risco says.

"I'm new in town. Who's that?"

"It's a defense group for political prisoners," Ruth says.

"Ah, bullshit," Gilbert says. "Don't tell *mentiras* to the dude." He swigs from his bottle and points it at her. "She's a commie."

"Gilbert thinks all white radicals are communists," she says.

"Hey, *ese*," Gilbert continues. "So what are you writing about?"

"Eh, well, you know, I got a connection and I'm looking for something good. A cousin of mine told me you guys were going to have a strike."

"You want to write about our strike for the New York *Times*?" Risco asks.

"Fuck the New York *Times*," Gilbert says. "What the *movida* needs is a brown-assed fighting lawyer. If you want to write anything, write it for *La Voz*. Here, *ese*, have a shot." He hands me the bottle."

I laugh. "I guess the Episcopalians are pretty liberal," I say to the fat priestly pirate.

"Hey, *ese*, I ain't no fucking priest!"

He pulls the black tunic over his head and throws it in the corner. Underneath I see a sweatshirt with a vicious plumed serpent silk-screened onto the front. The same Aztec god is featured in posters around the office. And printed under the design, in rough block letters: CHICANO MILITANTS ORGANIZATION.

"What kind of cases do you handle?" Ruth asks.

"Criminal. . . . Dope busts and such."

"Chicanos?" Gilbert asks.

"No political cases?" Risco says.

"Yeah, I've had some Chicano clients. And all legal cases are political. Politicians make the laws and we break them. Every dope bust is a political event."

"But you can't get too far with that, can you?" Risco says with a smile.

"The *vato*'s a flower child!" jeers Gilbert.

"Fuck you, man! I'm Chicano!" I am beginning to get mad. And what I am saying scares me. I have no idea where my words will take me.

"Come on, *ese*, they don't get Chicanos up north," Gilbert continues with the same sneer.

"How many peaches have you picked, priest?" The basement is getting hot. Gods on the wall snap their fangs

*The Revolt of the Cockroach People*

and drool. But Ruth cools it.

"Gilbert hasn't done anything except paint a few pictures and write a few poems," she says.

"And smoke a lot of weed," Risco smiles.

"What!" Gilbert jumps up and pokes his serpent with his thumb. He sounds angry, but clearly he is joshing with his comrades. He even draws me into the routine. "Shit, those guys don't know. I keep telling 'em . . . Man, when I was in the melon strikes in South Texas . . . Shit, *ese*, just ask old Cesar Chavez how I tore up those Texas Rangers." He paces around the room, waving his hands wildly. I like him; he has imagination.

"Gilbert has an imagination," Risco says. I nod, passing him the wine.

"You're all a bunch of lousy commies," Gilbert says. "You don't know shit from marbles."

"Here, *ese*," Risco says, holding up the bottle. "You get thirsty talking so much." Gilbert retrieves his bottle and hooks it on his thumb. He waits beside me and Risco gets serious. He still smiles, all his teeth shine, but it is different.

"Let's see a bar card, Buffalo." I lug out my wallet and show him. "OK," he says, after checking it against the driver's license, "you're a lawyer. But you're here as a writer, right?"

"Right."

"You want to write about the strike," Risco goes on. "You probably want interviews, pictures, the works, right?" I see where he is heading.

"If possible," I say.

"Without us knowing a damn thing about you," Risco finishes and smiles up at me brightly.

"Hey, *ese*," Gilbert says to Risco. "Don't give him a hard time yet." He turns to me. "You want to write for *La Voz*?"

"You might not like what I say."

"Shit, man, nobody likes my writing either," Gilbert says. "You come to the demonstration tomorrow. It's free to the public. After that, we'll see." Risco nods his head in agreement.

"Do you guys expect any trouble?"

Ruth and Risco look at Gilbert. Nobody says anything for a moment.

"We'll see what happens," Ruth says finally.

"OK, ese," Gilbert says, putting his arm around my shoulder. "You meet me at nine o'clock tomorrow at the hot dog stand in front of Garfield. OK?"

"Fine," I say.

I take one more drink of the lousy dry wine and shake hands again all around. As I leave the strange brown people in the basement, I know I am on the track of a story at last.

I think of calling Stonewall for his connection, but decide to hold off until the blood starts pouring in the streets. I am fairly confident the New York Times won't be interested unless there's a little gore. The whole so-called Chicano Movement seems to me nothing but another splinter from the old Civil Rights era. I doubt I will see anything different from what I saw and worked with in the campaigns of Willie Brown and Phillip Burton in San Francisco. I'd been around for the early Negro pushes for more jobs in the car lots and banks. I'd been there when Mario Savio and other badmouths got their start at Sproul Hall in '65.

I even marched with the Berkeley Barbs down Telegraph Avenue until a few Hell's Angels showed up in black leather boots, stood in a line before a thousand men women and children, and shunted the whole shitload of us down some side street because we were afraid of a confrontation. My soul sickened at the decision, but I have to admit I agreed with it. Even so, that marked the end of my organized radical career. I went back to wine, women and law school. Now, some two foggy years later, I meet up with a fat pirate, a toothy Cuban and his white chick, and right off they invite me to a Blow Out. After three months of nothing in a city I hated.

Well, not exactly nothing. I was drinking again, partly because I decided it was my personal heritage and partly because nobody can learn Spanish sober. It is just too sensual a language, too rolling and flowing to want your tongue stiff and dry. With a little beer, picking it up again was easy. Booze helped my writing some, but as yet, nothing worth writing about turned up. I still stay away from the dope, mostly because just to think about those days with Stonewall mushes up my brain. I have a little bread saved from the Public Defender's Office. I won every case but they fired me for insubordination.

What they really fired me for was my new name, Buffalo Zeta Brown. General Zeta was the hero of an old movie classic, *La Cucaracha*. A combination of Zapata and Villa with Maria Felix as the femme fatale. It suits me just fine. And Brown Buffalo for the fat brown shaggy snorting American animal, slaughtered almost to extinction. I feel right at home. So now a frog asks me to a Blow Out? It may be something or nothing, but why not? I am a free buffalo in a horrible place, looking for a little excitement. I still don't believe a damn thing.

The next morning, I get there early. I sit in Cronie's eating a burrito. I am surrounded by young kids who chatter and twist, sucking on straws and licking ice cream cones. Young girls with their hair teased up into frizzy beehives. Young dudes in navy surplus bellbottoms. All the kids wear black leather boots. Today, all the older boys wear brown berets cocked on their slick black heads. Everybody in sight has on a button, CHICANO LIBERATION FRONT printed over two crossed rifles. The burrito tastes good; I understand the dialect the kids are talking, which also makes me feel good.

"Hey, *ese*, do you think those *vatos* will blow it when the *jura* comes?" A little kid in a white T shirt with a blue knitted beanie is speaking to another kid dressed exactly the same. I notice they both have tattoos on their arms.

"*Pues, ¿quién sabe?* You know how those *putos* are, *ese*."

The picnic tables are crowded with these *vatos locos*, these Chicano street freaks. They pick at bowls of green *chiles curtidos*, washing the hot fire down with coke. The jukebox is blaring out Latin jazz by Willie Bobo. Everybody, including me, is grooving.

A loud buzzer sounds from across the street. I bet it can be heard two blocks away: nine o'clock. Some of the students pick up books and lunch bags and start to drag themselves toward the school.

"Hey, where are you guys going?" people ask.

"We ain't supposed to go. . . . We're supposed to be on strike, *ese*."

Across the street, the huge lawn is crowded with Chicano students and skinny trees. The broads are fantastic. I am eye-popping the incredible asses, the slim waists and the bulging breasts of these savage wenches who move with graceful twists. Since I have come to LA, I still have not touched a woman of my own culture. I swallow my milk and feel my pants bursting with heat.

"WALK OUT, WALK OUT, WALK OUT, WALK OUT . . ." I hear the shouts.

Several men in khaki field jackets and brown berets call out for the students to leave the lawn area.

I strain to spot Gilbert or Risco, but all I see are hundreds of young kids milling around, looking toward the entrance of the green buildings. Here teachers are bunched, ordering kids inside. I leave Cronie's and walk through the crowd on the sidewalk.

A group with picket signs is beginning to march around the front of the school. The signs are the ones I saw yesterday at *La Voz*. A young bearded man carries a bullhorn and tells the people to march in a thin circle on the sidewalk. "Stay off the lawn," he tells them.

"CHICANO POWER!" they shout into the sunny skies.

Another buzzer sounds off. Then a bell begins to clang.

"Hey, that's the fire alarm!" someone shouts.

I look to the building . . . BUZZZZZZZZZ.

Students who have gone inside now pour out of the drab ugly buildings. Smiles and laughter fill the air.

"Come on, *tapados*! Walk out!" Strikers are shouting at these students who remain on campus, in formation with their teachers.

"You bunch of *vendidos!* Blow out!"

"Walk out, you pussies, walk out!" the bearded man shouts through the bullhorn.

And then I see Gilbert. He is on campus with Risco, Ruth and several others. I watch the fat frog move between students and approach the wire fence. A tall Indian with huge shoulders and a red headband moves beside him. Risco and the others rendezvous with Gilbert and the Indian in front of the wire gate. Suddenly the gate is opened! I see it swing out and then Gilbert is lost in the crowd. The students break formation and charge out shouting whistling and waving their hands in the air.

"VIVA LA RAZA!"

The teachers try to stop it. They stand at the gate and try to shoo them back in. But the Chicanos are too many. The front of the school is a madhouse of excited Cockroaches.

Fire engines, sirens and red flashes of light come next. Black and white police cars are rushing to the scene. Big burly cops with shotguns on their shoulders jump out of the cars.

Several cops go up to the bearded man with the bullhorn and talk. They push him. He does not resist. The cops clear the sidewalk in front of the school. The demonstrators are chased across the street. I am surrounded next to Cronie's.

"*¡Pinche puto!*" they scream at the cops.

"*¡Cabrones marranos!*"

"Pigs! Filthy Pigs!"

The cops begin to prod slow students with their clubs. Then there are a couple of swings. I see a kid with a blue beanie strike back. Down he goes. A long black club strikes him down like a twig.

"Sit down, everybody . . . Just sit down on the street," the bullhorn bellows.

First one, then two, then a hundred students and Chicano Militants are seated in the middle of Whittier Boulevard. The cops are ordering them to clear out. But nobody moves.

"Chicano Power!" they shout back at the Law.

From out of a school window I see smoke. Chaos! The helmeted firemen are hauling limp hoses to the fire. A heavy metal trash can comes flying out another window! A cop car heads toward the seated students.

From out of the sidewalk crowd of a thousand, eggs and bottles fly through the air. Splat! An egg hits the car. The windshield is yellow with yolk.

The cops are beginning to swing harder now. I see a girl in an orange poncho go down. A cop picks her up and she swings her purse in his face. Several boys rush to her defense but are beaten back by other cops. Some students are being taken into the wagons now. The cops are beginning to arrest demonstrators with picket signs. I stand and stare. What can I do? I am carrying my Goodwill Industry briefcase, but this is not a court of law. This is no book. I have no license to practice on the streets. What the hell can I say? What in God's name can I do?

"Let's go to Hazard," I hear the man shout through the bullhorn.

"Yeah, let's go and talk to Hayes," I hear someone say.

"What's up?" I ask a kid about four feet tall.

"That's where they got the school board offices."

"Come on, *vatos* . . . on your feet. Let's go see Hayes."

Like a disorderly army, the students and the Chicano Militants pick themselves up from the street and walk toward the sidewalk crowd behind the bullhorn. I am caught up with them. I march along, looking for Gilbert and Risco. A thousand young Chicanos and I are marching together away from Garfield. The cops remain behind.

"Viva Zapata!" through the bullhorn.

"*¡Que Viva!*" roars the crowd.

"Viva Pancho Villa!"

"*¡Qué Viva!*"

"Viva Cesar Chavez!"

"*¡Qué Viva!*"

"Viva Corky Gonzales!"

"*¡Qué Viva!*"

"Viva Reis Lopez Tijerina!"

"*¡Qué Viva!*"

We swell through streets of dogs and cats and trash, narrow jungle paths of garbage cans, beat-up jalopies, mudholes and dogshit. A thousand kids streaming through a barrio of palm trees and Mexicatessens.

"MENUDO EVERYDAY," the signs say.

And then I remember that menudo is the stew made only on holidays, at Christmas time, for a wedding, a baptism and on those days that the fathers have tripe, corn and lime for the morning-after hangovers. But here they make it *everyday*. It would make a good title for a short story. Not just on Saturday and Sunday, but *everyday*.

"Hey, *ese*, you got a cigarette?"

I look down. It is another four-foot *vato loco* with a blue beanie. He looks around ten. He has a scar on his forehead and a tattooed arm, a Mexican Eagle perched on a cactus.

"Sure, man," I say and hand him the pack.

"Can my *camarada* have one?"

I nod. Why not? Why not contribute to the delinquency of these minors who've walked out of school and told the cops to stick it? If they can burn a trash can, break a window, throw an egg or two. . . .

Tears are in my eyes. I am breathing with difficulty. I am in the midst of the first major public action by the Chicano community. They have picketed before, they have been arrested before, if you can believe the chauvinistic articles in *La Voz*. But never on this magnitude. They have never walked down the streets of their own barrios and shouted at the drunks on the corners, "Hey, *ese*, come on, *carnal*. Join up with us!"

The little kid passes the cigarettes around to his friends, none of whom is more than five feet by a hundred pounds. And I am walking with my head tall and my fists clenched, with tears slithering unashamedly down my cheeks. I am remembering Mr. Wilkie and my own grammar school fiasco. And now, twenty years later, here I am giving cigarettes to scrawny children, kids who dare to act without their parents' permission, at the risk of being clubbed and busted by uniformed monsters.

All around me is a new breed of savages, brown-eyed devils who shout defiantly to the heavens. And what am I to do? Is all this just to write some story? Do up-and-coming great men march at the command of a wretched voice over a bullhorn? Is this the place for a lone buffalo? Will they bust me for passing out Camels? I am divided against myself, torn in two.

I wander away from the sweep of the crowd, stumbling off in a daze. I cannot stop my tears. In the distance, bells ring, sirens and horns blare at a bunch of kids on their way to revolution. I have been here three months now and all I have seen is uninteresting, too distorted to put down on paper.

The great lawyer has been fired. His fantastic name seems like a pile of bleached bones on a smoggy desert. My head aches and my heart pounds with anger and fear. What shall I do? To whom shall I turn for advice?

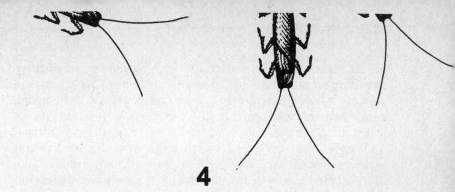

# 4

Delano is a pint-sized farming town, not too far from Riverbank where I was raised as a peach picker. It was built along the railroad line running from Los Angeles to Sacramento. The Atcheson Topeka and Santa Fe laid five hundred miles of steel rails, and the gandy dancers unwittingly served as racial separationists. Steel forever marked the line of demarcation between the races: Delano, Madera, Merced, Livingston, Hughson, Turlock, Modesto, Riverbank, Waterford, Escalon, Salida, Manteca, Tracy, Stockton, Lodi, Sacramento, Marysville and on up into the north country. One side of the tracks for Chicanos, the other for Okies. It was that way when I came to California in the summer of 1940 at the age of five. And it was still that way in the spring of 1968 when I arrived to visit Cesar Chavez.

All through law school, my secret dream had been to work for Chavez and the *campesinos*. I never really fancied myself as a lawyer, but as long as I was on my way to being one, it sure as hell wasn't going to be an ordinary job. My fantasies ran to the vineyards and orchards at Cesar's side, a union organizer rather than a courtroom attorney. But, by the time I passed the bar, I was fed up with politics, organization, with just about everything. I indulged myself with psychic ashes. Now I wanted to show the world. I wanted to write. And if I had to be a lawyer to make some bread, I still wanted to be the best at it.

The Farmworkers Union had purchased a forty-acre ranch on the outskirts of town. The land is clean and brown. Corn has just been planted. An immense barnlike building houses the union hall and also a service station for the use of members. Near one corner, field women have built a chapel. When I arrive for my appointment, the men are all out pruning the trees and tying back the grape buds. A light rain had fallen the night before, bringing out full rich smells.

I know that for twenty-five days now, Cesar has not tasted a morsel of solid food. He has starved himself like Ghandi. He believes that physical resistance to oppression only produces lesser men. Self-defense by design only creates violent characters. A revolution accomplished by brute force generates but another brutal society. By way of example to his followers, he gives up his flesh and strength to their cause. The height of manhood, Cesar believes, is to give of one's self.

"You can only stay a minute," the woman in brown sandals informs me. We are inside the chapel. Everything, including the altar, is homemade. Rough deep brown wood for benches. Bright paper flowers cover the back of the white and green altar. An oil painting of *La Virgen de Guadalupe,* the patron saint of the *campesino,* hangs above the flowers. A bronze madonna with a bronze child in her arms is their principal deity. There is no Christ in the homey green temple.

The woman leads me to a door at the rear of the chapel. Her thin dress and sandals rustle like soft spirits. She opens the door and whispers with her eyes how I must not disturb him too long. I enter and close the door behind me. It is very dark. There is a tiny candle burning over a bed, illuminating dimly a wooden cross and a figure of *La Virgen* on the wall. My ears are buzzing. There is a heavy smell of incense and kerosene. I don't move. I hear nothing. I no longer have any idea of why I have come or what I will say.

"Is that you, Buffalo?" The voice is soft, barely audible. He coughs.

"Yeah, Cesar?"

"Sit down."

I approach the bed and finally make out the frail form. It leans toward me, offering a limp hand. There is so little life left in him. I hear his short breaths but can barely detect the outline of his features against his skull. He struggles to keep his eyes open, then lies back and sighs.

"This is really something," he murmurs. "Do you know how long I've been waiting for a Chicano lawyer to come up here? But I knew the day would come."

I have no idea what to say, what he is expecting. Finally I manage something.

"Hey, Cesar . . . I always wanted to come down here, but . . ." Would he understand my confusion? "But . . . I dropped out for a while."

"And now you're back?"

"Well . . . that's what I've come here for. I need your advice."

And then there is silence. His breathing becomes regular. Perhaps he has fainted from weakness. I sit beside the bed, gritting my teeth and balling my fists. I can hear the sputtering of the candle.

"Buffalo?"

"Yeah, Cesar. You all right? Should I leave now?"

His eyes open and he sighs again deeply. "No, I'm OK. How about you? How you doing?"

"OK . . . I'm down in LA now. I've been there for a few months, trying to write."

"I know. I've heard from Risco."

"Oh, yeah? . . . Well, I've sort of taken some cases. The guys that got busted during the Blow Out last month." He must have heard the question in my voice.

"You're *with* Risco and Ruth, aren't you?" he asks gently.

"Yeah . . . Well, that's what I want to talk to you about."

"Those two are great organizers," he says proudly. "They used to run our paper before going down south. I keep up."

There is silence again. In the darkness, I think again of his words. The Father of Chicanos, Cesar Chavez, has *heard* of me.

"Buffalo?"

"Yeah, I'm here, Cesar."

"So how are things in LA?"

"All right, I guess."

"Are you guys trying to get the *viejitos* to join you, too?"

"Well, you know how old people are. Besides, I'm not doing much organizing myself. I'm kinda confused."

"Look," he says, a little stronger. "I *know* LA is a graveyard for organizers. You, personally, Brown Buffalo, a Chicano lawyer, have got to help those kids. Nobody else is going to do it. The Militants are doing a terrific job. Aren't you satisfied?"

"Oh, yeah." I think about his philosophy of non-violence. "I didn't know if you would approve," I say lamely. I don't know how to explain to him where I'm at.

"Listen, *viejo* . . . It doesn't matter if I approve or if anyone approves. You are doing what has to be done. ¿Que mas vamos a hacer?"

"It's not exactly what you do . . ."

"So what? I'm a man, just like you, no? Each of us has a different role, but we both want the same, don't we?"

Role? Want the same? "I guess . . ."

"Come on, *viejo!* Don't be so . . . They tell me you are one hell of a lawyer. Don't give up so easy, hombre."

"But I don't want to be a lawyer!" Finally I get out a part of it.

"So?" he says, leaning up again. "Who in his right mind would *want* to be a lawyer, eh?"

Again he falls back. I hold my breath until I can hear his own breathing. Now it is my turn to sigh deeply as I wipe tears from my squinting eyes. The door opens behind me. The woman puts her fingers to her mouth to indicate my time is up. I arise to leave.

"Buffalo?"

"Yeah, Cesar."

"You go back to LA and take care of business, OK, *viejo?*"

"OK, Cesar . . . And you take care of yourself."

"I'll be fine. You tell them I said hello."

"OK, Cesar. Adios."

I walk slowly back through the chapel. This time I notice a sign hanging by the door. I read it through the tears that still flow gently:

*LA VIDA NO ES LA QUE VIVIMOS,*
*LA VIDA ES EL HONOR Y EL RECUERDO.*
*POR ESO MAS VALE MORIR*
*CON EL PUEBLO VIVO,*
*Y NO VIVIR*
*CON EL PUEBLO MUERTO.*

(Life is not as it seems,
Life is pride and personal history.
Thus it is better that one die
and that the people should live,
rather than one live
and the people die.)

Lopitos
Acapulco, Guererro, 1960.

I know then and there that nothing matters anymore. It no longer matters to me what I have been or not been, whether ashamed or evasive or alone. It does not matter that I have fried my brains with dope or never touched a brown skin in tenderness; it is unimportant that I poisoned brothers in Panama with the gringo's venomous Christ-shit. The toilets I washed for black liberation, the handbills, the doorbells and registered voters, everything I knew *then* had nothing to do with me, now *really doesn't*. Those battles are nothing to me. I feel somehow that, this afternoon, I have met my destiny. But its terms are not Cesar's. I decide to accept some of the misdemeanor cases from the Garfield Blow Out. I figure it will take maybe three months to do the job. After that, I will split to Acapulco, write about the whole struggle and get in touch with my Chicano soul.

It is April, 1968. The next day Cesar broke bread with Robert Kennedy, brother of the man who dreamed Cockroach dreams some years before.

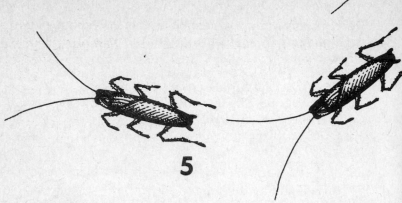

# 5

My office is the shitty green room in the Belmont Hotel overlooking Third and Hill Streets. A huge Goodwill Industries junk shop looms directly across the street. A cable car chugs up the hill with slick lawyers and their rich clients who park in the flat lots behind my hotel. It costs them a nickel to escape us. The courthouses, the city hall, the county buildings and federal offices are within a couple of blocks from where I live with cockroaches, winos, pimps, whores, junkies, fags, yoyos with bloody noses and bad breath. The newspaper vendor shouts out daily headlines in Spanish. I can see a Mexican restaurant, a couple of bars advertising mariachi music direct from Tijuana, many liquor stores and a shop that sells day-old bread. Down the block, the Farmer's Market is open to thousands who come from across the river to buy green chiles, tamales, *carnitas*, *tamarindo*, *nopales* and all the vegetables that Chicanos use.

I have been working on the briefs for Gilbert, Risco, Ruth and the others whose cases I've taken since my return from Delano. I've had new business cards printed up with the same design of Huitzilopotchtli which Chicano Militants wear on their brown berets:

> Buffalo Z. Brown,
> Chicano Lawyer
> Belmont Hotel, L.A.

The first day I went into court on a case, a simple disturbing the peace matter, I left my card with the clerk. I merely asked the judge, a short faggoty Mexican, for a continuance of the matter until I had time to prepare my briefs. I planned to challenge the statute on the grounds that Chicanos had a constitutional right to demonstrate their beliefs even if it disturbed the peace and quiet of the neighborhood. When I returned to my room, I received a call from the judge. He told me he didn't appreciate my business card.

"Some local attorneys have asked me to refer the matter to the State Bar, Mr. Brown."

"I'm terribly sorry, Judge. I'd never insult the dignity of your court with my tasteless business cards."

"Oh, I'm not against you calling yourself a Chicano lawyer. But it could be misinterpreted, it could be in violation of the canon on ethics. . . . We're not supposed to advertise, you know."

"Yes, sir . . . uh, if I may, Judge . . . Isn't this telephone call . . . isn't it *irregular* for a judge to phone an attorney when there's a matter pending before him? I don't want to do anything that might result in a mistrial. . . ."

He apologized quickly and told me that he was acting as a friend, not an official.

"I understand, Judge. And I'll never use that card again . . . Uh, that is, in your courtroom . . . But you can tell those local lawyers that I'll call myself any goddamn thing I want!" I slammed the phone in his face and continued to type my brief.

Today is Friday, May 31, 1968. I am chain-smoking cigarettes and thinking clearly as I work on a brief that will go to the Supreme Court when the telephone rings. It is Ruth.

"Hey, man, can you get right out here?"

"Where are you, at the office?"

"Yeah. Hurry! The pigs are coming in. Can you get down?"

"What do you mean?"

"Right now. They just parked outside. They're coming in. Hurry!"

I rush down to my '56 blue Plymouth which I bought from Public Defender fees. I scramble through traffic onto the San Bernardino Freeway and fight my way through the cars, the trucks and the smog, over ten of the ten thousand miles of paved roads in the County of Los Angeles. It takes forever.

By the time I arrive at Father Light's Episcopal Church, the place is quiet. Ruth is alone with her fury. The office has been turned upside down, totally trashed. She tells me that the cops have arrested Gilbert, Risco and Mangas, the broad-shouldered Indian who helped Gilbert cut the locks to the wire gates at Garfield.

"The bastards just tore up the place . . . They said they were looking for evidence of conspiracy . . . Those motherfuckers pushed me around when I tried to stop them. . . Can they do that, Buff? I mean, can they just bust in and take your stuff?"

"They can do what they want, Ruth. They got bigger guns than you or me."

I tell her to call up the office of the Chicano Militants. She talks to someone and then turns to me in disgust: "They've been there, too. Same thing as here. . . . those filthy bastards!"

"Jesus! . . . Uh, look . . . I'll go down to the jail . . . I'll find out what's going on. You stay here and call as many people as you can . . . Tell them to meet me here this evening. I'll see what I can do."

I run out to my car and pile back on the freeway. trying to tune in some news station. Soon I hear it:

*"Thirteen Chicano Militants have been indicted by the Los Angeles County Grand Jury on charges of Conspiracy to Disrupt the Schools. Chief Reddin and District Attorney Younger have stated that all have been apprehended and are being held in custody without bail. The Grand Jury charges them with having conspired to riot in connection with the school strikes in East Los Angeles of last March."*

I drive with my eyes blurred from the smog and the news. My heart is beating furiously. I am sweating like a pig when I arrive at the downtown Police Sty, Parker Center, only four blocks from my hotel. They call it the Glass House because the block-square building looks like solid glass, a cute architectural trick. But behind the glass there are concrete walls and iron bars. The prisoners cannot see the daylight.

"Who do you want to see?" the booking sergeant asks from behind a wire screen. He scowls at my levi's and cowboy boots.

"Eli Risco, Gilbert Rodriguez, Mangas Coloradas . . ."

"There's no bail on those guys. You better check it out with their lawyers."

"I'm not here for bail. I'm their attorney."

He looks down again at my levi's and cowboy boots. "You? You're an attorney?"

"Here's my bar card."

He checks it three times, stands up and looks me over from head to toe. He scratches his head and says, "All right, which one do you represent?"

"There's thirteen?"

"Yeah."

"I represent all of them."

He nods and gives a short chuckle. And then he buzzes the door and it opens and I am inside the jail, behind bars. I walk up the stairs and tell the deputy who I am.

He brings out Gilbert, Risco, Mangas and ten others. I don't know all of them. They all appear to be Chicanos, but some are dressed in militant gear while others are dressed in coats and ties. Risco introduces me. I shake hands with them through the green iron bars of the holding tank.

"Hey, ese, you got any cigarettes on you?" Gilbert says.

"No man. I'll bring you some next time."

"Hey, Buff, can you call my ruka?" Henry, a kid with a goatee asks.

"And my jefita, too," another one asks.

"Hold it up, you guys," Risco says. "Let the lawyer talk."

Thirteen of them stand and stare at me. What can I do for them? They are in and I am out. They wear shadows while I wear a blue turtle-neck.

"Jesus, what the fuck happened?" I ask.

They laugh. "That's a Chicano lawyer for you," a kid with a suit says.

"Hey, man. Can they hold us without bail?" Mangas asks.

"*Pues,* they're doing it, ain't they?" Henry says.

"Did they tell you anything?" I say.

"Sure, *ese.* They said they were going to get even with us for what we done at the schools."

"Yeah, the dude that took me in says he seen me at Lincoln."

"They showed me a picture of me picketing Roosevelt."

"All right . . . hold it. . . . Look, you guys . . . the first thing . . . you guys need lawyers, right?"

They all look at me with a twist. They stare me down.

"Hey, *ese,* I thought you said you was a righteous lawyer?"

"I am, goddamn it. But . . . Hey, man, this is a felony bust! The booking slip says you've got *fifteen* counts against you!"

"Ah, fuck them *putos, ese!* We didn't do shit!" Gilbert yells.

"Come on, Gilbert," Risco says. "This is serious."

"You bet your ass it's serious. . . . Do you realize . . . that's forty-five years in state prison . . . three for each count."

"Hey, Buffalo, come on, man . . ." mumbles a kid with a pock-marked face and heavy glasses.

"Forty-five years! Jesus fucking Christ!" They explode furiously. Risco calms them. We are all silent for a moment. We are taking measure of one another. My guts and head are stewing in adrenalin. They are waiting for me.

"Look, you guys . . . yeah, I'm a lawyer. I've done a few preliminaries. I've done some divorce work and a few dope cases. . . . I've practiced law for about . . . well, I practiced in Oakland for a few months before I took a vacation."

"You mean before you became a flower *vato!*" Gilbert shouts.

"Yeah, all right . . . Anyway, I don't have the experience . . . Jesus, man, forty-five years!"

"Well, fuck it, *ese*. I don't want no fucking *gabacho* lawyer!"

"Me neither. I want me a righteous Mexican!"

I nod my head and sweat it out. Thirteen defendants? Forty-five years?

"I have a friend who's a lawyer . . . He works for the ACLU," Muñoz says. He is a student.

"Fuck the ACLU!" Gilbert cries out. "I don't want no fucking white-ass liberal to talk for me. . . . You do it, Buffalo. Just don't cop out on nothing cause I ain't copping to shit!"

I stand back and observe them all. I who have been running around with my head hanging for so long. I who have been lost in my own excesses, drowned in my own personal confusion. A faded beatnik, a flower *vato*, an aspiring writer, a thirty-three-year-old kid full of buffalo chips is supposed to defend these bastards? With forty-five years of *their* lives riding? My knees feel like pillars of smoke blowing out from under me.

"Hey, Buff, ain't you got no gum on you?"

"Jesus, Gilbert . . . Shut up!" I shout.

"That's the way, *ese*, tell us what to do," Henry says from the rear.

"All right . . . all right, you bunch of creeps! Do you guys really want me to be your lawyer? I ain't promising nothing. Except that I won't cop out to nothing."

"Viva La Raza!" Mangas shouts, his head a foot above the others.

"¡Qué Viva!"

"All right you, knock it off or you'll have to go back to your cells!" the slimy deputy shouts to us.

"Now . . . the first thing. . . . Do you guys want to do it *heavy*?"

"Fuck yes, *ese*."

"What do you mean?" Risco says.

"Well . . . the school strike was one thing. You know, it's not the first time that someone's been arrested for disturbing the peace at a school . . . but this is different."

"What are you driving at, Brown?" Risco says.

"Look, man . . . why should they indict you guys for what you did? I mean, it wasn't *that* heavy. . . . A week of strikes by several thousand kids isn't worth all this trouble. . . . Can't you see?"

"Shit, we know that, man. This whole *movida* is just to put us out of business."

"Yeah, but why *now?*"

"What do you mean?"

"Why did they wait until two months after the thing? Why on *this* weekend?"

"Come on, man. What's up?"

"Well . . . what were you planning to do this Saturday and Sunday?"

"I was going to go work with McCarthy's campaign."

"Ah, you *tapado* . . . I'm getting out the vote for Kennedy."

"Fuck you, *ese.* Chicanos ain't working for those sellouts."

"Wait, man. Can't you see it?"

"Yeah, I see what you're driving at. . . . Next Tuesday is the election," Risco says.

"And didn't both Kennedy and McCarthy send you guys telegrams of support? Didn't you guys have a meeting with them? Aren't the Chicanos supporting either Kennedy or McCarthy?"

"Well we sure ain't supporting that fucking Nixon, *ese.*"

"That's what I mean. . . . The arrests just happen to coincide with the California Primary. This will make both those guys look bad because they've come out publicly in support of you."

"Shit, that ain't nothing new, *ese.* Those *putos* are always gonna move us around when they want," Gilbert says.

Again we are silent. Again we each try to figure it out.

"So, it's up to you. This is a political set-up. They're trying to fuck up the election in LA and put the Chicanos out of action at the same time. If you guys want to fight back, let's do it along those lines. This is a fight against the government, the Grand Jury, the judges, the DA and the Chief of Police."

"All right, Buffalo," Risco says. "I read you . . . I think we ought to have a picket line."

"Right on, *carnal*."

"Yeah, man. Let's picket the goddamn school board."

"No, man, let's picket City Hall."

I say, "Why not Parker Center? Why not have a weekend vigil right outside Glass House?"

"A police station? Hey, man, we've never done that!"

"It's dangerous, *ese*."

"But that's where it's at, man. They got you guys locked up in here like dogs. . . . How about it?"

"Well . . . I doubt that the college students will join in this," Muñoz says.

"Fuck the college sellouts!" Gilbert roars.

"Come on, Gilbert," Henry says. "We need all the help we can get."

"And you'll defend us all?" Risco says.

"I'll defend you guys as long as you want me to. . . . You can get somebody else whenever you feel like it."

"Not me, *ese*. I want you, period," Henry says.

"*¡Viva el Búfalo Café!*" Gilbert shouts.

"Who?" I am startled myself.

"Pues . . . Ain't he Brown? You know: *Café?*"

"Yeah . . . *¡Viva el Búfalo Café!*"

They lift their arms to the air, clench their fists and cheer me on. They give me notes and messages for their friends and families. I promise to return as soon as I can.

"We've decided to go on a hunger strike until we get out," Risco says.

"You have, you Christian!" Gilbert roars.

"Look Buff, you tell the people out there . . . You tell them we want them outside this building on the sidewalks, and that none of us are eating until they free us. . . . Except Gilbert."

"Hey, man. I'm game, if you want."

"Viva Gilbert Rodriguez!" they shout.

I ring the buzzer and the deputy opens the door for me. I lift my fist to them as I walk out of the cell.

I rush back to *La Voz*, where the CMs, the college students, the wives, girl friends and other partisans are waiting for news. I tell them of the plan to hold a demonstration at the Glass House. There are shouts and lifted arms of defiance. But the college students and their advisers are against the idea.

"We shouldn't even be talking about it," a well-dressed kid says.

"Yeah, man, you want us to get busted for conspiracy, too?"

"And how do we know someone here isn't a . . . spy?"

Everyone looks at one another. There is an edge, a tenseness.

"There's no law that says we can't have a picket line," I say.

"Then why are those guys in jail?" a law student asks.

The eyes are all on me, the lawyer without much experience. They want to see my credentials. They want to know why there's no bail. If it's unconstitutional, as I have told them, then why is it happening? Is it possible I don't know what the fuck I'm talking about?

"Listen, all of you . . . I've been to see them and they want a picket line. . . . Risco says they're going to be on a hunger strike until they get out. . . . Now if you guys don't want to, that's up to you . . . but *I'm* going to be at the Glass House tomorrow morning at nine and I'm going to try to get as many people as I can to be there with me."

"I'm with you, Buff," Ruth says.

"Me too, man," a tall bearded man in a green field jacket says. I look at him and nod.

"I'm Black Eagle, man," he says. We clasp the power handshake and I notice his green eyes.

"That's enough to start. Let's get on the phones and start calling up every single organization in town."

"Hey, my old man's in there, goddamnit! I'm going!" a tall girl with lustrous black hair shouts to me. I look at her. "I'm Henry's old lady. My name's Ester."

"Me too, Buffalo . . . I'm Joe's wife," an Anglo girl with a baby in her arms calls to me.

"Well, not me. You guys are just asking for it," the adviser to one of the college groups speaks out.

"You guys do what you want!" I yell back at him. "I've got work to do."

Some people walk out of the office. Those that remain get on the phones. Some are making posters; some are drafting leaflets explaining about the arrests. Ruth whips up an organizational storm. I realize I have stepped off a cliff.

We work through the night, listening to the news every hour. The bust is the number-one item. We have made the headlines for the first time. Throughout the week of the Blow Outs and afterward, we sought media exposure. For two months groups of students, parents and teachers have met nightly to form an Educational Issues Committee. An Armenian Baptist preacher from Tijuana, Vahac Mardirosian, has gone before the school board weekly to explain the students' demands: a simple insistence upon their dignity as a people. That's what the demands boil down to. But the press and TV ignored the issue right along with the school board. The Blow Outs were buried in the back pages. We were nothing but a bunch of outside agitators, radicals, communists and racists. But now that the racist-agitators are in jail, charged with Conspiracy, now it is *news*.

With sleep in my eyes, bones rag-down tired, I drive to the Glass House next morning, my car packed with picket signs. Slowly, in pairs, in small groups, the people begin to arrive. We are standing outside the entrance to the Glass House which handles the best equipped police force in America. Cops await us in a line at the entrance. They allow me into the jail because I am the attorney. I've told the men we are outside. The building is closed to all the rest. The police stand with hands on their holsters, feet spread apart, waiting for us to attack. But all we do is walk around in a circle.

"Old McDonald had a farm-E-I-E-I-O"
"Old McDonald had a pig-E-I-E-I-O."

"With an oink-oink here, oink-oink there. . . ."

The militants throw birds, raspberries and kisses to the tight formation of blue. There is an air, an excitement, a feeling of rally, parade and rebellion on the streets. The cops stare down at us grimly. They say nothing.

We are joined by a contingent from the Black Panthers, then another group of blacks, this one from US, with shaved heads and African togas. Both groups march up to us, give the power salute and join the picket. Rose Chernin, a little old lady in tennies, and Dorothy Healey, a Communist Party official, come up to me and introduce themselves.

"If you think it'll be embarrassing to your group, we'll leave," Dorothy says. She is a beautiful woman with flaming sunset hair.

I put my arm around her and squeeze. "Listen, Dorothy, you can march with me anytime . . . and besides, the Chicanos are ten times to the left of the Communists now."

She twinkles her green eyes and joins the bandwagon.

I walk around and talk to everyone. I tell people to stay in line, get off the streets, don't walk on the lawn, quit throwing birds to the pigs, move it along, move it along, we can't block the road, we've got to keep moving or we'll be arrested.

I am the self-appointed marshal of the parade. I bark out my orders like a fired-up captain. Except for a couple of seasons with the Safety Patrol in Riverbank Grammar School and a short stint in the Boy Scouts, I have never been a drill sergeant. Even in the Air Force, I never got to give anyone orders. And except for one year with the Junior Varsity Football Team of Oakdale Joint Union High School, I never got to be captain of anything. And then I got clobbered in the mouth and needed thirteen stitches for telling Walter Brown to get over the ball. Now it is different. For five solid hours we march around the entire block. There are five thousand of us in support of the East LA Thirteen, the name that I have chosen for the cast.

"Let's go to Placita Square now!" I shout. We are to rally there.

Black Eagle relays the order to groups on the other

blocks. We are on the streets now and walking toward the small square, a designated historical monument. It is a rotunda, a square with trees and a small stage with a canopy. Old men in baggy pants, bearded winos with short dogs in brown bags, kids with skinny legs, men with faded skin, black and brown faces, all kinds hang around this park. And yes, the place is historical: right across the street from Olvera Street, the original site of old LA, when the Mexicans and *californios* were in power. Bronze figures, salted with birdshit, stand proudly in the park.

*EL PUEBLO DE LA REINA DE LOS ANGELES*
  *On this spot a battalion of Mormons*
  *from the Sixth Calvary in Salt Lake*
  *City defeated the last contingent*
  *of Indians and Mexicans in the*
  *war between Mexico and the United*
  *States of America. 1848 A.D.*

The plaque is under a monument of horsed figures driving away *bandidos* and near-naked savages. As I pass I spit on it. The person behind me does the same. A black militant passes and tells the statue to go fuck itself.

On Olvera Street, the vendors of Mexican food, Mexican clothes, serapes, ponchos, glass dolls, leather boots, dresses for dancing *corridos*, the old Mexican men and women sell their wares to the tourists. Vendors and tourists alike are staring at us as we crowd into the square. We have set up a microphone and have asked the various community leaders to speak. I am first.

I rise to the stage and look down upon the hundreds below. My tired eyes have not closed but to blink for thirty-six hours. The people are staring up at me, waiting for my words as I hold the mike in my hand. I remove my dark glasses and I begin to cry.

"The East LA Thirteen are behind those bars up there. Are they in jail because they rose to speak out against the educational system in this country? Do you think they have been rousted from their offices and their homes like a bunch of criminals simply because they got thousands of

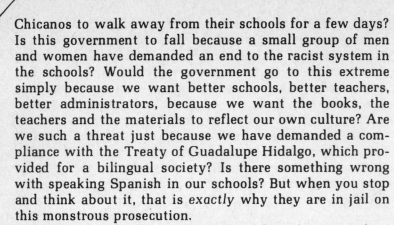

Chicanos to walk away from their schools for a few days? Is this government to fall because a small group of men and women have demanded an end to the racist system in the schools? Would the government go to this extreme simply because we want better schools, better teachers, better administrators, because we want the books, the teachers and the materials to reflect our own culture? Are we such a threat just because we have demanded a compliance with the Treaty of Guadalupe Hidalgo, which provided for a bilingual society? Is there something wrong with speaking Spanish in our schools? But when you stop and think about it, that is *exactly* why they are in jail on this monstrous prosecution.

"Imagine, forty-five years behind bars because of an idea. A life sentence for disturbing the minds of people in power. For that is all they have done. They have only *said* things. They are not being prosecuted because of any violence. They are not charged with throwing eggs or bottles or setting fires. They are charged with having planned, organized and executed a *demonstration*. The DA isn't saying that they incited anybody to riot. He doesn't claim that they told anyone to throw anything. And he doesn't say that they threw anything themselves. Only that they *conspired* to tell people to walk away from their schools. Period.

"We most emphatically agree with the prosecution. We did, in fact, plan, and we did, in fact, execute a demonstration at five Chicano High Schools in March of 1968. So what?

"If that makes us criminals, then criminals we are. Outlaws and rebels against any government of men that would make it a crime to speak out against injustice? We are definitely that.

"I represent the East LA Thirteen. I am the chief counsel for these men. I will be needing a lot of help in the days to come. We will need lawyers, law students, leg men, secretaries, and the support of anyone who is in agreement with our position. And to be honest, even if you aren't in agreement, but you simply want to help out of the milk of human kindness, then join up with us.

"Unless we all band together and fight against this type of political persecution, we are all doomed. If Evelle Younger can throw you in jail for speaking out against racism, he can just as easily throw you in jail for speaking out against the regime presently in power.

"Thank you for coming out and . . . Viva La Raza!"

"¡QUÉ VIVA!"

"Long Live The East LA Thirteen!"

"Power To The People!"

"CHICANO POWER!"

I stop early and let Ruth speak about the election conspiracy. I am too wrecked to continue.

Five days later, the night of the California Primary, I am partying with Gilbert and Pelon, a friend of his. We drink beer from plastic cups and eat cold hot dogs at the campaign headquarters of a liberal white lawyer running for DA against the incumbent, Evelle Younger. Gilbert and the other twelve defendants are on the street again. The large office is filled with whites who have been helping us over the weekend with our campaign.

A few days ago, we formed a Chicano Legal Defense organization. I am the chief counsel. Richard Alatorre, a dapper Chicano with connections in the McCarthy campaign, soon approached us. The good Senator wishes to make a large contribution to the defense of the East LA Thirteen. Immediately afterward, the young *honcho* heading Kennedy's wagon in the barrios told us RFK has the same idea. Both men want our support. They are neck and neck in the crucial primary leading to the Democratic nomination. As LA County goes, so goes the state; and Chicanos make up fifteen percent of the county.

After we consult, I tell the representatives: "If both camps give an equal amount, say, ten thousand each . . . then each man can issue his own press release. . . . But only if *both* give. We are not going to be used by anyone. Our people are divided between these two men and we are not going to divide them more."

"Hey, *ese*, you think we're pigs?" Alatorre says.

"Senator Kennedy wouldn't do something like that either," his young politico says.

Then, yesterday, we went to court. The judge finally set bail at a thousand dollars a head. On the strength of the politicians' pledges, everybody went into hock and sprung our men from the joint. Now we are waiting for the checks to arrive. They have already issued press statements but, so far, no cash. At the party, we listen to the election returns, wondering if the loser will renege.

"Shit, *ese*, if those *putos* don't come through. . . ." Gilbert says.

We are staring around, trying to con some short blonde with braces into hustling up some broads for us. I have appeared on television several times over the weekend, and some of the young white liberal chicks want to meet me, the blonde tells us.

"Hey, can you get one for me, too?" Pelon asks. He wears the only blue beanie in the crowd.

"If any broad wants to meet a member of the East LA Thirteen," Gilbert says.

Suddenly I hear commotion. "Look, look!" a girl screams.

People are rushing to the television set on top of the desk. "Ladies and gentlemen. . . ."

"Oh, my God, look!"

Girls are screaming, men are running around. There is commotion and confusion and congestion, both on the screen and in the room. . . . *Ayyyy!*

"Ladies and gentlemen . . . Senator Kennedy has been shot by a man . . . Ladies and gentlemen. . . ."

The announcer is reporting the assassination live. The screen flashes scenes of the sandy-flaked kid on the floor, blood on his shirt, his eyes white.

"Eyewitnesses report that the man has run out into the lobby. . . . Police have apprehended him . . . but they are looking for others who may have been in conspiracy with him. . . . The eyewitnesses say the man is a young Mexican-American, a Latin-type person. . . ."

"Hey, Gilbert, did you hear that?" I say.

"Yeah, *ese*. What do you think?"

"Let's get the fuck out of here, man."

"Come on, Pelon," he says.

We say nothing to anyone. We simply walk out and get into my faded jalopy. We drive silently toward East LA. We are carrying a case of beer in the car. And we are paranoid. We feel the chills down our necks. I am sweating. We are afraid to say anything.

"Hey, stop."

"What?"

"Isn't that a roadblock up ahead?"

But it is too late to turn back. I come to a halt before two uniformed cops standing with shotguns in their hands and a police wagon across the road with flashing red lights.

"All right, boys, let's see some ID." The pig pokes his head through the window.

"Have you caught those bastards yet, officer?" I say.

"What? . . . Uh, no. We're checking out . . . Say, where are you fellows from?"

"I'm from Beverly Hills, officer. These two men are my clients. I'm an attorney. I'm driving them back to their homes. The judge took away their driving privileges . . . heh, heh. That's why I'm driving this, uh, car of his." Nobody from Beverly Hills would own a piece of junk like my car.

I hand him my bar card. He looks it over carefully. Then he pokes a flashlight into the back seat. Gilbert has put my briefcase over the beer.

"Ain't you the lawyer for those, uh, fellows that got arrested?"

"I guess you saw me on TV."

"Listen, Brown . . . You better take your boys back to East LA. Things are pretty hot right now."

"Thanks, officer."

We drive away very slow. We pass the hotel where the murder has taken place and then head back to Tooner Flats.

"Jesus, *ese* . . . that fucking pig, I wanted to smash his nose," Gilbert says.

63

"What are we going to do?" Pelon asks.

"What is there to do?" I say.

"I don't know, man. I know Cesar and the *campesinos* dug him . . . but he's just another *gabacho* as far as I'm concerned."

"Me too, man," Gilbert says to Pelon. "But, you know, I still *feel* bad."

"Ah, you anarchists can say what you want," I say. "But without that man and his organization, there ain't no chance for us anymore. . . ."

"What do you mean, man?"

"He was the last hope for the Chicano. . . . I don't mean him, personally, but the whole white liberal bit, it's dead now. McCarthy lost tonight, too. It doesn't matter who killed him; liberals choke at violence. You watch and see. This will insure the election of that motherfucker Nixon."

"Jesus, you're right, *ese*," Gilbert says.

"What are we gonna do, *ese*?"

"What the fuck *can* we do?"

"Shit, I feel like throwing a bomb or something," Gilbert says.

"Who you gonna bomb?"

"What the fuck does it matter?" Pelon says.

"That's the way I feel, too." Gilbert says.

"So what are we gonna do?" Pelon says.

We drive and listen to the live broadcast from the Ambassador Hotel. The reports make it pretty clear that Kennedy has only a few hours of life left. We drive in silence. Tears are in my eyes. My chest is heaving air in gulps.

"Shit, *ese*, there ain't nothing we can do. Let's go get some weed from this *ruka* I know up in Lincoln Heights."

"That sounds better than nothing," Pelon says.

I drive in the darkness and I know, I can feel it in my bones, that the ante has been upped.

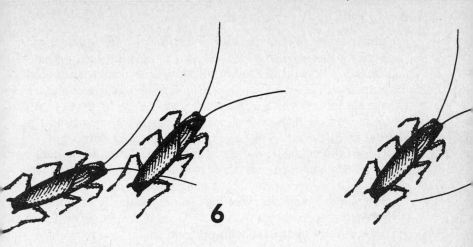

# 6

We got the ten grand from McCarthy, but the check bounced. Alatorre straightened it out finally. We didn't have the nerve to ask the Kennedy people for their dough; I told their man to forget it. McCarthy's ten was split between *La Voz* and the Militants, some going to me for legal fees. I promised Mangas and Gilbert a weekend in San Francisco with my share. But instead, I flew up alone to visit an old friend from my beatnik days. It was an impulse decision. Maybe I needed some distance from my present goings-on.

Ted Casey met me with a bagful of Savage Henry's blue acid and said, "Here, spic, take this magic to those creeps and see what happens." It seemed perfectly natural that he should say it and I should hear it and nothing should happen. I am where I am, always. When I got back to LA, I invited my friends out to the desert to share the drugs and prepare for the trial, a bare fortnight away.

Now we stand at the edge of a lake, a murky lake of green crud at the bottom of a dead sea, waiting for the acid to hit. I am with Gilbert, Black Eagle, Mangas and Lady Feathers, a Chicano princess. We are in the desert twenty-five miles and two mountain peaks from Edward's Air Force Base. Edward's is one home of the Strategic Air

Command, which keeps the B-52s afloat for doomsday. Lake Elsinore is around the bend in the hills but, around us, there is no green. Everything is yellow and brown and silent. The sun is hot and white. The sky is blue. We are sweating in our white underwear and we are ready to jump into the black lagoon. Lady Feathers has gone around a corner of dirt road to change into her bathing suit.

"Here she comes!" shouts Mangas, the Chicano prince.

We turn and see her fine bronze flesh poured into a white suit. She wears a headband of many colors. Her face is sand-baked sex; her legs and breasts bounce along with each step.

"All right, I'm ready," she giggles.

Mangas stretches his long arm to her. "Come here, baby."

She clobbers him with a right to the midsection. "Have a little class, ese."

"Don't act so white, squaw," Mangas says.

Lady Feathers has recently left Black Eagle. She has since taken up with Mangas, the six-and-a-half-foot-tall, light-skinned vato who calls himself an Indian, an ex-boxer who once sparred with Ingemar Johansson. Through the CMs he obtained a scholarship to UCLA and took up acting. Lately, he has been extremely worried about the arrest and the upcoming trial. The first time I met him was the day the judge released him on a thousand dollars bail. He told me straight off that he knew I was on acid. He had heard of my reputation as a dope lawyer and he wanted to know if I could get him a cap or two. I hope the trip will relax him.

"All right, you guys, let's get the party going," Lady says.

"Jesus, Armida, are you going to gang-bang us?" Black Eagle says.

"Fuck you, ese. You've had your chance. . . . I thought we were going to have a meeting. Aren't we here to prepare for the goddamn trial?"

"Let's take a swim first," Mangas says.

"How long's it been?" Gilbert asks.

"About fifteen minutes," I say.

"Will it hit me just like that, *ese*?" Lady asks.

"Just relax, *esa*. It'll come to you. You'll know when it takes you," I tell the woman of my dreams and my fantasies. I have known her since I first came to the infernal city. She was with Black Eagle then, though I didn't meet him until the Glass House caper. I told both of them about acid and they told me about Chicano culture. Black Eagle is a former guard for the USC Trojans who now teaches English as a second language to the Chicanos in Watts. I had been away from my people for so long that I had forgotten many of our tribal rites and customs. But over the months they have not ceased to instruct me.

In the course of our discussion, I found that some Chicanos in the city have a misconception of gringos that we farmworkers could never have. They don't quite realize they have an enemy while, in the country, the Chicano *knows* from birth he is a lowdown cockroach. In the cities, only the lowriders, the *vatos locos*, are in tune with this. Which is why I have spent all my off-duty hours drunk with the likes of Gilbert, Pelon and the Chicano Militants, all politicized lowriders.

"I call this orgy to order," Mangas says.

"Hear, hear!"

"The first meeting of the, uh, Brown Buffalo Party will hereby come to erection," the tall Indian says in his actor's voice.

"Can we all vote?" Gilbert asks, leering.

"Just don't get any funny ideas, *ese*," Lady Feathers says.

"I want to make a motion," I say.

"OK, man."

"I move that this party not have any rules."

"I second that, *ese*," Gilbert says.

"I third it," Black Eagle says.

"The motion carries. . . . The Brown Buffalo Party is hereby . . ."

"We're free to do what the fuck we want!" Gilbert shouts.

We stand and move toward the water. The acid has taken hold.

We slush through mud, our black legs dripping ooze. The water is warm, the wind is kind and gentle while the sun shines brightly. Mountains of sand and stone, brown and yellow bushes; no trees, nothing but stillness and calm; no ants, no bugs, no birds.

We are sitting at the shoreline contemplating our legs of mud and laughing in sensuous abandon at my brown stomach. I am fat again. Mangas is lifting stones high above his head and casting them into the muddy waters at his feet. Gilbert is puffing on a reefer.

"Hey, *ese*. Is this stuff supposed to *do* something?" Gilbert asks. The black frog who geezes with Pelon in the garages and alleys of East LA wants to know if the LSD is supposed to make him silly like Mangas or like Buffalo Z. Brown, who is sitting contemplating how he has ended up at the edge of Lake Elsinor in the company of such strange Chicanos.

Black Eagle says, "I think we can run our own country."

"You can't even fix the sink, *ese*," Lady Feathers says.

"I wouldn't mind being Chief Justice for a while," the lawyer says.

Gilbert stands in his khaki pants. He refuses to run around in white underwear while a regular *chola* looks on. Stretching his arms to the winds, Gilbert says, "Shit, *ese*, if we *make* it, all I want is the top of that mountain."

"Just get me a color TV," Lady Feathers says.

"Yeah . . . and a cheese sandwich," the Brown Buffalo says.

"You guys are full of *caca!*" Black Eagle shouts, diving back into the primordial ooze.

Just then we hear a roar in the distance. A fat prolonged growl. We lift our eyes to the clouds and see a small plane coming down the valley.

"Hey, I think it might be the owners!" Mangas yells.

"Will they get pissed?" Black Eagle asks.

Mangas is picking up his shoes and his pants. "Yeah, we better make it quick. It's him."

I am standing, staring at the sun and at a black gnat in my eye. It belches yellow smoke and I hear my friends shouting to me. But I am waving at the man with the red cap whose face I see when the blue bird from the sky swoops down over us. The man shakes his fist at me.

"Come on, *ese*. They'll be coming back!" Gilbert shouts.

"Yeah, you'd better come, Buffalo," my secret love says.

But I am immovable, staring into the distance. "It's just a speck," I say to them.

"Hey, man. They'll come back. They shoot at trespassers!" Mangas shouts to me.

They are all on the path at the side of the lake, starting to run into the bush. I have seen this paranoia before. I've taken this stuff with Stonewall and the hippies a million times, and usually somebody gets bent out of shape for a while. Bad trips are not uncommon. The devil simply grabs you by the neck and twists it off like a chicken for Sunday's dinner. I laugh at my friends.

And then I hear a new roar, not a plane but a machine gun coming around the bend in the lake. I turn to see a motor boat coming at full clip toward me, standing in my skivvies with my head full of acid madness.

"Hey, you. Get the hell off my property!" a man with a shotgun yells.

I stare at the red boat, at the three men all with rifles pointing at me.

"Hey, you fucking greaser, you better get out of here before we shoot your ass full of lead."

"Fuck you!" The gods are testing me.

*Bang, Bang, Bang!*

Bloop, Bloop, Bloop. Little piddle-puddles in the water before my eyes, at my legs.

I whirl around and begin to run. Up the path. Run.

Laughter in the back. To my heels the bastards are laughing. Big croaking laughs. Stomps in the stomach. Whiskey belly laughs. "Hot damn, but did you see that fat greaser run?"

I run up the hill. Into the sun. Struggle to breathe; strain at the hot lump in my burning chest; the wind is hot into my flaming red cheeks.

I stop at the crest. I turn and see the red motorboat skiffing away, around the bend. I am in total confusion. It is the lake at Chapultepec in the Valley of Mexico and I am scanning the water for the bodies of dead Spaniards. Where are the white horses they came on? Where are the long boats and where is the White Man of whom Quetzalcoatl spoke? And the woman in downtown LA who read my fortune and said to beware the same White Man in a red boat? Where is she now?

Suddenly I hear another roar. This one is a ROAR. It is a giant black bird floating above my head in the sky. It is ominous and evil and its wings wave in the wind from the weight of the bombs it carries in its belly, to rain havoc on those who simply want to swim in a dirty lake and have a little fun with some friends. It is a giant death box. It has wings big enough for a thousand men to stand and stomp with brown brogans while the band plays John Philip Sousa's "Stars and Stripes Forever." It is passing me by, heading in the same direction the red boat went.

*Ayyyyyyyyy, Ayyyyyyyyy, Ayyyyyyyyy!*

I lift my fists to the skies and shriek at the monster.

*Ayyyyyyyyy, Ayyyyyyyyyy, Ayyyyyyyyy!*

I lift my voice and I spit at the bird, flying at the speed of sound to kill brown babies and fine women and brothers that only want to pick up a chunk of earth and sift it through their fingers.

I lift a pebble in my hands. I pick up a rock. I throw them both after the bird. I run and I stumble and I pick up more and I throw them to see if I can strike the black bird before it can drop those bombs on downtown LA and East LA and downtown Mongolia or Saigon or Haiphong or Quang Tri or Tooner Flats and Lincoln Heights or wherever Cockroaches live.

*Ayyyyyyyyy, Ayyyyyyyyy, Ayyyyyy!*

And soon it is gone. I am on the ground. My face to the earth. I kiss the dirt. I eat the sand. I roll over so that I am flat on my ass, stretched out with my palms to the skies. It has been a fine day. And I am at peace. Content with my

*The Revolt of the Cockroach People*

commitment to the earth. . . . It has been a good omen that
the Party of the Buffalos should open with such a *bang,
bang, bang, you're dead!*

My preparations for the trial rose to new levels. Instead
of going to trial, I filed a brief with the Court of Appeals
demanding that the trial be stopped on the grounds that
the indictment was constitutionally defective. Under the
First Amendment, we had the right to march and verbally
protest, and evidence that minor acts of violence had occurred at the site of the planned demonstration was not
evidence of a criminal conspiracy. Unless, of course, the
Grand Jury had been told that the Chicano Militants had
also *planned* to set off fire alarms, burn trash in the toilets
and throw eggs at the police cars.

In those early days, however, the cops didn't have undercover agents. No one with such knowledge had testified. The court granted a temporary restraining order.
They told us to hold off until they looked into this can of
worms based on the transcripts of the Grand Jury hearing.
It would be a year before they could rule on the matter. A
year of waiting. A year of fear at meetings. A year of demonstrations. Of pickets at the School Board, pickets at the
police stations, pickets at City Hall, demonstrations at
poverty program offices, marches to the welfare offices.
Throughout the year 1969, we marched more miles than
those men on white horses who came in galleons to take
over land and people some five hundred years before. We
marched more miles between downtown LA and Brooklyn
and Soto Streets in East LA than the blacks had marched to
Selma. I became a professional drill sergeant during that
wretched year.

And, of course, I met the creme de la creme! . . .

A Doctor Francisco Bravo has been calling me for two
weeks. He leaves messages with Ralph, the old Okie clerk
downstairs. I've not answered because of the message he
left the first time. It said, "Dr. Bravo called and wants you
to meet with him and Mayor Yorty."

"Fuck that *tío taco*," Gilbert said when I told him.

"He's the owner of the Pan American Bank," Risco said.

"But maybe he can help us," I said.

Risco and the others laughed at my foolishness. So I didn't call back. But, after his third try, I called to see what he really wanted.

"Oh, Mr. Brown I'm so glad you've called," a whining voice says.

"What does Yorty want?"

"Well, the Mayor would like to meet with you and see if he can do anything to help the situation in East LA."

"You mean the arrests?"

"Just a general conversation."

"He wants to size me up?"

"Heh, heh . . . No, no, Mr. Brown. The Mayor is a fine person."

"If you'll get Reddin and Younger there, we'll be glad to meet."

"Oh, I can't promise that. . . . As you know, the Mayor and the District Attorney are from different parties."

"Well, you see if you can set it up and let me know."

He lets me know immediately. The Mayor has invited me and two other persons of my choosing to meet with him this afternoon. I have already called all thirteen defendants to gather at City Hall before the appointment for a preliminary rehearsal.

At one o'clock, we are inside the white castle we have seen on "Dragnet" for so long: concrete, granite, marble and dark wood, long flights of steps vanishing to fairytales of Supervisors, Councilmen, and the Lord Mayor of the nation's flattest city.

When the last defendant has arrived, the short redheaded secretary ushers us into the Mayor's chambers. Two palace guards stand erect beside the door and say nothing. The royal furniture is plain-jane Sears & Roebuck. There are a few books for looks on a shelf above the little balding Okie who sits behind the brown desk with his feet crossed. He wears brown wing-tipped shoes and a pair of white socks that barely clear the ankle, gray suit and a

*The Revolt of the Cockroach People*

narrow blue tie. Before he opens his mouth, I know he's a hick.

"Howda you do? I'm Sam Yorty," he says, rising.

I look down on him and wonder how such a short guy could have been elected mayor of the world's biggest armpit.

"I'm Brown."

He reaches for my hand. I turn quickly and sit down.

"And this is Chief Reddin."

I turn to see a tall graying faggot with wet white skin in a black toy soldier's uniform. He twinkles his slice-of-lime eyes with that icy glare only effeminate men can produce.

"Mr. Brown?" His lips crack open.

"This is the East LA Thirteen that your men arrested," I say to Yorty.

"Whatcha say there, Mayor," Gilbert calls out.

Henry giggles. He has taken reds and now is slumped in a chair, eyes and feet twisted. *Anda pingo.*

"Howdy, Sam," Mangas calls out.

"Howdy fellers," Sam says.

Doctor Bravo looks like a bowling ball. He speaks in a low voice, a man of authority, the only Chicano millionaire in the state: "Now, Mayor, I invited Mr. Brown and his clients . . . heh, I actually thought only a couple were coming, but you don't mind, do you, Mayor?"

"No, no, Francisco, this's just fine. . . . Like I've told you over the years . . . uh, some of you fellers might not know it, but Doctor Bravo here has been in this game a long time. . . . He was fighting for Mexicans a long time before some of you were probably born. . . ."

"He's a sellout," Gilbert calls out from the rear. Everyone pretends they didn't hear him.

"And like I was saying, I've asked Doctor Bravo to bring you fellows here . . . I'd like to see what I can do."

"About what?" I ask.

"About the problems that you people are interested in."

"Will you ask Evelle Younger to dismiss the conspiracy charges?"

"Now, Mr. Brown, you're a lawyer, you understand I can't do that."

"Why not?"

"Why, Mr. Brown, come on. You know that I've got absolutely no authority for doing something like that. Why, Evelle's in a different administrative department than me. . . ."

"Tell the pigs to quit vamping on us," Henry says.

"Now, Mr. Mayor, I won't stand for this," Reddin says.

"Now, Tom, fellows, let's try to be civil."

"OK, Yorty, what is it? What do you want to talk to us about?"

"Like I said, can't we try to get together and see what we can do? I'm willing to do it if you fellows are."

"What specifically do you have in mind?"

"Well . . . I just don't see what you fellows keep on holding so many demonstrations for. I know you got the right to do it. . . ."

"If they're peaceful, Mayor," Reddin says.

"It's the pigs that start the trouble," Gilbert says.

"Mayor?" Reddin says. He pushes at his brass buttons.

"Now, Tom . . . What I want to know is . . . what do you think it's going to get you if you keep marching around the police stations, the school boards . . . you know?"

"That's our business, Mayor. . . . Now do you have something specific? Or are we here just to size one another up?"

"Come on, Brown, come on! . . . I'm trying to tell you . . . I'm telling you, that picketing thing is over. . . . All you're doing is getting your own people in trouble. Now look . . ." he leans over toward me and lowers his voice, "the blacks picketed for years . . . for years. They marched and they did the very things you people are doing now . . . but you know something, and this is the honest-to-God truth . . . they didn't get a thing until they had Watts! That is a fact! And I'm telling you, until your people riot, they're probably not going to get a thing either! That's my opinion."

I stare directly into the wrinkled narrow green eyes of Sam-the-Straightshooter, a short John Wayne with a sincere simple honest smile. He is not blinking. He is telling me the *truth*.

But I do not know *why* he is telling me the truth.

"And that's what you wanted me to come over here for?" I can't believe it.

"That's about it, Brown. Just so we can know where we both stand."

"Let's go, you guys. I've had enough of this shit."

Everybody stands up. Reddin is seven feet tall, a hulking giant fag with slime eyes. He looks like he'd like to bite my nose off.

We are walking out the door. Yorty, Reddin and the two guards are watching us leave with their mouths open. We have no manners. We are absolutely without class.

Passing a table, I see a vase with small flags of many nations. Black Eagle is at my side. We both see it at the same time.

"Should we, *ese*?" he says.

I pluck it out of the vase. I hand the ten-inch flag of *La República Mexicana* to Black Eagle.

"He shouldn't have this thing in here."

"Fuck no, man. Viva La Raza!" Black Eagle shouts as we pass beyond the immobile guards.

"*¡Qúe Viva!*" the others shout back.

We are walking down the hall, past the secretary, past the guards at the entrance. Black Eagle is leading us with the Mexican Flag held up over his head and we keep shouting "Viva La Raza!" over and over as we march out of City Hall while suited lawyers and busy people are suddenly confronted with this Hollywood madness.

"CHICANO POWER!"

Such incidents didn't win us anything you could point at, but at least we had some fun and kept our spirits alive. So when, in the late fall, the Chicano Law Students asked me to help them take on the Holy Roman Catholic Church, I joined in with my customary abandon and went right for the throat. . . .

Six law students and I walk into the holy mahogany office of The Reverend Monsignor Hawkes. He is perched like a gargoyle at his huge desk. Two younger priests stand officiously at either side. The office is lined with books. He is also a lawyer, an ecclesiastical lawyer.

What do you want?

We'd like to talk to Cardinal McIntyre.

The six students stand behind me. They are only second-year law students, at Loyola on scholarships. The Catholic Church and The US Government is paying the tab and so they tremble slightly. It's all right for me, they say. I'm already a lawyer. If we blow it, nothing will happen to me. But for them? Who knows? Maybe the Monsignor will have them expelled.

"Sorry, but the Cardinal is busy," the gargoyle with the whiskey face says. He expects us to leave immediately. He looks at his two black pillars. They too have red hands. All three look as if they whack it at least twice a day.

"Well, I'd like to make an appointment."

He looks up from his papers. Leaning back into the posh chair, he clears his throat and lights up a pipe. He uses two matches before he speaks.

"Your name is, uh, Mr. Buffalo?"

"No, sir. It's Mr. Buffalo Z. Brown."

"Ah, yes. But, of course. You're, uh, the attorney, right?"

"Among other things . . . I'm also a Roman Catholic."

"Yes, uh, well . . . what can I do for you?"

Once again I run it down for him.

"But what do you want to talk to him about?"

I turn to Tony, the secretary of the CMs. He says in his broken Chicano accent, "We want to see about more scholarships. . . . There's a lot of dudes who ain't got the bread to make it into law school and we . . ."

"And who are you, sir?"

"He's a student at Loyola," I intervene.

"Can I have your names, please?"

We give him our names. He'll notify us by mail when the Cardinal will have time to talk with us.

The two bodyguards escort us out the door into the long corridor. We thank them and head toward the exit. Suddenly I stop. I see a sign over a door: Office of The Cardinal.

"Hey, you guys really want to talk to the Cardinal?" I say to them.

Seconds later, we're right in the Cardinal's main office. A woman under a blue wig is trying desperately to get us out. We've told her that we're not leaving until we see the holy man. She is making frantic phone calls. When suddenly, out of an imposing door, the man himself appears. He is a regular mummy. He could be the original *vato loco* with his red beanie. He has jowls and robes of red, a hard beak and a trembling voice.

"Yes, what do you want?"

I rush up to him. "Uh, Cardinal, we've come to speak to you about some problems."

He stares me straight in the face. He glares at me. I assume someone has told him who I am. He sticks a trembling hand out to me. The ancient palm is down, pointing to the ground. He waits for me to kiss the big blue ring on his bony middle finger. Either finger or ring was blessed by the Pope.

Instead, I take his hand and shake it. He explodes:

"Sir! . . . Perhaps you've never been taught manners! . . . But let me say this! I know who you people are! I have kept up with your shenanigans in the paper. . . . And let me say this! I shall never meet with the forces of evil. . . . We *know* who is behind you. And we can take care of you, remember that!"

He turns and waddles right back into his office. The blue wig opens another door and five beefy cops walk in. They carry clubs.

"All right, all of you, clear out. Now."

So three weeks later, on December 24, 1969, some three hundred Cockroaches gathered at the newest monstrosity in the archdiocese to protest corruption within the Church and to seek reparation for the conquest of our lands. And in two years now, I still had not written one single word for myself.

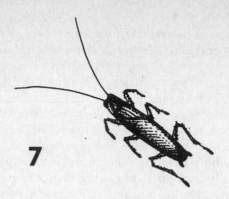

**7**

Christmas Day, seven hours after the arrest of the St. Basil
Twenty-One, we returned, this time without picket signs
or candles. I am still numb, grim from my conversation
with Stonewall. While the Faithful inside pray and count
their beads, we march silently in front of the church and
demand the release of our prisoners.

The media turn out in full force. Chicanos have not
fought inside a temple since the Spanish conquistadores
invaded the shrines of Huitzilopochtli in the Valley of Mexico. We make headlines without the assistance of Stonewall and his liberal white connections. McIntyre heaps
it on us. We are the rabble at the foot of the cross, calling
for the death of Christ. We are agents of the devil and communists to boot.

"Actually, we're Jewish underground," I say with a
straight face. The man taping the conversation has told me
he is from the biggest newspaper in Tel Aviv. He doesn't
smile.

A team with cameras tells us they are making a film on
America. They are from Berlin and want me to explain the
purpose of our demonstration. I tell them that the Church
and government have combined to exterminate us. "We
are the Jews of Nazi America," I tell the people of Berlin.

A reporter from *Life* wants to know if any of our members are affiliated with radicals. How do I answer the charges
of the Cardinal and the Chief of Police?

"Well . . . yes, I belong to some violent organizations,"
I say.

"Is this for publication?"

"You can tell the whole world, mister."

"Well . . . ?"

"I'm an American citizen . . . Nixon is my leader."

But my flippant answers don't satisfy the probing of the media. Unable to understand the obvious, they keep coming around for more. I stand under the glare of hot white lights and repeat myself to the citizens of Los Angeles and Beirut, to the people in Akron and New Jersey, even to the blokes in England.

My secretary, Rosemary, has the shakes when I come in the day after Christmas. The first hour of work she received three telephone calls, all from Chicanos. The anonymous callers threatened to bomb my office. They told her to tell me if I didn't stop saying such horrible things about their religion, we wouldn't have any place to work. I tell her not to worry. She looks at me and begins to cry.

"I'm not worried about *them*," she says. One of the calls was from her brother in Albuquerque. Chicanos in New Mexico take their Catholicism very seriously.

I tell her to take a week off but she just shakes her head and says she'll wait it out.

Two weeks of bad vibes. Meetings with groups within the community of East Los Angeles, meetings to explain why we had chosen to move against the Church. "The Church," the Cockroaches of old say to us, "is the only institution we can turn to for help. It is our religion, don't you understand? We are a very religious people."

I try to explain: "But we aren't against religion, we're not attacking religion," I tell them. "It's the power of the church, the administration of funds. We want the Church to become more democratic. We want them to become more involved in social-action programs. The people make up the Church. They should be the ones who control it."

But they won't have it. All but the most fanatic amongst us separate themselves from the struggle against the Church. There is talk of violence and of political expulsion from the community where I'd worked for some two years as the militant spokeman, lawyer and playboy.

79

We have to find some way to counter the bad publicity. We make headlines for two weeks, looking worse each day. Newsmen pry deeper and deeper into our organizations, endangering the precarious financial base. Many of us work for programs dependent upon the government or some charitable organization for support. The Militants earn most of their coins from the Poverty Program. They are "community organizers." My own office, Chicano Legal Defense, is funded by the Ford Foundation.

I begin to receive inquiries from men in New York who claim to be members of my board of directors. They want to know what I am up to. How can they explain my actions when the question of refunding comes up next month? They ask for a work schedule of my cases. How many suits have I filed in the past six months? Why am I spending so much time defending criminal defendants in political cases? Don't I know that Congress is about to put a stop to the political activities of various Legal Aid attorneys? Don't I know that certain congressmen mean to withdraw the tax-exempt status of charitable organizations who fund groups constantly involved in radical politics?

So to hell with the plush offices. To hell with the fat checks, the IBMs, the Xerox machines, the filing cabinets, the secretaries and the free telephones.

I quit my job and walk out of the Belmont lugging my files, my posters and my souvenirs to the basement of Father Light's Episcopal Church. I set up shop alongside the Chicano Militants and La Voz. My volunteer law students come with me.

"What are we going to do?" one of the law students asks.

We sit around a work bench twiddling our thumbs. Ruth is pouring us coffee and Gilbert is painting a banner with a figure of Christ dressed like a greaser.

"We've got to do something fast to get back with the people," Risco says.

"Why don't we have a fast?" I jest.

"Cesar's tried that one already," Risco laughs.

"So what?" Gilbert says. "Jesus did it before he did."

"You mean a real one, without eating?" says Pelon. He has on his usual white T shirt and blue beanie.

"And no Thunderbird, either," I say.

"Are you guys serious?" Ruth asks.

"Why not?" Risco says.

And so it blossoms into a full-fledged escapade. The Chicano Militant Catholics, as we come to be called by the press, send out invitations to all the organizations in East LA. Three days later we are back once again at St. Basil's. We tell the world we will engage in a three-day fast outside the church to show our commitment to non-violence. Everyone laughs in our faces.

So now I am sitting cross-legged on my Indian blanket in the parking lot of a Jewish temple. Black and white pebbles stick into my ass through the blanket. Chicanos are still arriving, straggling into the chained-up lot three and four at a time. An hour ago, Black Eagle, Mangas and I were the first to appear. We looked helplessly around the dirt lot next to the church. This construction site was our chosen battlefield, which we scouted and planned on. But now it has been leveled. Stacks of lumber that would have shielded us from the wind are gone. Gone is the scrap wood to fuel our night fires. I know Sergeant Armas has his eye on us from his command post on the sixth floor of the FEDCO Building.

A hundred of us show up. Wind whips sand into our faces. We stand around, feeling dumb. The bastards outfoxed us again! As usual, our planning, our "conspiring," was done in open meeting. We forget about the infiltration of our group by Armas' boys. Now look where it gets us.

"Let's go over and camp across the street at the Jewish Temple," I suggest.

"I guess you weren't kidding about being Jewish underground."

It is the same skinny blonde Israeli who interviewed me on Christmas Day. We are heading toward the parking lot of the Temple.

"I'm sorry, I can't talk. I'm not giving out interviews today."

"Why not?"

"We're on a fast. . . . I'm just tired of talking. Sorry."

I step it up as we pass St. Basil's. The bright sun cuts through the waves of stained glass in sheets of red and purple and blue light. The building, for one moment . . . is it, in fact, beautiful? Is it a work of art? Are we on the right target?

"Are you trying to set an example of some kind?" The brash kid is on my back again.

I nod my head and stare straight ahead. Up ahead, the orange oval soft plaster Temple is surrounded by green plants, elegant palm trees with white trunks. It appears to be an old-folks' home.

"Didn't you people do this once before? Aren't you connected with Cesar Chavez' Farmworkers?"

Black Eagle takes the reporter's arm and leads him away. He reports that I have decided not to give any more interviews during the three-day fast. We aren't going to eat for three days. So I decided not to talk for those days, either. Moreover, I am not a *lawyer* during the fast, I had told them. If anybody gets arrested, so do I. I am tired of answering or not answering the same questions. I am tired of being a legal spokesman, a leader who is always exempt from danger. And as I sit and ponder this decision, I wonder how Cesar Chavez felt when his stomach started growling on the first day of *his* fast.

The media come, take their pictures and then leave us on our own. A man in a brown suit comes along and asks us what we're doing. He holds some position in the Temple. We explain our situation.

"But what have you got against the Jewish People?"

"Nothing. . . . We need your help."

"But you can understand our position, can't you?"

"Are you refusing us *sanctuary*?"

"We don't want to get involved in a political dispute," he says.

"But this is a religious dispute," we say. He disappears

into the Old-Folks' Home.

We lounge around smoking cigarettes, laughing and waving at the passing tourists. Someone has brought a twenty-five-foot banner announcing our fast. Lupe Saavedra, the hard-faced militant poet of Aztlan, joined with Gilbert and Pelon to make long posters of Chicano art, revolutionary slogans to hoist to the wind for the passing cars.

The man in the brown suit turns out to be the local rabbi. He is on our side, he confides in us. But not all of the congregation, he says, is as liberal as he is.

"But *they* should understand about religious persecution," we tell him.

"I'll see what I can do," he says and leaves us again in the lot.

Half an hour later he returns for the second time. He asks to speak to the leader: "Who is Mr. Brown?"

Mangas point to me. Gilbert laughs. I am still sitting cross-legged on my blanket. Earlier a young girl brought me a twelve-inch God's Eye, a cross webbed with strands of colored wool. She and two friends set the cross in front of me, stood back and said, "Now you look like a *real* guru."

"Uh, Mr. Brown?"

I stare straight into the God's Eye. I nod my head. I have been in a sort of trance for two hours.

"Mr. Brown isn't talking," Gilbert says.

"What? Well, who's the leader?"

"We are all leaders," I say.

"Well ... What I want to say to you ... all of you ... I've spoken with my Elders. . . . And you are all perfectly welcome to stay here for your fast. But could you please move over to the lawn next to the wall? We'll need this parking space for tonight's services."

"Chicano Power!" Black Eagle shouts.

"Viva La Raza!" the group echos.

We get up, move out of the rock garden and onto the soft green lawn. A brick wall now serves as our shelter from the bitter Santa Ana winds.

David Hippie brings out his guitar. He is called "Hippie" because he cannot speak his mother tongue. I was in that position a few years ago. Seven fine broads are at his side. They sing songs of the Mexican Revolution which they learned from their grandmothers. A kid with long hair and a headband plays a harmonica. Saavedra is passing out mimeographed sheets with the words to the revolutionary songs and *corridos*. Gilbert stands in his faded wrinkled khakis and recites his Aztec poetry to another group. "Flowers to the kings of Mexico!" the black frog yells.

Beds are being made. Blankets are being stretched along the brick wall. We are digging in while the sun is still high and the cars and buses of white people pass and stare at us. We push away debris. We clean up the fifty yards of lawn alongside the sidewalks. This will be our retreat for the next three days. And already my stomach is hurting.

Three hours of songs. Three long hours of words and cigarettes. We have no coffee, no food, nothing but cigarettes. The rabbi brings us a five-gallon drum of water. We can have refreshments if we want, he says. Thanks. We can use the toilets inside the Temple if we want. Thanks. "Good luck," he says.

Two blocks away stands the FEDCO building. We can see Armas' men peering at us from the sixth floor. Police cars prowl the area. The Black and White are out on the streets. But they have agreed to keep a "low profile." They are simply not visible. But we know they are there, looking down on us, waiting for something to go wrong. Or waiting for night so they can move in and clear the area of vagrants and litterbugs and disturbers of the peace. But we are together. And, when the sun sets, we lean against each other, wrap ourselves in blankets and sing songs of love and war and peace.

"Hey, Buffalo. . . . Do you have any more blankets?"

I look up and try to make out features. It's night. The street lights show the outlines of a young pretty girl, the one who brought me the God's Eye. I had fallen asleep. I sit up and see two more teeny-boppers. Our group is quiet now. Only low voices here and there and the guitar strumming softly.

"No . . . but you can have this one," I say.

The girls giggle. They have on bellbottoms and light sweaters. It is incredibly cold out.

"Come on. We can share it."

They sit down next to me and I pull the blanket over their legs. We lean against the wall and chat.

The tall dark-haired one is Rosalie. Veronica is the shortest, sixteen years old with red hair and a soft chest. Madeline has hornrimmed glasses and a cute little ass. They are cousins. They all chew gum and talk fast without missing a beat.

"Wait till we tell John about this," Rosalie says. And all three laugh loudly and hit one another.

"Are you really stoned?" Veronica asks.

"What do you mean?"

They look at each other. Did they say the wrong thing?

"What is it?" I say.

Rosalie finally says, "Isn't that why you've been . . . just sitting?"

"You look spaced out," Madeline says.

"Hell, no . . . I've been . . . I'm fasting."

They giggle and slap me on the back.

"Come on, Buff . . . We know. Gilbert told us."

"What the hell you guys talking about?"

"You big phony. . . . You get *loaded,* don't you?"

"Yeah, sure . . . But not now."

"Why not? I thought we were just supposed to be fasting," Veronica says.

"Yeah! The *others* are smoking," Rosalie points out.

And then it hits me. *Jesus H. Christ!* I've been sitting and staring blindly into space for nearly a whole day. While people have been singing and laughing and enjoying the spectacle of it all, I've just been playing the part of some middle-aged phony-ass mystic. Who in the shit ever said that revolution has to be a drag? Why can't one be serious and have fun at the same time? Who said you have to suffer and be depressed? For two weeks now, since my talk with Stonewall, I've been grim as death, guilty. Fuck it!

"Do you guys have any dope?"

After an embarrassed giggle they bring it out. Two joints left, they whisper to me. They suggest we smoke it. Where? Right here. Everyone else is doing it. What? Are you guys crazy? There's cops right across the street.

"We'll just swallow it if we see them coming," Rosalie says.

Goddamn! Here I am, sitting on a blanket on Wilshire Boulevard, surrounded by danger and bright starlight, and three teeny-boppers want to share a joint with me under a blanket!

"Why not!"

"The Buff is a *winner*, I told you!" Rosalie says.

Soon we are under the blanket. It covers us like a tent. We take quick short puffs and swallow the forbidden smoke. We laugh and giggle and we forget about the revolution raging on outside the pup tent. We are in a dark closed world of our own.

They have grown up together as sisters. Their parents are divorced or separated or scattered, so they were living together with a grandmother in San Jose when they heard about the Christmas Eve massacre. They saw me on TV and decided to come down and join the revolution. Isn't that how the women did it when Zapata and Villa took to the hills? Isn't that what young girls are supposed to do?

Son of a bitch! Look at this! I am in a pup tent with three gorgeous broads. Three tender Chicano babes. I, who have never been with even one without payment.

For two years now I've sniffed around the courthouse, I've stood around *La Voz* waiting for one of these sun children to come down on me, to open up to my huge arms and big teeth. And yet I've not scored once. How many times have my pants been hard? How many times have I gone to bed wet? Alone? How many times have I shouted "Viva La Raza!" waiting for a score? And how many times have I desired to taste of that same warmth that is Lady Feathers, my mother, my sisters, my aunts and my cousins? And now, thanks to the Pope, thanks to the media and thanks to the revolution, at last I have a brown babe for my hurts. *Three* of them under the same blanket!

I caress a leg and it holds still, waiting for my hand. It is firm and soft and warm. I reach for a soft arm. It comes into mine easily. There is no hesitation. And then a moist lip to my ear. Zingo! I laugh.

"You're too much, Buff," one of them says.

"Scoot over," another orders.

Jesus, but this can't be. This can't be happening. I reach for a breast. It is small. Wonderfully small and firm. It fits into my palm. A brown pear in my hand. God Almighty! *This* is the revolution!

"Shall I light up the other one?" Rosalie says.

"Not now, stupid!" Madeline shouts.

Veronica is huddled on my right shoulder. She sticks her nose in my neck and the goosebumps come out.

"Hey, you guys . . . Jesus, what are you *doing?*"

They giggle and snuggle and squeeze my arms. I push the blanket away and bolt upright.

"How's it going, *ese?*" Gilbert says.

He and Black Eagle are standing over us, laughing in the starlight.

"Are you out of mourning, Brown Buffalo?" Black Eagle asks.

"What?"

Everyone around me is in stiches. They have been watching us move under the blanket. David Hippie strikes a chord.

"Don't say I never turned you on to a connection, *ese!*" Gilbert roars.

"You guys mind your own business," I say.

"You going to keep all of them?" Black Eagle asks, hungry.

I look at the three teeny-boppers. They are chewing gum. Their eyes are at half-mast. They lean into me.

"Why not?" Veronica says.

And with that we return to our fasting. We hoist the blanket and I take turns at them. I will touch one and kiss another. I will rub a soft face and suck a hard breast. While one tickles my side, another will stick her tongue into my left ear and the other one will be under my arm. Three cousins and a big uncle all tangled in the sack together. But the blanket is not big enough to undress. We cannot fuck. Not now. Later, after the battle. But for that night, while the winds rage outside our tent and the cars honk their horns and people yell insults to our demonstration, for that night I am filled with the youth of three *cholas* who want me to take care of them all. Can they stay with me after the fast? Are they welcome at my house?

"Can you guys cook?"

"Sure. I can make hot dogs and stuff like that."

"Will you keep the house clean?"

"Rosalie knows how to clean house," Madeline says.

"That's good enough," I say. "Now let's smoke that last joint and get back to it."

The night is long and the bodies are warm. I am filled with a strange longing for peace and quiet. I think of my long-lost plans for Acapulco, the few months in LA grown to a few years.

We camp out for three days without incident. By the time it is over, the papers have told the world about the non-violence of the Chicano Militants. They omit my antics under the big top, thank God.

On Sunday morning we march into the service at St. Basil's. We hear a stupid sermon and receive Holy Communion without confessing our sins to anyone but ourselves. The priest says nothing to us as we march out, hair in our faces, grass in our teeth, all dirty and gummed up from three days on the street.

I am now living in a small apartment on Sixth Street, not too far from Cronie's and Garfield High. I take the girls home with me and force them to call their grandmother. They tell her that an attorney has employed them and not to worry. She agrees to let them remain in Los Angeles.

"Do whatever he tell you," the grandmother advises. They assure her they will. *Ayyeeee!!!*

That week Pope Paul fires Cardinal McIntyre.

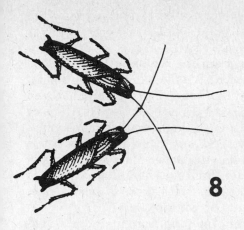
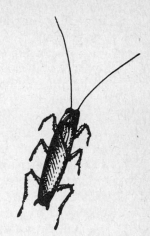

# 8

The week after McIntyre got the ax, I first encountered death as a world of art.

It is early one morning when the family of Robert Fernandez arrives. The sign outside the basement office only announces *La Voz*, but these strangers come in asking for me. Via the grapevine, they have heard of a lawyer who might help them. Nobody else is around. It is just them and me:

"We gotta have someone to help us, Mr. Brown. The deputies killed my brother."

A hefty woman with solid arms and thick mascara burnt into her skin is talking. She says her name is Lupe. She is the spokesman, the eldest child in a family of nine. The woman beside her is the mother, Juana, an old nurse. Juana is still in shock, sitting quietly, staring at Gilbert's paintings hung on the wall. John, Lupe's husband, sits on her other side. His arms are crossed, bright tattoos over corded muscle. He wears a white T shirt and a blue beanie, the traditional garb of the *vato loco*, the Chicano street freak who lives on a steady diet of pills, dope and wine. He does not move behind his thick mustache. He too sits quietly, as a proper brother-in-law, a *cuñado* who does not interfere in family business unless asked.

"Why do you say they killed your brother?" I ask.

"*¡Porque son marranos!*" Juana cries out and then falls

back into silence. Aztec designs in black and red meet her glazed eyes.

I ask for the whole story. . . .

Robert was seventeen when the weight of his hundred and eighty pounds snapped the bones and nerves of his fat brown neck. He, too, lived in Tooner Flats, a neighborhood of shacks and clotheslines and dirty back yards. At every other corner, street lights hang high on telephone poles and cast dim yellow glows. Skinny dogs and wormy cats sniff garbage cans in the alleys. Tooner Flats is the area of gangs who spend their last dime on short dogs of T-Bird wine, where the average kid has eight years of school. Everybody there gets some kind of welfare.

You learn about life from the toughest guy in the neighborhood. You smoke your first joint in an alley at the age of ten; you take your first hit of *carga* before you get laid; and you learn how to make your mark on the wall before you learn how to write. Your friends know you to be a *vato loco*, a crazy guy, and they call you "ese," or "vato," or "man." And when you prove you can take it, that you don't cop to nothing even if it means getting your ass whipped by some other gang or the cops, then you are allowed to put your mark, your initial, your sign, your badge, your *placa* on your turf with the name or initial of your gang: White Fence, Quatro Flats, Barrio Nuevo, The Jokers, The Bachelors, or what have you. You write it big and fancy, scroll-like, *cholo* print. Grafitti on all the stores, all the garages, everywhere that you control or claim. It's like the pissing of a dog on a post. And underneath your *placa*, you always put C/S, "Con Safos," that is: *Up yours if you don't like it, ese!*

There is no school for a *vato loco*. There is no job in sight. His only hope is for a quick score. Reds and Ripple mixed with a bennie, a white and a toke. And when your head is tight, you go down to the hangout and wait for the next score.

On the day he died, Robert had popped reds with wine and then conked out for a few hours. When he awoke he was ready for more. But first he went down to Cronie's on

*The Revolt of the Cockroach People*

Whittier Boulevard, the Chicano Sunset Strip. Every other door is a bar, a pawn shop or a liquor store. Hustlers roam freely across asphalt decorated with vomit and dogshit. If you score in East Los Angeles you score on The Boulevard. Broads, booze and dope. Cops on every corner make no difference. The fuzz, *la placa, la chota, los marranos, la jura* or just the plain old pig. The eternal enemies of the people. The East LA Sheriff's Substation is only three blocks away on Third Street, right alongside the Pomona Freeway. From the blockhouse, deputies come out in teams of two, "To Serve And Protect!" Always with thirty-six-inch clubs, with walkie-talkies in hand; always with gray helmets, shotguns in the car and .357 Magnums in their holsters.

The *vato loco* has been fighting with the pig since the Anglos stole his land in the last century. He will continue to fight until he is exterminated.

Robert had *his* last fight in January of 1970. He met his sister, Lupe, at Cronie's. She was eating a hamburger. He was dry, he told her. Would she please go to the store across the street and get him a six-pack on credit? No, she'd pay for it. Tomorrow is his birthday so she will help him celebrate it early. Lupe left Robert with friends. They were drinking cokes and listening to the jukebox. Robert liked *mayate* music, the blues. They put in their dimes and sip on cokes, hoping some broad, a *ruka*, would come buy them a hamburger or share a joint with them.

I know Cronie's well. I live two blocks away with the three cousins. I know if you sit on the benches under the canopy long enough, *someone* comes along with *something* for the evening's action. This time the cops brought it.

By the time Lupe returned with a six-pack, two deputies were talking with Robert and his friends. It all began, he told her when she walked up, just because he shouted "Chicano Power!" and raised his fist.

"The cop told me to stay out of it, Mr. Brown. I told him Robert is my brother. But they told me to get away or else they'd arrest me for interfering, you know."

Juana says, "Tell him about the dirty greaser."

"Oh, yes. . . . We know this pig. He's a Chicano. Twice he's arrested Robert," Lupe says.

"Yes, Mr. Brown!" Juana could not restrain herself. "That same man once beat up my boy. He came in one day, about a year ago, and he just pushed into the room where Robert was sleeping. He dragged him out and they held him for three days. . . . They thought he had stolen a car. . . . But the judge threw the case out of court. That pig hated my boy."

Robert had been in jail many times. He'd spent some time at the Youth Authority Camp. But he'd been off smack over a year now. He still dropped a few reds now and then. And yes, he drank wine. But he was clean now. The cops took him in from Cronie's, they said, to check him out. They wanted to see if the marks on his arms were fresh. But anyone could tell they were old.

Lupe appeals to John:

"That's the truth, Brown," the brother-in-law says. "Robert had cleaned up. He even got a job. He was going to start working next week."

"And we were going to have a birthday party for him that Friday," Juana says.

The deputies took Robert and told Lupe not to bother arranging bail. They told her he'd be released within a couple of hours. They thought he might just be drunk, but mainly they wanted to check out his arms. They said for her not to worry.

An hour after he was arrested, Robert called his mother. The cops had changed their minds, he said. They had booked him for Plain Drunk, a misdemeanor. The bail was set at five hundred dollars.

"He told me to call up Maldonado, his bail bondsman. Robert always used him. I could get him out just like that. All I had to do was make a phone call and then go down and sign, you know? The office is just down the street. I didn't even have to put up the house or anything. Mr. Maldonado always just got him out on my word!" the mother cries.

*The Revolt of the Cockroach People*

Juana had called the bail bondsman before she received the second call. This time it was a cop. He simply wanted to tell her that Robert was dead. He'd just hung himself. And would she come down and identify the body.

"He was so cold, Mr. Brown. He didn't say he was sorry or anything like that. He just said for me to wait there and he'd send a deputy to pick me up," she says bitterly.

"I went with her," John says. "When we got there I told the man right away that they'd made some mistake. I told him Robert had just called.

"Then they brought in a picture. And I said, 'gracias a Dios,' I knew him. It wasn't Robert, it was somebody named Sanchez. But that lieutenant said there was no mistake. He said the picture just didn't come out too good. . . . But Juana told him, 'Well I should know, he's my son.' And I told him Robert wouldn't do a thing like that. He'd never kill himself. He was católico, Señor Café. He even used to be an altar boy one time. And he was going to get married, too. He was going to announce it at his party. I talked to Pattie and she told me. She said they were going to get married as soon as he got his first paycheck."

"Pattie is pregnant," Lupe says. "You might as well know, Mr. Brown."

"So what happened after that," I ask.

"We had the funeral and they buried him last week," Juana says.

Lupe says, "We just got the certificate last night. It says he killed himself. Suicide, it says."

"That's a goddamn lie," John says. "Excuse me. . . . But it is."

"How do you think he was killed?"

"I know," Lupe says. "At the funeral . . . you tell him, John."

"Yeah, I was there. I saw it."

Doris, another sister, had discovered it. At the funeral, while the others sat and cried, Doris had gone up to get her last look at the body. She bent over the casket to kiss him. Tears from her own eyes landed on the boy's face. She reached over to wipe the wetness from his cheek when she noticed purple spots on the nose. She wiped away the tears and the undertaker's white powder came off his face. It was purple underneath. She called John over and he verified it. They began to look more closely and noticed bruises on the knuckles.

"We told the doctor at the Coroner's Office," John finishes. "But he said not to worry about it. It was natural, he said."

"Anything else?"

"Just what Mr. de Silva told me," the mother says.

"Who's that?"

"Andy de Silva. . . . Don't you know him?"

"You mean . . . *the* Andy de Silva? The man who makes commercials? Chile Charlie?"

"Yeah, that's Mr. de Silva."

I know of him. He is a small-time politico in East LA. A bit actor in grade B movies who owns a bar on The Boulevard. And he considers himself something of a spokesman for the Chicano. He served on Mayor Yorty's Chicano Community Board as a rubber-stamp nigger for the establishment. He and his cronies, the small businessmen and a few hack judges, could always be counted upon to endorse whatever program the Anglo laid out for the Cockroaches. He had been quoted in all the papers during our uprising against the Church. He had agreed with the Cardinal that we were all outside agitators who should be driven out on a rail.

"What did Andy say to you?" I ask.

"Well, I don't even know him. I used to go to his meetings for the old people. Anyway, he called me the next day after Robert died. He said, 'I heard about your boy and I want to help.' That's how he started out. I was so happy to get someone to help I told him to do whatever he could. He said he was very angry and he would investigate the case. He said he would have a talk with the lieutenant and even with the captain if necessary.

"What happened?"

"He called me back the next day. He said he had checked it all out and that the captain had showed him everything, the files and even the cell. He said not to make any trouble. That Robert had hung himself."

"Did he say how he knew about it?"

"Yeah. I asked him that, too," John says.

"He said his nephew was the guy in the cell with Robert."

"His nephew?"

"Yeah, Mickey de Silva . . . He's just a kid like Robert. He was in there for something. . . . Anyway, Andy said his nephew told him that Robert killed himself."

"But we don't believe it," Lupe says fiercely.

"Can you help us, Señor Brown?"

I pick up the phone and dial the office of Thomas Naguchi, the Coroner for the City and County of Los Angeles.

"This is Buffalo Z. Brown. I represent the family of Robert Fernandez," I tell Naguchi. "And we want to talk with you about the autopsy. . . . Your doctor listed it as suicide. However, we are convinced that the boy was murdered. We have information unavailable to the pathologist conducting the autopsy. I plan to be in your office this afternoon. I'm going to bring as many people as I can and hold a press conference right outside your door."

"Mr. Brown. Please, calm yourself. I can't interfere with the findings of my staff."

"I'll be there around one."

I hang up and tell the family to go home, call all their friends and relatives and have them meet me in the basement of the Hall of Justice. They thank me and leave. I then call the press and announce the demonstration and press conference for that afternoon. I know my man. And since Naguchi can read the newspapers, my man knows me. The afternoon will be pure ham.

Naguchi has been in the news quite a bit. He was charged with misconduct in office by members of his own staff. They accused him of erratic behavior and incompetence. They said he took pills, that he was strung out, and hinted that perhaps he was a bit nuts. After the assassination of Robert Kennedy he allegedly said he was glad Ken-

nedy was killed in his jurisdiction. He was a publicity hound, they contended. He was removed from his position of County Coroner. He hired a smart lawyer and challenged it. The Civil Service hearings were televised. The white liberals and his own Japanese friends came to his defense. He was completely exonerated. At least he got his job back.

A month prior to the death of Fernandez, both the new City Chief of Police, Judd Davis and the Sheriff of LA County, Peter Peaches, announced they would no longer request Coroner's Inquests. The publicity served no useful purpose, the lawmen stated. Since the only time the Coroner held an inquest was when a law enforcement officer was 'involved in the death of a minority person, they contended that the inquest merely served to inflame the community. Naguchi made no comment at the time of this statement, although his two main clients were emasculating his office.

When we arrive at the Hall of Justice, the press is waiting. The corridor is lined with Fernandez' friends and relatives. The television cameras turn on their hot lights as I walk in with my red, white and green briefcase, the immediate family at my side.

"Are you making any accusations, Mr. Brown?" a CBS man asks.

"Not now, gentlemen. I plan to have a conference with Dr. Naguchi first. Then I'll speak to you."

I hurried into the Coroner's Office. The people shout "Viva Brown!" as I close the door. The blonde secretary tells me Naguchi is waiting for me. She opens the door to his office and ushers me in.

"Ah, Mr. Brown, I am so happy to make your acquaintance."

He is a skinny Jap with bug eyes. He wears a yellow sport coat and a red tie and sits at a huge mahogany desk with a green dragon paperweight. The office has black leather couches and soft chairs, a thick shag rug and inscrutable art work. It seems a nice quiet place. He points me to a fine chair.

"Now, Mr. Brown, I'd like you to read this." He hands me a typed sheet of white paper.

I smile and read the paper:

*The Corner's Office announced today that it will hold a second autopsy and an inquest into the death of Robert Fernandez at the request of the family through their attorney, Mr. Buffalo Z. Brown. It will be the first time in the history of the office that an inquest is being held at the request of the family.*

*Thomas A. Naguchi*
*County Coroner*

I looked into the beady eyes of Mr. Moto. He is everything his men say. "I've been wanting to meet you, sir," I say.

"And I've heard about you, Mr. Brown. You get a lot of coverage in your work."

"I guess the press is interested in my cases."

"Would you be agreeable to holding a joint press conference?"

"Sir, I would be honored. . . . But one thing . . . If we have another autopsy, the body will have to be, uh. . . ." I am coy.

"Exhumed . . . We will take care of that, don't you worry."

"And who will perform the autopsy?"

"I assume the family will want their own pathologist."

I looked down at his spit-shined loafers. I shake my head and sigh. "I just don't know. . . . The family is extremely poor."

"I understand, sir. I offer my staff, sir."

"Dr. Naguchi . . . would it be too much to ask you, *personally*, to examine the boy's body? I know you are very busy. . . ." It is my trump card.

"I would be honored. But to avoid any . . . problems, why don't I call up the Board of Pathologists for the county. I will request a panel. Yes, a panel of seven expert pathologists. It will be as careful and as detailed an autopsy as we had for Senator Kennedy. And it won't cost the family anything . . . I have that power."

I stand up and, walking over to him, I shake his hand.

"Dr. Naguchi, I'll be glad to let you do all the talking to the press."

"Oh no, Mr. Brown, it is your press conference."

He calls his secretary and tells her to bring in the boys. When they arrive with their pads and cameras, he greets them all by their first names. He is better than Cecil B. DeMille. His secretary has passed out copies of his statement. He tells them all where to sit and knows how many lumps of sugar they want in their coffee. Then he introduces me to them and stands by while I speak.

"Gentlemen, I'll make it short. . . . We have reason to believe that Robert Fernandez died at the hands of another. The autopsy was inconclusive and we have since found some new evidence that was not available to Dr. Naguchi's staff. . . . The Doctor has graciously consented to exhume the body and hold a full inquest before a jury. On behalf of the family and those of us in East LA who are interested in justice, I would like to thank Dr. Naguchi."

After the press leaves, I reassure the family and all the arrangements are nailed down.

The following Tuesday, I again enter the Hall of Justice. Above me are Sirhan Sirhan, the mysterious Arab who shot Kennedy, and Charles Manson, the acid fascist. Both await their doom. I am told to go straight down the corridor, turn right and the first door to my left is where I'll find Dr. Naguchi and his seven expert pathologists. The light is dim, the hard floors waxed. Another government building with gray walls, the smell of alcohol in night air.

I open a swinging yellow door and immediately find myself inside a large dark room full of hospital carts. Naked bodies are stretched out on them. Bodies of red and purple meat; bodies of men with white skin gone yellow; bodies of black men with blood over torn faces. This one has an arm missing. The stub is tied off with plastic string. The red-headed woman with full breasts? Someone has ripped the right ear from her head. The genitals of that spade are packed with towels. Look at it! Listen! The blood is still gurgling. There, an old wino, his legs crushed, mangled, gone to mere meat. And there, young boys die too. And there, a once-beautiful chick, look at her. How many boys tried to get between those legs, now dangling pools of red-black blood?

Don't turn away from it, goddamnit! Don't be afraid of bare-ass naked death. Hold your head up, open your eyes, don't be embarrassed, boy! I walk forward, I hold my breath. My head is buzzing, my neck is taut, my hands are wet and I cannot look away from the dead cunts, the frizzled balls, the lumps of tit, the fat asses of white meat.

I have turned the wrong way. Backtracking, I find the room with Dr. Naguchi and the experts.

The doctors wear white smocks. They smoke pipes. Relaxed men at their trade. They smile and shake my hand. In front of us, the casket is on a cart with small wheels. On a clean table we have scales and bottles of clear liquid. There are razor-sharp tools, tweezers, clips, scissors, hacksaws, needles and plenty of yellow gloves. The white florescent light shines down upon us. It reminds me of the title of my first book: *My Cart for My Casket.*

"Shall we begin, gentlemen?" Dr. Naguchi asks the experts.

The orderly, a giant sporting an immense mustache, takes a card and a plastic seal from the casket. He booms it out to a gray-haired fag with sweet eyes who sits in a corner and records on a shorthand machine.

"We shall now open the casket, Coroner's Number 19444889, Robert Fernandez, deceased."

We all gather close to get the first look.

The body is intact, dressed in fine linen. Clearly, Robert was a bull of a man. He had big arms and legs and a thick neck now gone purple. Two experts lift the body and roll it on the operating table. It holds a rosary in the hands. The orderly removes the rosary, the black suit, the white shirt, the underwear and brown shoes. The chest has been sewn together. Now the orderly unstitches it. Snip, snip,

snip. Holding open the rib cage, he carefully pulls out plastic packages from inside the chest cavity. I hold my breath.

"Intestines." The meat is weighed out.

"Heart . . . Liver . . ."

A Chinese expert is making notations of everything. So is the fruity stenographer.

There is no blood, no gory scene. All is cold and dry. Sand and sawdust spill to the table.

"Is this your first autopsy?" a doctor with a Sherlock Holmes pipe asks me. I nod.

"You're doing pretty good."

"He'll get used to it," another one says brightly.

When the organs are all weighed out, Dr. Naguchi says, "Now, gentlemen, where do you want to begin?"

Sherlock Holmes asks, "Are we looking for anything special?"

"Treat this as an ordinary autopsy, Dr. Rubenstein. Just the routine," says Naguchi.

"Circumstances of death?"

"Well, uh . . . Mr. Brown?"

"He was found with something around his neck."

"Photographs at the scene?"

"No, sir," a tall man from the Sheriff's Department says.

"Self-strangulation? . . . or . . ." Rubenstein lets it hang.

"That's the *issue*," I say. "The body was found in a jail cell. The Sheriff claims it was suicide. . . . We, however, believe otherwise."

"I see."

"We have reason to believe that the boy was murdered," I say.

"Nonsense," the man from the Sheriff's Department says.

"Now, gentlemen, please. . . ." Naguchi oils in.

Dr. Rubenstein is obviously the big cheese. He comes up to me and says, "You think there was a struggle before death?"

"It's very possible."

He ponders this and then announces: "Gentlemen, we will have to dissect wherever hematoma appears."

"What's that?" I ask.

"Bruises."

I look at the body closely. I noticed purple spots on the face, the arms, the hands, the chest, the neck and the legs. Everywhere. I point to the face. "Could *that* be a bruise?"

"There's no way to tell without microscopic observation," Rubenstein answers.

"You can't tell from the *color*?"

"No. . . . The body is going through decomposition and discoloration . . . purple spots . . . is normal. You find it on all dead bodies."

"Are you saying we have to cut out all those spots?"

"That's the only way to satisfy your . . . yes."

"Well, Mr. Brown?" says Naguchi. "Where do you want us to begin?"

I look around at the men in the room. Seven experts, Dr. Naguchi and a Chinese doctor from his staff, the orderly and the man from the Sheriff's . . . they want *me*, a Chicano lawyer, to tell them where to begin. They want *me* to direct them. It is too fantastic to take seriously.

"How about this? Can you look there?" I point to the left cheek.

Without a word, the Chinese doctor picks up a scalpel and slices off an inch of meat. . . . He picks it up with the tweezers and plunks it into a jar of clear liquid.

"And now, Mr. Brown?" says Naguchi.

I cannot believe what is happening. I lean over the body and look at the ears. Can they get a notch from the left one?

Slit-slit-slice blut! . . . into a jar.

"Uh, Dr. Rubenstein? . . . Are you *sure* there's no other way?"

He nods slowly. "Usually, we only try a couple of places . . . It depends on the family." He hesitates, then says, "Is the case that important?"

"Would you please take a sample from the knuckles . . . here?"

No trouble at all, my man. Siss-sizz-sem . . . blut, into another jar.

The orderly is precisely labeling each jar. Dr. Naguchi is walking around like a Hollywood mogul. He is smiling. Everything is going without a hitch. He touches my shoulder.

"Just tell us what you want, Mr. Brown. . . . We're at your service."

"Would you please try the legs? . . . Those big splotches on the left."

"How about the chin?"

"Here, on the left side of the face."

"What's this on the neck?"

"Try this little spot here."

"We're this far into it. . . . Get a piece from the stomach there."

Cut here. Slice there. Here. There. Cut, cut, cut! Slice, slice slice! And into a jar. Soon we have a whole row of jars with little pieces of meat.

Hrumph! Yes, men? Now we'll open up the head. See where it's stitched? They opened it at the first autopsy. See the sand fall out from the brain area? Yes, keeps the body together for a funeral. No blood in here, boy. Just sand. We don't want a mess. See that little package? That, my lad, is the brain. I mean, it was the brain. Well, actually, it *still* is the brain . . . it just isn't working right now.

Yes, yes! Now we pull back the head. Scalp-um this lad here. Whoops, the hair, the full head of hair, now it lays back, folded back like a halloween mask so we can look *into* the head . . . inside, where the stuffings for the . . . Jesus H. Christ, look at those little purple blotches. . . . You can tell a lot from that, but you got to cut it out . . . Then cut the fucking thing out, you motherfucker! This ain't Robert no more. It's just a . . . no, not a body . . . body is a whole . . . this is a joke . . . Cut that piece there, doctor. *Please!*

Uh oh! Now we get really serious. If he died of strangulation . . . We'll have to pull out the . . . uh, neck bone.

Go right ahead, *sir!* Pull out that goddamn gizzard.

Uh, we have to . . . take the face off first.

Well, Jesus Christ, go ahead!

Slit. One slice. Slit. Up goes the chin. Lift it right up

over the face . . . the face? The face goes up over the head. The head? The head is the face. Huh? *There is no face!*

What do you mean?

The face is hanging down the back of the head. The face is a mask. The mouth is where the brain . . . The nose is at the back of the neck. The hair is the ears. The brown nose is hanging where the neck. . . . Get your goddamn hand out of there.

My hand?

That is the doctor's hand. It is inside the fucking face. I mean the head.

His hand is inside. It is pulling at something. What did he find in there. What *is* it?

He's trying to pull out the . . . if we put it under a microscope, we'll be able to make some strong findings. It's up to you. . . .

Slice, slice, slice . . . No dice.

"Give me the saw, please."

Saw, saw, saw, saw, saw . . . No luck.

"Give me the chisel and hammer, please."

The goddamn face is gone; the head is wide open; no mouth, nose, eyes. They are hanging down the back of the neck. God! With hammer and chisel in hand, the Chinese doctor goes to town. Chomp, chomp, chomp . . . Hack, hack, chuck, chuck, chud, chomp!

Ah! Got it!

Out it comes. Long, gizzard-looking. Twelve inches of red muscle and nerve dripping sawdust. Yes, we'll dissect this old buzzard, too.

How about those ribs? You want some bar-b-que ribs, mister?

Sure, *ese.* Cut those fucking ribs up. Chomp 'em up right now!

"How about the arms? Is there any question of needle marks?"

Yes, they'll claim he was geezing. Cut that arm there. Put it under your machine and tell me later what I want to hear. Tell me they were *old* tracks, you sonofabitch . . . And try the other one.

Why not? The body is no more.

Should we try the dick?

What for? What can you find in a peter?

Maybe he was raped, for Christ's sake. Or maybe he raped someone. How should I know? I just work here.

I see the tattoo on his right arm . . . God Almighty! A red heart with blue arrows of love and the word "Mother." And I see the little black cross between the thumb and the trigger finger. A regular *vato loco*. A real *pachuco, ese*.

And when it is done, there is no more Robert. Oh, sure, they put the head back in place. They sew it up as best they can. But there is no part of the body that I have not ordered chopped. I, who am so good and deserving of love. Yes, me, the big *chingón!* I, Mr. Buffalo Z. Brown. Me, I ordered those white men to cut up the brown body of that Chicano boy, just another expendable Cockroach.

Forgive me, Robert, for the sake of the living brown. Forgive me and forgive me and forgive me. I am no worse off than you. For the rest of my born days, I will suffer the knowledge of your death and your second death and your ashes to my ashes, your dust to my dust . . . Goodbye, *ese*. Viva la Raza!

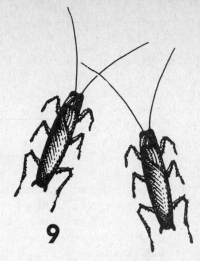

## 9

"I *can't* say for sure. I'm just not positive. If you ask me, I'll say that in my opinion, the physical evidence is *inconclusive.* We can't determine if death was caused by his own hand or the hand of another."

Dr. Rubenstein explains his findings to me. We are in his plush office in Beverly Hills. The wall behind his brown desk is papered with licenses from all the *best* schools. An *expert* investigative pathologist.

"How can you account for the break in the ribs?"

"Obviously something, or someone, or even his own hand. . . . How can you expect me to tell you who or what did it? We're trying to be *objective,* Mr. Brown. . . . But, of course, it seems more probable, from what you've told me, the other factors in the case . . . I would *vote* that the boy was murdered, if that's what you want me to say. But not as a scientist."

"The police report says they gave him heart massage, they tried to revive him after they cut him down."

"Exactly! . . . That's what I mean! . . . You know, Mr. Brown, you know that's what those bastards will argue . . . that the rupture was caused by the hand of the ambulance driver."

We go over all the alternative theories. But when I leave the doctor's office, I know that I will have to prove Robert's murder by testimony from the mouth of a direct witness.

A Coroner's Inquest is an official proceeding where a group of eight men and women vote to direct the Coroner as to what is the cause of death. But it is not an adversary proceeding. I cannot participate as a lawyer. There is no cross-examination. As the representative of the family, I can only *assist* the Coroner's Hearing Officer, Norman Pitluck, in his role of "referee." It is Pitluck, a man with thick glasses and a big nose, who calls the witnesses; he questions them; he instructs the jury. There can be no talking by counsel for the family or from the DA's representative, just from Pitluck. But he has invited us to bring anything to his attention that we feel is relevant. If I know of witnesses, I should give him their names. If I have a question, either before, during or after the hearing, I should write it out on a piece of paper and hand it to him. But I can say nothing to the jury. That is state law. Period.

I go with Gilbert to find de Silva, the movie actor. Chile Charlie has a big mustache, a big stomach and a big dog. When we walk up through the garden, a ferocious German shepherd leaps out at us and is ready to tear us to bits but is stopped by the appearance of his master. De Silva is a three-hundred-pound ex-*vato loco* who became famous by acting like a dumb greaser. His arms are as big as my legs.

We stroll together in the hills behind Tooner Flats. He was expecting me, he says. And he was ready to help.

"You just tell me what you want, Buff. That's what I'm here for."

"Listen, Andy, I appreciate it. . . ."

But I am at a loss where to begin. How do you tell a man that you suspect his nephew of murder and you want him to help you make the kid confess?

"I've been trying to get a hold of Mickey. . . . He's your *familia*, right?"

"Oh, sure. . . . Did you call him?"

I've been calling him all week, I explain. I left half a dozen messages, even talked to his mother. But still I have not spoken to him.

"I guess the kid's scared," de Silva says.

"You tell him that if I were him, I'd get myself a lawyer. He's in trouble no matter what. He was there."

"Oh, I don't think he has any problems . . . I already talked to the captain . . . They're not going after him. He's clean."

Gilbert says, "Yeah, ese, but we want the dude to help us. . . . If he's so clean, then how come he don't answer Brown's calls?"

De Silva looks only casually at the black frog. His only response, his only acknowledgment of Gilbert—a duplicate of de Silva thirty years ago—is a slight nod.

"Listen, Brown, don't you worry, I'll have that kid call you. I'll get him down to see you . . . Even if he done something."

"No, Andy. If he's involved, you better get him a lawyer."

"Listen, Brown. You don't know my familia. . . . You don't know how it was around here before. . . . We ain't like the new militants, man. If we do something, we say it right out. We aren't afraid to admit when we whip somebody. . . . And the kid's my nephew. . . . If he did it, you'll find out."

I thank him and pump his hand. We clasp the power shake.

"I don't know, ese," Gilbert says back in the car. "Those de Silvas are mean dudes." But I tell him he is too skeptical.

"What's that, ese?"

I thought about it. "Shit if I know . . . it's one of those gabacho words that have no meaning."

The hearing room is downtown, a courtroom in the old Hall of Records. The new Hall of Records stands right in front. The hallway is crowded with spectators. All the family and the Militants with their guerrilla outfits are out in full force. They stand along the edges of the crowd, heads hunched over, looking out the corner of their eyes. They are perpetually on guard, with dark glasses to cover their motives.

I walk in with Rosalie, Madeline and Veronica hanging onto my arms. (All the girls masquerade as my nieces in court.) They have fought over who would carry my briefcase. I told them to alternate. Then they fought over who would carry it the first day. Madeline insisted that she had the *legal* right: she was seventeen, the oldest of the three.

Veronica bases her argument on rights of prior possession: she has the briefcase in her hand.

"How about me? I'm the youngest," Rosalie says.

"Jesus, I've never asked! How old are you?"

"I'm San Quentin Quail, Mr. Winner," Rosalie says. She is also the tallest of the bunch. And after a week of jumping back and forth, I decided that she would be the one. Her long brown hair and the tender peach skin, the black eyelashes of a young girl, fresh breath always smelling like bubble gum. Those soft pears, those two fine lovely pears . . . Shit! She is fifteen years old. I am thirty-five.

I arrive early to talk with Mickey de Silva. His uncle promised to have him meet me prior to the hearing. We take the elevator to the eighth floor. Neither of them is there. I asked Gilbert to call me when proceedings begin. I descend to the lobby and talk with the Militants. Then Gilbert comes down with a message: Andy's wife told him she didn't know *where* Andy is or when he'd be back. There is still no answer at Mickey's house.

I enter the courtroom. We can see downtown LA through the windows. The smog and the hot sun fall upon the flat roofs of old buildings. Sounds of jackhammers, machines, trucks, buses, people, a busy place of work and movement.

In front of the spectator's gallery, three television cameras cast hot white lights at me as I walk through the swinging gates into the counsel area. I sit at a long empty table. Ralph Mayer, a short thin Jew from the District Attorney's Office, sits at an identical table to my left. In front of the judge's bench, the same fag from the autopsy revs up his shorthand machine. Four men and four women lounge in the jury box. Everyone waits for Norman Pitluck, the hearing officer.

*The Revolt of the Cockroach People*

Finally he appears wearing a plain brown suit. He hides behind glasses and he has nervous hands, always in motion, rubbing together, one finger playing against another. He briefly explains the nature of the proceeding to the jury and the press.

The first witness is the doctor who performed the initial autopsy, a heavy Italian without interest in the matter. He describes the body of Fernandez, the condition of the corpse and his examination.

"In my opinion, the deceased met his fate by strangulation. Death was caused by asphyxiation," the Italian says.

At that instant I hear the buzz of a rolling camera behind me. The white lights get brighter. KMEX, the Spanish language station, is televising it straight through. The other two—one is Channel 9, a local conservative station, the other is Channel 4, an NBC outlet—are selective. When something occurs that tickles their interest, cameras roll.

Pitluck is satisfied with the doctor's answer. He looks at Mayer and me. I wave my sheet of questions. He calls us to the bench and reads aloud both our lists, asking if either has any objections to the other's inquiries. None. Then he begins again on the witness.

"Now, Doctor, this is a question from Mr. Brown, the attorney for the family . . . On what facts do you predicate your opinion that death was caused by strangulation?"

"The injuries to the neck, the bruises on the skin and the ruptures inside."

"Could those injuries have been inflicted after death?"

"It's possible, but not probable."

"Why do you say that?"

"Well, the deputies found a belt and a piece of cloth around the boy's neck when they found the body. . . . It just doesn't make sense. . . ."

"Objection! This man is not qualified to testify to what others may have seen!" I shout, standing and pointing my finger.

"Mr. Brown. Please sit down. You may not speak in front of the jury. If you have an objection, come to the bench."

Both Mayer and I approach the bench. My objection is based on the rule of evidence which prohibits the words of one witness coming in through the mouth of another.

"But heresay evidence is allowable in a hearing, Mr. Brown. This isn't a criminal case, you know."

"We're here to get to the truth of this matter. . . . Hearsay testimony is unreliable. It's within your power to limit him."

"And it's also within my power to permit him . . . Let's proceed."

I sit down again and listen to Pitluck. Before each one, he tells the witness which lawyer framed the question. And then he asks it in a manner suggesting the answer he wants.

"Can you give us your opinion as to whether the hanging was caused by his *own* hand or by another?"

"In my opinion it was caused by his own hand . . . From the position of the body and the bruises on the neck, I would say that. . . ."

"Objection. OBJECTION!"

Once again we approach the bench. I tell Pitluck that the doctor is engaging in pure speculation and in argument. He is an expert pathologist, not an eyewitness and not a lawyer. Pitluck says, "But, Mr. Brown, the doctor is simply giving his opinion."

"But he's not qualified to give this kind of an opinion. He wasn't there. He didn't even examine the scene of the crime."

"But he can still give his opinion . . . Overruled. Let's proceed."

Every question of mine produces statements that would influence any jury to lean towards a finding of death by suicide. Naturally, so do Mayer's questions. It's clear that Pitluck is in the game with the Sheriff and the DA.

The Chicano deputy who arrested Robert takes the stand. He sits stiffly in his nearly pressed khaki uniform, cap in hand. He says he arrested the boy because he was drunk and because he had heroin tracks on his arms. He took him to the station without incident. The boy seemed depressed but offered no resistance. It was possible that Robert was still under the influence of drugs.

I jump up shouting, "Objection! This is improper." I feel like a jack-in-the-box.

"Your behavior is improper, too, Mr. Brown. Sit down and keep still or you will not be permitted to assist in this proceeding."

I run up to the bench and begin to argue before Mayer arrives. "He's not a chemist. He's not a doctor. There is absolutely no evidence that Fernandez was under the influence of heroin. He's prejudicing the jury."

"And you are attempting to do the same thing with your outbursts."

"Brown thinks he's in one of his political trials," Mayer says.

"Yes, Mr. Brown. This isn't a criminal case, I keep reminding you. And this is certainly not the place for politics."

"What in the world are you talking about? I'm trying to find out what happened as much as you are . . . Do you think I would prefer to find that the boy was murdered rather than to find that he committed suicide?"

"Of course. Then you can make your wild accusations to the press," Mayer says.

"You're nuts," I shoot back.

"All right, Mr. Brown. One more statement like that and I'll have to ask you to leave. We're supposed to be *lawyers*, you know."

"And that's exactly what I'm asking you to do. I'm asking you to proceed with the normal rules of evidence that we both learned in school!"

"Let's get back to it," Pitluck says.

The deputy then testifies that about an hour after he had booked Robert for drunkenness and for "marks," he placed a prisoner in the cell adjoining Robert's.

"The body was hanging from a bar on the door to the cell. I ran to the front and called the jailer. We entered the cell and cut him down."

I submit my questions to Pitluck.

"What part of the belt or strip of blanket did you cut?"

"Well, actually I didn't cut anything. I meant I *untied* the knot."

I ask Pitluck to show the jury the belt and cloth. They are still tied together in a noose. The deputy doesn't know who has tied them back together. And he cannot explain how Robert could have tied the noose more than seven feet off the floor without something to stand on. No, there were no chairs in the cell to his knowledge. The bunk was screwed to the wall, far away from the door.

During the afternoon session, Pitluck calls the jailer to the stand. He confirms the deputy's story. However, he admits that it is uncommon for arresting officers to place the suspects in their cells. Usually suspects are turned over to the jailer.

"I don't remember exactly why he did . . . I think we were pretty busy around that time. He was just giving us a hand."

He repeats how they called the ambulance. An orderly attempted to revive Robert. They stretched him out in front of the cell and thumped on his heart for nearly ten minutes. But he was DOA when they got him to the coroner's lab.

"Why didn't you take him to a hospital?"

"He was already dead. There had been no detectable breath for nearly half an hour."

"Are you a doctor? Can you say *when* a person is dead?"

"No, sir. He just looked dead to us."

The next man to testify is a black prisoner, brought into court wearing prison blues. His thin eyes are rolling around when he takes the stand. He crosses his hands in front of him and waits for the lead from Pitluck.

He had seen Fernandez around an hour before he was cut down by the jailer. He was a trusty. As part of his duties, he passed out blankets and pillows to the prisoners. He specifically remembered giving Robert a clean one upon his arrival. In the mornings he would pick up the soiled blankets if the prisoner had left.

"Did you pick up a blanket from Fernandez' cell the next morning?"

The young black kid stares right past us. He looks into the white lights of the television. The question is repeated.

"Uh . . . I can't remember . . . I think I did. I always have to count out the things I leave . . . but. . . ."

I get up and walk over to the table next to the court reporter. I remove a blanket from a paper sack. I then write out the questions for Pitluck.

"What do you do with blankets if they're torn?"

"I turn them in to my supervisor."

"Do you ever let torn blankets remain in the cell after the prisoner is gone?"

"No, sir."

I then turn and face the cameras. I unfold the blanket and hold it outstretched. A strip is cut out from its center, making an unmistakable hole.

"Have you ever seen this blanket?"

"No, sir."

"Did you know that something unusual had occurred that night?"

"Everybody in the tank knew that someone had . . . we knew what had happened."

"Did you enter that cell the following day?"

"Yes, sir."

"Do you remember the event?"

"Yes, sir."

"You knew you were standing in a cell where a death had occurred the night before?"

"Yes, sir."

I stretch the blanket out again. Pitluck continues.

"Did you see this blanket?"

"No, sir . . . I, uh . . ."

"Did you remove any blankets from that cell?"

The young man looks at the sergeant next to the DA. He squints from the lights.

"I removed two . . . One from the prisoner in the bunk next to Fernandez. And the other one was the same one I gave to Fernandez the night before. But it wasn't cut up."

There is total silence in the court. I have no further questions for him. He looks me straight in the face as he passes by. I know I have just sent him to hell. The jailers will walk all over him. I nod my head and whisper my thanks. He has just exposed a murder.

I rise and ask Pitluck if we can measure the hole in the blanket for the record. A ruler is handed to me by a blonde clerk. I flatten out the blanket on top of my counsel table. The hole measures sixteen and a half inches long by two inches wide. I then ask Pitluck for the strip of cloth tied to the black belt.

*The cloth is twenty-four inches long by two inches wide!*

The audience gasps. The TV lights burn into my face and the grind of the cameras sizzles my head. It is *impossible* to match up the hole in the blanket with the fatal strip. The hole is a straight cut. The edge of the noose is torn and jagged. Pitluck calls me to the bench.

"Mr. Brown, I don't want you to make any statement to the jury about this. You may not argue. They have seen the evidence, it is for them to draw their own conclusions."

"I don't need to argue, sir. It is evident what is going on here."

"One more statement like that, Mr. Brown . . ."

"Mr. Pitluck . . . let me tell you something . . . You are not a judge. You yourself said this is not a court . . . So if you're trying to scare me with contempt, you don't have that power. . . . And if you want to remove me, go ahead. . . . Just don't forget that you work for Dr. Naguchi."

Pitluck glares at me. He removes his glasses and breathes deeply. Then he turns and informs the jury that they are excused for the day. He says nothing to me.

The reporters rush to me. They want to hear my accusations.

"The jury and the public will have to judge for themselves . . . The District Attorney is sitting right next to me . . . You should ask him if he's going to investigate the possibility that someone has been at least tampering with the evidence. You *know* what I think."

I go to speak with the Fernandez family. Of course, they

knew it all the time. But they wonder what the finding will be. I comfort them, assuring Juana and Lupe that Robert will be vindicated.

That night Gilbert and I go out looking for de Silva. He owns a bar on Whittier Boulevard, about three blocks from Cronie's.

"I've got my gun, just in case," Gilbert says as we drive down the street of sin. The frog has again transmogrified to Corsican pirate.

"Ah, come on, man."

"You don't know these *vatos, ese.* That de Silva is a stone hood. I ain't taking no chances."

The bar is dark, locked up. There are no signs as to why it is closed, nothing. We ask a man in the restaurant next door if he knows anything.

"The joint's *closed?* I hadn't noticed . . . You got me. Maybe Andy is sick."

We drive to his house, but get only ferocious barking in response to our knocking. We call the number we have for the nephew. A woman answers. She knows nothing. She hasn't seen him for some time. And please quit bothering her. If she sees him, she'll give him the message. With a chill, I realize that I am on the track of some murderer.

The following day a psychologist testifies. He'd "investigated" the case, he says. He is a chic bearded man with thick glasses. A "psychological autopsy," he tells us, is something new. He has read all the reports from the doctors, the Sheriff and the Coroner. Then he talked with members of the Fernandez family to get the background of his client, who just happens to be dead.

"Fernandez was a Chicano. A poor boy. He had a history of drug abuse. He'd been in jail an average of three months of every year since he was twelve. He'd never held a steady job. He had numerous women companions, drank heavily, took amphetamines and depressants, reds and bennies in street language . . . and we know that he had been using heroin in the past. He had no job and he had a pregnant girl asking him to marry her. He had a promise of

115

a job, but the fact remains that he hadn't held a steady job in his life. In my opinion, Fernandez could very well have committed suicide."

I write my questions as fast as possible. I scribble them out in a rage while the witness sits comfortably in his smugness.

"Are you qualified to give expert opinions as to mental conditions?"

"I'm not a psychiatrist, if that's what you mean."

"Have you studied 'psychological autopsies' in a school?"

"No, this is a relatively new field. I'm one of the few licensed psychologists who is specializing in this area."

"And you can give an opinion about a person whom you've never seen? You can actually tell us about his probable state of mind, based only on the testimony of others?"

"In my opinion, I can. Yes."

"Goddamnit, I object!" I shout. I stand up and scream at the court. "This man is not only unqualified . . ."

"Mr. Brown, please sit. . . ."

"He's also a quack! . . ."

"Mr. Brown, please leave the courtroom!"

"You'll have to throw me out!"

Pitluck turns to the jury and asks them to disregard my outburst. He summons me to the bench. I am ready to bite off his nose.

"Now, Mr. Brown . . ."

"If all you're going to do is bawl me out, forget it. I've told you, I don't give a damn about your proceeding."

"Now, Mr. Brown . . . I agree that the witness's testimony is rather self-serving. . . ."

"It's also premised on a racist view. . . ."

"There he goes," Mayer chortles.

"What do you mean, sir?"

"That idiot is saying that because Robert was a poor screwed-up Chicano, he probably committed suicide."

"How is that racist? Never mind. Let's get back to work. Do you have any more questions of this witness?"

"Not that you'd permit me to ask."

The doctor is excused and, as he walks out of the courtroom, spectators hiss at him. "*Puto! Tapado!*" The cameras take it all down. The courtroom is buzzing with emotion.

"Now we will have testimony from our last witness," Pitluck announces. "Bailiff, please bring in Mr. de Silva."

The big kid lumbers in with his nose to his chest. He keeps his eyes on Mayer throughout the testimony.

He'd been arrested for auto theft on the same day that Fernandez died. He was asleep on a bottom bunk when they brought Robert in. There were two bunk beds in the cell. He was awakened by the sound of bed springs. When he raised his head, Fernandez was standing on top of the other bunk bed.

"He asked me if I had a pencil. He wanted to write his name on the wall. I told him no. We talked for a while. Then I fell asleep. When I woke up a little later, I heard some noise . . . It was the police. They were taking Fernandez out of the cell . . . I didn't see nothing."

His voice is low and soft. Pitluck has to ask him twice to speak louder. I submit my questions to Pitluck.

"I object to those questions," Mayer said.

"Which ones?"

"Those that . . . This one that says, 'What is the status of your case?' And the one that says, 'Were you offered immunity or protection by any law enforcement officer?' And this one that says, 'Why did you refuse to speak with the attorney for the family?' This witness is not on trial. The jury isn't interested in that."

I look Pitluck straight in the face.

"If you don't ask those questions, I'm walking out right now."

"Mr. Pitluck . . . If you permit Brown to do that . . . I'll report it to the Bar. He's making a mockery of our procedures."

"Oh, you're full of shit, Mayer."

"Mr. Brown . . . if you use any more foul language . . ."

"Jesus, Norman, get off your high horse. We're talking about a murder here."

"Let's get on with it . . . I'll ask Brown's questions."

We return to our tables. Just as I am seated, I catch a glimpse of my three little teeny-boppers. They smile and Rosalie blows me a kiss. The Militants give me the power salute, clenched fists in the air. I look *mean* for the cameras.

The hearing continues. De Silva contends he never knew I wanted to see him.

"My case was dismissed and nobody said nothing to me," Mickey answers another question.

"Was it 'formally dismissed,' or did they not file a complaint?"

"Well, I'm not a lawyer . . . They just cut me loose."

"And has anyone told you how to testify?"

"No, sir. The Sheriff just said to tell the truth."

"Anything else, Mr. Brown?" Pitluck inquires.

I rush to the bench. It is an impossible procedure. I can't anticipate everything he will say. I ask Pitluck to permit me to cross-examine.

"Under the code, Mr. Brown, the procedure is left up to the hearing officer. We've always used this method. I see no reason to deviate from it."

"But we're not getting the whole truth here. Even if it is a suicide situation, we are not getting at the truth."

"That's my ruling. Do you have any other questions?"

I do, but he sticks to his story. He heard nothing. He saw nothing. Even though he was two feet away from the death, he couldn't help us.

After he finishes, the muscle-bound sergeant who brought him in walks out with him. He is gone. There is nothing more I can do.

The jury goes out to deliberate. An hour later they are back. The cause of death, the jury says unanimously . . . was suicide.

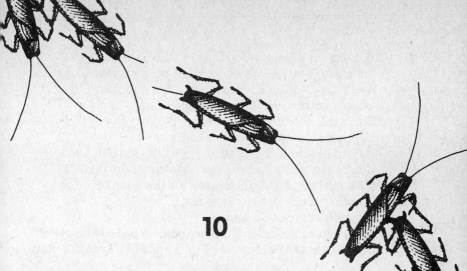

# 10

"Let's stop for a beer, *ese*," Gilbert says.

We are driving down the freeway to my house on Sixth Street where Gilbert now lives. Pelon is at the wheel. The Fernandez family lives down the street from me. They invited me over for supper, but I am too weary. I left the courtroom in a rage, bawling in front of the reporters. One of them, a heavy graying Chicano, had introduced himself. His name was Roland Zanzibar and he wanted me to call him tomorrow about an interview for KMEX. I rushed past him with Pelon, Gilbert and the girls.

Foul air and burning rubber and oil flush into the blue Mustang. The girls are in the back, singing. I bought them ice cream and soda pop before we got on the freeway. Usually, on our way home after court, I buy a six-pack of beer, but this time I have intentionally not bought any.

"We can't drink when we're on duty," I say to Gilbert.

"We got more work to do? I thought the thing was over," Pelon says.

"You think I got them to cut up Robert's body for *that*?"

"But what else can you do, *ese*?" Gilbert asks.

"Well, aren't you the one that's been telling me how heavy you are?"

"What do you mean?"

"Haven't you been talking for over a year about taking some *action*?"

"You mean . . . a *movida?*"

"We got to start somewhere . . . I'm for it now."

"*Ay, ay, ay! ¡Viva La Raza!*" Gilbert shouts.

"What's going on?" Madeline pipes in.

"You keep out of this, *mocosa*," Gilbert says.

"Up yours, fatso!" Rosalie shouts.

"Hey, Gilbert. They've got to get into it, too."

"You're not going to let the *chavalas* in on this?"

"Why not? Isn't revolution for all the people?"

"Jesus, Buffalo, you're nuts, *ese.*"

"I know . . . Are you game?"

Gilbert gives me a long queer look. "You serious, *ese?*"

"If I got to do it alone . . . I'm gonna get even for Robert."

He puts his arm around my neck and clasps my hand.

"It's about *time*, man! I've been waiting for this. Right, Pelon?"

"You know me, Gilbert. I'm game for anything."

We drive to a service station and purchase a gallon of gas in a tin can and two quarts of oil. We stop at a store and I tell Veronica to go buy a box of large tampax. She tries to dump the job on Rosalie.

"No, you do it. . . . Rosalie, I want you to get a box of Tide soap."

We take our ammunition and go home. Gilbert shows us how to make a molotov cocktail. He puts all the ingredients before him and sets about it as if he were a master chef making a gourmet dish. Two parts gasoline mixed with one part oil and one part soap. You put it in a bottle, stick the tampax into the neck, and tape it shut with the string sticking out. Before you throw it, light the string and then heave it so it'll break upon contact. The molotov is the poor man's napalm. The soap and the oil make the goo stick and burn deeply into the target.

The girls hang around and giggle during the production.

"Let's take a toke before we go, *ese*," Pelon says.

"No dice. We got to be sober," I say.

"Shit, *ese*. I mean just one joint."

"We're going to do this one right, man. No dope. No

booze. We got to do it on balls alone."

"OK, man. You're the boss."

I order the girls to turn off the record player. I ask them to sit down. They just laugh and fall to the floor.

"If I don't come back tonight, you call my lawyer. Here's his card. . . . Tell Herringbone I might be in jail and to check it out. And you guys stay put. After we leave, I want you to get rid of all this junk here. Go throw the gasoline can and the rest of the oil in somebody's garbage can . . . No, better yet, walk to Cronie's and ditch everything in the garbage can in the women's toilet. Wipe off all fingerprints and use gloves. . . . Understand?"

"What are you guys gonna do, Buff? Snuff a pig?"

"We're going to try to do *something*. . . . I'll let you know if we make it."

"Shit, *ese*. Don't be so dramatic. We're gonna do it," Gilbert says.

I grab two coats and ties from my closet. I throw them to Gilbert and Pelon. "Here, put this stuff on."

"You nuts, *ese*? I ain't wearing no fucking tie."

"Yes you are. We look suspicious enough without your *vato loco* uniforms. . . . Put them on. . . . And don't forget your gun."

We laugh at Gilbert when he emerges from the bathroom with combed hair, a coat and tie. He looks like a dumpy grocery-store clerk. We load the two bottles of liquid death into the car and drive off, searching for doom and destruction.

"What's the plan, *ese*?" Gilbert asks.

We are in the Mustang, driving along Whittier Boulevard in search of a target. It is late at night. Pelon is driving. Gilbert, twirling his tie, rides shotgun and I am in the rear. We are listening to the radio. The announcer gives a report of the inquest. I curse and Gilbert flips it off.

"Yeah, man. Who we gonna hit?" Pelon says.

"Just keep going. I'm trying to think."

We pass women coming out of endless bars. Gilbert sucks his teeth and yells to them, "Hey, mama, you're looking good!"

"Hey, man, that one was fine . . . I'd sure like to get down on something like that," Pelon says. He holds his head up and tugs at the tie.

"Come on, you guys. We got to get serious."

We continue to drive east in silence.

"How far we going, man?"

"We've got to find something, or someone . . . I'm trying to think."

"Hey, man, why don't we just find a pig and shoot the sonofabitch?"

"Pigs got guns, too," Pelon says.

"So what, ese? You think I'm scared?"

"I didn't say you were . . . but why does it have to be a cop? Shit, I'm for shooting any fucking gabacho we see. What difference does it make?

"Hey, you guys. I'm trying to . . . And we can't just shoot anybody. You think we're a bunch of hoods?" I ask.

"I'm a stone anarchist myself," Gilbert says.

"I don't give a shit about politics myself," Pelon says.

"I know. You're just a vato loco."

"No he's not, ese. Pelon here is an outlaw, just like me."

"You're full of shit, Gilbert. I'm no crook. I just don't like gabachos."

"But you like white girls, don't you?" Gilbert says.

"I like all viejas, ese. You know me."

"That's why I say let's find us a pig; I'll shoot the bastard."

"No, Gilbert. . . . You've got it, uh . . . we've got to find a target that . . . look, if we get caught . . . first of all, leave your wallets in the glove box. If they catch us. . . ."

"Don't talk that way, ese. You're making me nervous."

"Well, we've got to make plans, just in case. . . . We've got to find a target that's symbolic."

"You mean like the Bank of America?"

"Fuck no, ese. That's a hippie trip. The SDS is doing that."

"So what?" Pelon says. "They weren't the first ones."

"Hey, lawyer . . . What do we say if they catch us?"

"I was just thinking of that. . . . Don't say anything.

We'll wait until we get lawyers. . . . Don't say a word."

"We just got to give them our name and address," Pelon says.

"No. Don't even tell them that."

"I know! I'll tell them my name is Pancho Villa," Pelon says. Both of them break up. They pound their fists on the dashboard.

"I'll say my name is *Zapata!*" Gilbert roars.

"You're too fat, *ese*. They won't believe you."

"And you think they're going to believe *you?* You can't even grow a mustache yet."

"I don't give a shit what they think. . . . If I can just get me one *gabacho*."

"Hey, man. What name are you going to give?"

I think it through. "My own," I say. "Buffalo General Zeta Brown."

"Is that what that middle initial stands for?" whoops Gilbert.

"Yeah, man. Zeta fought with Villa and Zapata," Pelon says.

"Hey, Zeta. . . . Heh, heh. . . . How far are we going to drive, *ese?*"

I see the flickering of lights on the hills behind Tooner Flats. We are past the barrios and heading toward Rose Hills where Eldridge Cleaver grew up.

I lifted "Zeta" from a movie over two years ago because he was the closest thing to a Chicano Humphrey Bogart, the guy who always ended up with Maria Felix. The name I lived with for two years, the hidden name, an initial between two other words. And now there is no movie. Just me in the back seat with my rage and fear and two whiskey bottles full of vengeance because of another name, Robert Fernandez. Just a name, no body any more. My heart is pounding.

I have not killed since I was a kid. Where I grew up, in Riverbank, we had flies. We lived right next door to the world's largest tomato paste cannery. Each summer, the rotting red pulp brought tiny black buzzards by the millions. We'd have to line up at one end of the room and

chase and shoo them with towels until they flew out the windows. I could kill flies without compunction. But the few times I went fishing with my brother and the old man, I threw what I caught back in the river. Years later, when I was stationed in Panama, I once went on a canoe trip with a french horn player named Robert Peoples. We were gliding along, the sun was shining down on the Panama Canal, when I mindlessly aimed my twenty-two and shot a mud duck. His neck broke like a twig and he went under.

"What did you do that for?" Peoples asked.

I had no answer. That was in 1955. Now here it is, February, 1970, and I am out looking for a man to kill.

"We ought to find that *puto* that busted Fernandez," Pelon says.

"That Chicano pig probably did him in too," Gilbert says.

"Who, the cop? Or de Silva?" Pelon asks.

"What, you guys think Mickey did it?" I say.

"I keep telling you, Buff . . . uh, Zeta . . . They say the de Silvas are stone gangsters. . . . They say they're tight with the Maganas," Gilbert says.

"Who's that?"

"The Maganas, *ese*. The dudes who control the shit in East LA."

"I could use a little geeze right now," Pelon says.

"Ah, you *pinche tecato*," Gilbert says.

"You're not still shooting, are you, Pelon?"

"Fuck no, *ese*. I told you I was off that stuff until after the revolution."

"And you think they're going to let you shoot up after?" Gilbert says.

"I don't give a fuck what anybody says . . . I dig the stuff."

"Jesus, Pelon!"

"It's better than that bullshit LSD you guys take."

"You're *tapado, ese*. Acid is good shit."

"It just makes you crazy. . . . Look at Zeta. Look what it's done to him."

"What? What's it done to me?"

They both laugh and punch each other on the arms.

"I'll tell you, man. After the revolution . . . if anybody tries to stop me . . . I'm not going through all this just to. . . ."

Gilbert says, "Don't worry, *ese*. We'll fight the Militants after we finish off the *gabachos*."

"I'll stop geezing while we're at war, man. But afterwards . . . Man, I'm gonna shoot until my arms bust. And if anybody tries to stop me. . . ."

"Fuck it, *ese*. We'll just start another revolution."

"You guys are really a bunch of stone *vatos locos!*"

"I'm an anarchist, man. I keep telling you."

We stop at a small grocery store. We are out of cigarettes. Pelon goes in while Gilbert and I wait.

"Are we really going to kill a pig, *ese*?"

"I don't know, man. . . . We ought to kill someone that did something to us. . . . So that when, I mean, *if* we're caught we can say that we did it for the movement."

"That's why I say . . . Let's just find a cop."

"But we can't just shoot any cop."

"Why not?"

I can't answer him. Pelon jumps in.

"Hey, man . . . I just got an idea," Pelon says.

"Yeah? Well, let's get away from here. I don't want to get caught with these molotovs in here." Pelon pulls away, already talking. "Why don't we pull a job? I was just thinking . . . There's just an old man in that store . . . I looked in the register when he opened it. . . . It's stuffed with *feria*, *ese*."

"You mean, just *hold* the guy up?" I say.

"Yeah, man. Why not? We could buy guns with the loot," Gilbert says.

"Jesus Christ. You guys are a bunch of goddamn outlaws. . . . Fuck no, we're not going to pull any shit like that."

"Then what are we going to do, *ese*? It's getting late."

"Yeah, man, we don't want to drive all night. I'm getting thirsty."

"All right. Look . . . we can't just kill for the fun of it."

"Hey, I'm not kidding, man. I'm serious," Gilbert says.

"Me, too," Pelon says.

"If we knew that pig killed Robert . . . or that de Silva did it. . . ."

"Let's go throw the bombs at de Silva's joint," Gilbert says.

"No, goddamnit! We don't know for sure what happened."

"What, you think the dude hung himself?"

"No . . . But we don't know *who* did it."

"Shit, man. What difference does it make? You think the pigs give a shit *who* we are? When they bust us or whip us, you think they ask *who* we are?"

"And that's why we call them *pigs*, dummy. . . . I'm not going to be like them!" I shout.

"Well, why don't we just throw these bombs and think about *who* we're gonna shoot later?" Pelon says.

"That sounds pretty good to me," Gilbert says.

"OK. . . . Where are we going to throw them?"

"Hey, I got an idea," Gilbert says.

"What?"

"The Farmworkers are picketing Safeway Stores. Why don't we hit one of them?"

"But they're supposed to be non-violent," I say.

Gilbert and Pelon start to laugh. They shake their heads at me.

"All right, what is it? Don't tell me Cesar is into bombs."

"No, man. *He* isn't. But we are. So why not help those dudes? If they catch us we can say we did it for the *huelga*."

"Yeah, let's get the one over on Fourth. My *jefita* goes there. They're always giving her a bad time. Let's go there," Pelon says.

"All right with me," I say.

Pelon takes the cutoff and heads back toward East LA. We make plans as we drive back. Pelon gives us the layout of the entire shopping center.

"Gilbert, you take one to the front and I'll take one to the back. . . . Zeta can wait in the car."

"What? I'm going to throw one, too," I say.

"No, ese. You're supposed to be a lawyer. It would look bad."

"Fuck that, man."

"It's your car, too. If they stop us . . . I don't have a license. It'll violate my probation if they catch me driving."

I do not argue with them. It makes too much sense. Once again, as at the St. Basil's riot, I am left on the front lines without a position. My heart begins to beat furiously. We are not far from the target.

Pelon stops and we trade seats. I cruise slowly along Whittier and turn down Atlantic toward Fourth Street. We have all stopped talking. Gilbert and Pelon have agreed on the details: Gilbert is to walk to the front, Pelon to the rear. I am to remain parked in the alley where I can see both of them. When Gilbert reaches the front, he is to wait for my signal. When I see them both in place, I will blink the headlights once. Gilbert will light his molotov, throw it through the window and then return at a normal pace to the car. Pelon will fire about the same time. If anything goes wrong, I am to honk the horn and try to distract any approaching cops, even if it means drawing them away in a chase.

I sit alone. Gilbert is in my blue sport coat, waddling toward the front of the huge supermarket. Signs advertise a special on La Piña Wheat Flour. I can see Pelon walking carefully, casually toward the rear of the darkened store. He looks, is a young kid. I feel old as I sit and stare all around. My neck is twisted and tense. I feel cramps throughout my body. My eyes are strained from looking at every movement on the street. Every car that passes causes my heart to miss a beat. My breathing is coming in gasps now as I see Gilbert and Pelon in position.

I put my fingers on the light switch . . . I blink once.

I can see Gilbert's match glow. I can see him lighting the bomb. And then I see him crash it through the window. Buzzzzzz: an alarm!

Pelon tosses his cocktail. I watch flames explode against boxes and trash in the warehouse where the food is stored.

I look toward Gilbert. He is strolling, his arms hanging at his sides. He is on a Sunday walk in the park. . . .

BUZZZZZZZZZZZZZZZ. . . .

We didn't plan on a burglar alarm.

Pelon jumps in the car. He is gasping for air.

"Where the fuck is *Gilbert*?"

I say nothing. I have started the motor. We both look at the fat black frog. He walks as if he were taking a casual stroll down Whittier Boulevard digging on the *viejas*.

"Run, Gilbert! Come on, *ese!*" Pelon shouts out the window.

But Gilbert just keeps walking peacefully. My head is about to explode. The red-yellow fires are both blazing.

BUZZZZZZZZZZZZZ. . . .

Gilbert gets into the front seat and closes the door gently. "Let's go, *ese*," he says.

I rev up the engine and push away through the blackness of an alley with my lights off. Gilbert and Pelon are straining to catch a glimpse of their handiwork. We turn out into a street two blocks away and we are safe. I turn around and drive back toward the store, one anonymous car in a host of others.

"Viva La Raza!" Gilbert shouts.

"Chicano Power!" Pelon says.

My heart is still trying to claw out of my chest. I can't control the tears in my eyes. My hands are wet and itching with excitement. I am in a state of complete joy and delerium. The flames inside lick at the plate glass. I pound the steering wheel and shout, "Viva Pancho Villa!"

"Viva Zapata!" Gilbert shouts and pounds Pelon on the back.

"Look at that beautiful fire!" I say.

"Viva Zeta!" Pelon shouts.

"*¡Qué Viva!*" Gilbert bellows.

We drive back and forth in front of the flaming store until we hear the sound of a siren. We cruise slowly and innocently and laugh when the red fire engine passes us going the other way.

"Let's go get a bottle of wine," Pelon says.

*The Revolt of the Cockroach People*

"Yeah, let's celebrate!" Gilbert shouts.

"OK . . . but I got a question: how come you kept walking when you heard the alarm? Why didn't you run?"

The Corsican pirate says, "That was the *plan, ese.* We said I was supposed to walk."

"I know, man. I fucked up. But when I heard that alarm . . . I blew it," Pelon confesses.

"No, it was my fault," Gilbert says. "I should have thought about the alarm. We just weren't thinking."

"Ah, fuck it . . . We did it, we got away. So let's go celebrate," I say.

By the time we get back to the house, we are ready with booze and dope from Gilbert's cousin. The girls are waiting for us outside and throw themselves around my neck. They hang on to me as we go into the house. Gilbert and Pelon go into the kitchen and leave me alone with my three child brides.

"Did you get one, eh? Did you?" Rosalie screams.

"Come on, tell us, Buff. . . . How was it?" Madeline asks.

"It was great. . . . But, hey, Gilbert, Pelon!" I call them in.

They have already lit up a joint and opened the bottle of Thunderbird. "*They* did it," I say. I stand and salute them. I lift my glass to them and say, "These two soldiers of Aztlan fired the first round in the war."

"Ah, shit, *ese* . . . . It was nothing."

"Oh, look at *Señor Modesto,*" Veronica says. She has washed her hair and taken a bath. Her smell is soft and sweet. She walks up to Gilbert and puts her hands around his arms, feeling the biceps. "Let me see how tough you are."

Gilbert takes a step back. "Hey, girl. You better watch out."

"Why?"

Gilbert looks at me. "Hey, *ese.* Tell your *ruka* to watch out."

"What do you mean his *ruka*?" the sixteen-year-old redhead says.

"Well, aren't you?"

Veronica looks at me. I am sitting on a soft chair with my hands on Rosalie's hips. All of them stare at us. Madeline is sitting next to Pelon in the corner. No one speaks for a moment. They await my instructions.

"Hey, you guys. What am I? . . . Your father?"

"Can we?" Madeline asks.

"Oh, don't be such a winner," Rosalie says. She turns, faces me and plants her lips over mine, continuing to talk into my mouth. "Besides, I got this fat one already."

Gilbert doesn't wait. He grabs Veronica and throws his fat, short arms around her. She pushes him back. She puts her hands on her hips and growls at him. "Get away from me, you dog."

"Hey, Veron, what is it?" I ask.

"I hate to kiss a jerk with a tie on."

Gilbert rips it off and throws the coat on the floor behind the long green couch. He pulls her down and they sit and wrestle under the Sgt. Pepper poster the girls have stuck on the wall. Pelon looks at Madeline. She is reading a comic book.

"Don't get funny, Mr. Cool," she says to him.

"Are you serious, girl? You're just a baby."

"Fuck you, you old man."

"Old? You nuts? I'm just twenty."

"Really?" Madeline says.

And with that, she jumps and takes a diving leap at him, landing right in his lap. . . .

Soon we are all struggling for air on the floor. The shaggy carpet is our bed. I have turned off the overhead light. Now only the cozy purple lamp hanging over our potted marijuana plants shines down on us from the corner.

I think to myself, what would I say if the cops busted in on us right now? If someone saw the car—my car! With my license plates . . . What would I say about Rosalie? My girl friend. Fifteen years old, your honor. Yes, sir. I found her at a riot. And yes, that was me driving the car. I'm the one.

"Hey, Gilbert. What if someone saw us?"

"Heh, heh . . . tough luck, *ese*."

"Jesus, I just thought of it . . . The fucking cops might be looking for me right now."

I jump up but Rosalie grabs my leg and pulls me back to the floor.

"Take it easy, *ese*," Gilbert says.

"You can say that, man. But they won't be coming looking for you. It's registered in my name." I am working myself into a panic.

"So what, man? Just tell them somebody stole your car."

"Ah, come on, man . . . Just tell them you don't know who he is," Pelon says.

"Well, they're going to be looking for Buffalo Z. Brown, right?"

"Yeah."

"Well, just tell them your name is Zeta."

"Yeah, man. You're supposed to be *Zeta* now, remember?" Gilbert says.

"Zeta? Who's that?" Rosalie says, rubbing her eyes. She lies on her back, her long brown hair is under her and spread out like a rug.

"That's Buffalo's new name," Madeline says.

" 'Zeta?' What's that?"

"It's the last letter of the Spanish alphabet," I explain modestly.

"And it's a Greek letter, too," Gilbert says.

"How do you know?" Veronica asks.

"I saw a movie. But they called it Zee. . . . It means *He Shall Return*."

"That sounds like General Mac Arthur," I say.

"Who's that?" Rosalie asks.

"He's a general who . . . ah, never mind."

"General Zeta," she mimics Gilbert. She stands up and salutes me. "Rosalie Ranger at your service."

"*¡Mi General!*" Gilbert snaps. He jumps up and stands squat. Even when he sucks in his drooping belly, he still looks like a raunchy pirate. "*¡Mi General! ¡Estoy a sus órdenes, mi General!*"

"Goddamn, wouldn't it be too much if we had . . . our

own army!" Pelon shouts.

"*Mi General. Mándeme a matar gabachos. . . .*" Gilbert says.

"What do you want to kill the whites for?" Veronica says.

"You guys are too much," Rosalie says.

"Man, if I had a machine gun . . . I'd get even with those deputies who did in Robert."

At the mention of his name we are silenced. For some reason, we look at Pelon. "Hey, why don't we infiltrate the Sheriff's Department?" he says. "You know . . . join up and get the guns."

"Yeah, Zeta . . . We could join and find out who killed Robert."

I laugh at the decrepit black frog. There is no possiblity of visualizing him in a deputy's uniform.

"I'm too old. They wouldn't take me," I say.

"What do you mean?" Rosalie demands hotly.

"You've got to be under thirty, I think."

"Even to be the Sheriff?" she says.

"Uh . . . No, not for that. He's an elected pig."

"So why don't you run against him?" Rosalie says, cool as a cucumber.

"What? You mean, *me* run for *Sheriff?*"

"Why not, *ese?* We could sure use a Chicano Sheriff."

"That would be a trip, man," Pelon says. "Shit, you could get my brother Freddy out of jail."

We all laugh. I roll on the floor. They shout me on.

"Vote for Zeta!" Pelon yells.

"Who is Zeta?" Madeline asks. "Oh, yeah, I forgot. . . . Viva Zeta!" she screams.

I get up and put a record on the stereo. We light up another joint and listen to some Mexican music. I am thinking about the joke. My head is in a swirl. Joke? It is getting too heavy.

"Why not? Why the hell not?" I mutter.

"I'll back you up, *ese,* you know that," Gilbert says.

"Me too, man," Pelon says.

I look at Rosalie. "What do you think?"

"Well, it was my idea, you winner!" she shouts.

And it was . . . Seven hours later I visit the Office of the County Registrar and give her a bank draft for the filing fees. Then the six of us drive down to another office on Spring Street, near the courthouse. To the surprise of the clerk, I file my candidacy for the office of Sheriff of Los Angeles County, population seven million.

# 11

I walk into KMEX and ask the receptionist for Roland Zanzibar. He is the news director at the Pulitzer Prize-winning Chicano station. Soon he appears to greet me and we go into his office.

"I'd like to go over the crucial points of the hearing," he says.

He appears relaxed and after a brief conversation I feel that I have his confidence. The talk is warm and friendly and he seems genuinely interested in the subject. It is not simply another day of work for him. He gauges my own sympathies. He knows that the event has great meaning for me. And, from newspaper articles, I know he is regarded as a veteran journalist by his own peers. He has recently returned from Vietnam and has a weekly column in the largest newspaper west of Chicago, the Los Angeles *Times*. Stonewall comes off like an angry baboon in comparison.

We go into another room where he introduces me to his staff. From here, we go behind a stage into a sound-proofed room and meet the man with the camera.

"Ladies and gentlemen, we are in the studios of Station KMEX and we have Mr. Buffalo Z. Brown for this afternoon's program. . . . Good afternoon, Señor Brown. ¿Cómo está usted?"

For an instant I freeze up. It is the first time I've been interviewed in Spanish. I look into the loose smiling face of Roland Zanzibar, who wants to know how I am.

"Horrible. It has not been a good week. . . . It has not been a good century for us."

"Uh . . . Well, I assume that is partly because of the Coroner's Jury findings yesterday? . . . Mr. Brown, I should say, is the attorney for the family of Robert Fernandez, who was found dead in his cell at the East LA Sheriff's substation, and whose inquest we have been carrying live for our viewers. . . . Now, Mr. Brown, can you tell us what happened?"

I give the basic facts of the case first, and then my conclusion: "The refusal of the cell partner to speak with me and his testimony that he remembers nothing of a death—a violent death that occurred right next to him—that and the findings of the expert pathologists convince me that the boy was murdered."

"Do you have any suspicions as to the murderer?"

"If it had been another prisoner, particularly if it had been a Chicano or some other Cockroach, you can bet your boots the Sheriff would not have covered the way he did."

"'Cockroach' you say, Mr. Brown?"

"Yeah, the Cockroach People . . . you know, the little beasts that everyone steps on."

"Heh, heh . . . I see . . . And, uh, so you think the Sheriff was engaged in this killing. Sheriff Peter Peaches?"

"Not personally . . . but he is responsible for his men. He's the boss. . . . When I get in there, I'll see to it that those who are guilty are punished."

"When you get in there?"

"Yes, I have decided that the job is too important to be left to killer-dogs like Peter Peaches."

"Are you trying to say that you're going to run for Sheriff?"

"Yeah . . . you got yourself a scoop, Mr. Zanzibar. I just filed for the office before I came down to the station. . . . Here, this is my receipt for the filing fee." I hand him a slip of paper the registrar has given me.

"This is . . . uh, can you pick up this paper?" he says to the cameraman. "You are full of surprises, Mr. Brown."

135

"Yes, I am. . . . You will notice on the receipt that I have adopted a new name. . . . My name is now Zeta. I have given up my slave name. I do not intend to graze happily until I am slaughtered like Robert."

"I assume you're not, uh, pulling my leg, Mr. Brown, uh, Mr. Zeta. . . . Are you?"

"Mr. Zanzibar, I am dead serious. . . . The events of the past weeks have made me realize what historic moment I am living in. . . . No, sir, I am very serious."

"Yes . . . Now, what plans do you have for the campaign?"

"I intend to seek out the support of all Cockroaches."

"Yes . . . And what will be your campaign issues?"

"I have but one issue. I know there's no hope for actual victory at the ballot box. I have no money and no supporters other than a few ragged friends. We can hardly compete with the pros. My effort is an educational endeavor. I expect to carry my message to as many as are interested in my views. . . . If I were elected Sheriff, I would make every attempt to dissolve the office. The community has no need for professional killers. The law enforcement officers of this county, of this nation in general, are here for the protection of the few, the maintenance of the status quo. . . . The police are the violent arm of the rich and I would get rid of them."

"Do you think there is any legitimate function the Sheriff's Department can serve?"

"No, I would have a People's Protection Department. I would enlist the aid of the community to find ways to protect ourselves from the violence of our society. Obviously, the answer is not more tanks, helicopters and tear gas."

"Do you think that anyone would vote for you with a platform such as that?"

"Actually, I doubt it. Even most of my friends are too young to vote. But I'm going to try to get others to listen to me anyway."

And so it goes. When it is over, Zanzibar shakes my hand. He laughs at my outrage but it is sympathetic laughter. He encourages me to air my views. We go to a bar next door and, over a beer, he tells me about his job with KMEX. He is the only articulate Chicano in the business at the time, and he intends to bring the barrios to the public's attention. He invites me to call any events to *his* attention that I believe to be newsworthy.

' I tell him to come to the trial of the St. Basil Twenty-One. "I'm going to try to subpoena Cardinal McIntyre," I tell him. "It'll be quite a show."

"Ah, Zeta, you've really cut yourself a big slice. . . . Be careful, hombre. You know the dangers."

I thank him and promise to keep in touch. Then I drive to the downtown library where I begin to prepare for my biggest trial to date. I am the attorney for all twenty-one people arrested on Christmas Eve and charged with Inciting to Riot and Disrupting a Religious Assembly, a statute in modern times.

The trial is held in a special courtroom because of the large number of defendants, a spacious hall on the sixth floor where the Grand Jury normally convenes. The corridors are crowded with partisans of the St. Basil Twenty-One. Two of the defendants are Catholic priests who no longer work formally with the Church. Both of them are tall Anglos who have taken wives. Two others are former nuns. One is a Chicano teacher and the other is Duana Doherty, the redhead who rushed down the aisle in a mini-skirt to plead for help. Another, Lydia Lopez, is pregnant. Gloria, the woman with the golf club, tells me she has kidney problems and asks me to get permission from the judge to use the toilet without interruption of the trial. Law students and CMs sit around the double tables in front of the judge's bench. The judge assigned to the case is known as a liberal, a Jew called Nebron. He has bright red hair, pale skin and fat lips.

A jury of six men and six women is already empanelled. The judge orders the bailiff to bring in more marshals. I object that the jury may be influenced by the appearance of such force.

"I am more concerned with the safety of the witnesses

and the orderly procedure of this court, sir," he cranks it out to me.

"We have reason to believe there might be trouble," Ridder says. He is the special prosecuter, a squat punk with an ass like a duck.

"I don't want to hear any argument on this, gentlemen. I've made my ruling. . . . Let's begin."

The first witness is sworn in and takes the stand. He turns out to be the Irish cop who clobbered Gilbert in the vestibule. He tells us that, as a member of The Anchor Club, a Catholic men's group for law enforcement officers, he was asked by Monsignor Hawkes to provide ten ushers for Christmas Eve Mass. They had information, he says, that there would be a riot that night.

"Who told you there would be trouble?" I cross-examine.

"A detective from the East Los Angeles station . . . His name is Abel Armas."

"Did he tell you where he got his information?"

"No."

"Did you make any attempt to check it out?"

"No. I knew Sergeant Armas to be a reliable source."

"Did you know who the persons were that were supposed to start the trouble?"

"No . . . We were pretty sure it would be the same group that had picketed the Cardinal's office in the past months."

"What are the names or descriptions of those persons whom you suspected?"

"Well . . . You were one of those persons, Mr. Brown."

"You expected me to riot?"

"Or to encourage others to riot."

"Did you see me riot?"

"No, sir."

"Did you see me encourage anyone to riot?"

"No, sir . . . Your friends did all the rioting for you."

"And did any of your friends engage in any violence that night?"

"We did our duty. We protected the congregation and the church property from destruction by your group, sir."

The witness then details the arrests. He looks straight at Ridder and the man who sits next to him, Sergeant Abel Armas.

"Did anyone tell you what the plans were for that night?"

"Yes, that they were going to riot."

"Did you have any details on the subject?"

"No."

"And were you assigned to this detail by your superiors?"

"No. This was a *private* matter. We are all members of the church. We provide ushering service on special occasions."

"And do you always bring your chemical spray with you when you usher?"

"The Mace cans?"

"Yes."

"No. But this was a little different from the normal church service."

"Did you use your Mace?"

"I was forced to use it. Yes."

"And you were in a position to see every single defendant that night?"

"As head of the detail . . . It was my job to observe who was involved."

"And two months after the incident, you still have a perfect memory of all the events?"

"This isn't the first time I've done this, sir."

"How could you distinguish between the defendants and the other persons inside the vestibule."

"I knew who the ushers were."

"And you say that all the persons in that lobby—all hundred or so—that they all belonged to this group that was going to riot?"

"Yes, sir."

"How do you know that? Were they wearing some special uniform?"

"Yes. They were dressed differently."

"You can distinguish between, say, the members of the

congregation and the persons in the lobby by the clothes they wore?"

"Yes, sir. The rioters were not dressed for worship. And the ones doing the fighting, except for the priests, carried sticks and other weapons."

"I have no more questions of this, uh, so-called man."

"Mr. Brown, please come to the bench."

Together with the prosecutor and the blonde reporter with the little black box, we walk up to the front. Standing hunched up, we whisper with Nebron.

"Mr. Brown, I want you to treat every witness with respect. Do you understand that?"

"Uh, could you repeat that, please?"

"Yes, sir. I want you to be more lawyer-like with the witnesses."

"Even with those that perjure themselves?"

"Objection, your honor," the Duck says.

"Mr. Brown . . . Let's start over again . . . I want you to show respect for this court. Do you understand?"

"I speak English very well, your honor."

"Mr. Brown . . . You are bordering on contempt at this very moment."

"Your honor, I *am* contemptuous of liars. It's my nature."

"And I am contemptuous of *lawyers* who fail to show this court its proper respect. . . . I hereby hold you in contempt of this court. We shall deal with the sentence at a later time. . . . Now, let's get back to work."

"Thank you, sir."

I return to the counsel table and tell the defendants what has happened. "It's going to be heavy," I say.

Two other officers are brought before the jury. They describe the riot outside the temple after the Chicanos were driven out. One of them is a black cop. I remember him. Officer Bell, a handsome young black, is the one I saw shaking with nervousness on the outside steps. He speaks with a soft voice, giving bland general descriptions of the group. He remembers very little.

"And did you hear anyone yelling racial remarks at

you, sir?" the Duck asks Officer Bell.

"Objection," I say. Three members of the jury are black. I know that Ridder is trying to butter them up.

"Yes, Mr. Ridder. The question is vague. Please rephrase it."

"Did anyone call you a nigger?"

"Objection."

"Overruled."

"Well . . . someone did say 'nigger' to me."

On cross-examination, I ask him: "Officer Bell . . . Do you remember exactly what was said to you?"

"Yes, sir. The defendant Garcia said, 'Hey, man. You're a nigger just like us. Why are you doing this?'"

"Thank you. No more questions."

The cop steps down and walks to the rear of the courtroom.

"Right on, brother!" someone shouts from the spectators' gallery.

"Bailiff, take that man into custody," Nebron roars.

"Which one, your honor?"

"The one who hollered out just now."

"I'm sorry, I didn't see who it was."

"All right . . . Ladies and gentlemen of the jury, you will disregard the outburst in the courtroom. And you will be excused now. The court has some other business to attend to at this time. Bailiff, escort the jury to the jury room. The court is still in session. . . . Everyone will remain seated until the jury has left."

Three armed marshals lead the jury out. One of the jurors, a black lady with fine legs, smiles as she walks past. I tell Joe, one of the defendants, to keep his eyes on her. "She might be on our side."

"That's the one that Duana was talking about," he whispers.

When the jury has gone out, the judge says, "All right, now we can find out who hollered . . . Let me tell you people . . . First of all, this is a court of law. I don't know if you've ever been in a courtroom before, but from your demeanor, from your conduct, it appears that you haven't. . . .

If you want to be a spectator in this very serious matter, you'll have to observe the rules. . . . Now . . . Who hollered out?"

The people in the audience are smiling. There are nearly one hundred friends of the defendants. Half of them are Chicano Militants in the now traditional garb of khaki, olive-drab field jackets and black spit-shined boots. The others are Anglo kids with wild hair and patched-up levi's. There are also several priests and nuns who have come in support of the defendants. A row of neatly dressed law students rounds out the gallery.

"If I can't find out who made last outburst . . . I'll order this entire courtroom cleared. . . . Is that clear?"

There is a stirring in the crowd. People are looking at one another. But no one speaks up.

"All right . . . Since you don't know how to behave . . . Let the record show that this court has observed the conduct of the spectators and that it has noticed, on several occasions, that numerous persons have been talking, chewing gum and reading newspapers. It is the opinion of this court that the jury is being prejudiced, or might be influenced by these outbursts. Therefore, I order that all spectators, with the exception of the press and relatives of the defendants, that all other parties in this courtroom hereby be excluded from attending the rest of this session. Bailiff, clear the court."

"Just a minute, your honor. I'd like to be heard," I say.

"I've made my ruling, Mr. Brown."

"And I'd like to enter my objection."

"Your objection is noted."

"Well, your honor. I'd like to argue my objection."

"No, we don't need any argument on this . . . Bailiff?"

John Sanchez, the bailiff, is a crew-cut Chicano with striking white teeth. He sighs, shrugs his shoulders, and asks the people to leave. Several other marshals gather around him, hands on their guns.

"I'd like to note for the record, your honor. . . ."

"Mr. Brown, we don't need any more argument, I've ruled. My ruling is to insure your clients a fair trial."

"I know, Judge. But the record should reflect that there weren't numerous outbursts and that. . . ."

"Mr. Brown, if you continue to talk after I've told you to stop, I'll hold you in contempt once again."

"May I make a motion?"

"No."

"May I present argument as to what my motion would be?"

"No. We will continue with the trial. Bring in the jury."

"Your honor, I'd like to record an objection."

"We will proceed, Mr. Brown. Now sit down."

"Why do I have to sit down?"

The judge removes his glasses. He looks down on me. His green eyes glitter. "Because I have *ordered* you to sit down."

"But there isn't any reason for it. The jury isn't even in here. You're trying to intimidate me, Judge."

"Mr. Brown, I don't want to hear any more of your sass . . . Now, you sit down this minute or I'll have the bailiff remove you."

"I wish to make a motion for a mistrial, your honor."

"Not now."

I look at my clients. They only have eyes for me. We are *into* it, I tell them with my face. There is no turning back.

"I object to this court. I object to this judge. I object. . . ."

"Bailiff, take Mr. Brown into custody!"

"Your honor, may I be heard?"

"I've heard all I'm going to, Brown! . . . Bailiff? Take him away!"

The bailiff reaches for my shoulder.

"Hey, what is this?" says Joe, one of the defendants. He is a small wiry man, the new editor of *La Voz.* Joe is also a psychologist and a long-distance runner.

"You sit down, sir. Your lawyer will do the talking for you."

"What lawyer? You won't let him say anything."

"Cool it, Joe," I say.

"No chance, *ese.*"

"I've ordered you to sit down and shut up, young man."

"My name is Joe Ramirez, Judge. And I wish to be heard."

"I do too, Judge," one of the priests speaks up.

"I wish to be heard also, your honor," says Duana, the nun.

"Me too, sir." says Luis, the bite-sized ex-con.

"Now all of you listen to me!" the judge roars. "Bailiff, take *all* the defendants into custody. Take Mr. Brown with them. Your bail is hereby revoked and you are remanded to the custody of my bailiff until one-thirty this afternoon."

He stands and glares down at all of us. Five marshals rush to the front of the court, waving twelve-inch clubs. They position themselves around the judge.

"Your honor, may I make a motion?"

But he does not respond. He steps quickly from the bench and walks toward his chambers behind the courtroom.

"*¡Cabrón puto!*" cries out Victor, a student with a walking cane.

"All right, all of you . . . march."

"Aw, don't be so corny," I tell the marshal.

We are all laughing and shoving one another as we are placed in a large cell behind the court. There are two wooden benches. The yellow walls are covered with names, slogans, dates and other grafitti. It is nearly noon. Sanchez tells us, "Hey, what's wrong with you guys? You're just making it hard on yourselves."

"Ah, don't be so *tapado,* man," Luis spits out.

"Hey, get us some lunch," Victor tells him.

Soon he leaves. It is the first time I have heard of a judge locking up men and women in the same cell.

"Well, you guys asked for it," I say.

We are all sitting around waiting for lunch. A few guys are busy writing names and slogans on the walls, in *cholo* print.

"You think he'll make us stay in jail after court?"

"I doubt it. . . . Not if you guys keep your traps shut."

"We're not going to take this shit," Joe says.

"Yeah, me neither," says Ray, a long-haired musician.

"Look at *this,* will you? Ray is getting militant," Luis laughs.

"And he was just an innocent bystander," throws in Larry the priest.

"I used to be innocent until I met you guys," Ray says.

"Hey, Zeta, how's the campaign coming?" asks Chuck, the other priest.

"Yeah, man, I saw you on TV last week."

"It's going OK. . . . So far we haven't done anything." Everybody laughs.

"I'm going to get some of my friends to help," Duana says.

"Yeah, we've got a lot of people who would really like to get into it. . . . I guess you heard we, uh . . . left the order," says Josie, the other nun.

"I'll be glad to take all the help I can get. Just send them down to our office."

"Where's the campaign office?"

"At my house on Sixth Street."

"You'll get a lot of publicity from this trial, man."

"I know . . . Especially if we keep getting thrown in jail."

"It's OK with me, Zeta. I'll back you all the way," Luis says.

Soon Sanchez brings us our lunch. We have our choice of baloney or cheese sandwiches. They taste like different flavors of paint. We drink water from the faucet with our bare hands. There is no afternoon session. We are all released after lunch.

The following day, the headlines read, "*St. Basil Twenty-One In Contempt Along With Lawyer.*"

When we arrive in court, the media is there in full force. We are interviewed over every television channel in the area. When we enter, the bailiff is standing at the door. Each of us is searched. The women are taken behind a curtain and checked out by female deputies. Upon entering we are told by Sanchez that only alternate seats can be used. Judge Nebron, he says, has ordered that all spectators be separated. The crowd pushes and scuffles for position and the noise is swirling in my head when the court opens.

Monsignor Hawkes takes the stand. He tells the jury that he is the rector of St. Basil's. Wearing his robes, he still looks like a pock-marked gargoyle. His blustering hands are folded before him piously. A cross, a tiny silver cross, hangs from his neck. *Again* the jury is told that the church had information of a planned riot.

"Objection. . . . This is not a conspiracy prosecution. What was said by anonymous persons at some undetermined time and place can only serve to prejudice the jury," I say.

"Objection overruled. Proceed."

I cross-examine him. "Now, Father . . . Exactly who said what concerning a planned riot?"

"We had information, sir."

"Who told you?"

"I don't remember, sir, but we knew."

"What exactly did you know?"

"We knew, for example, that certain former priest would attempt to engage in a disruption of our services. We know these men from their prior activities with revolutionaries in Guatemala."

"What? Who are you talking about?" This is news to me.

"We know that one of the so-called priests that desecrated the host . . . we know that he attempted to overthrow the government of Guatemala."

"All by himself?" I say.

"Well, *you* opened it up."

"All right. Now who is the priest?"

"Blas Bonpane is the man's name. I didn't say he was a priest."

"Is he one of the defendants?"

"No, sir. But he was one of the priests, so-called, that gave wine to the children on that night."

"And you say that he tried to overthrow the government of Guatemala?"

"Yes, sir. At least that's the information that we have on him."

"And where did you get this information?"

"Oh, we have our news sources. . . . And it came out in the paper, too."

"And, based on this information, you told the so-called ushers to beat us up?"

"Objection. Defense is trying to put words in the witness's mouth."

"Sustained."

"And you say that he is a 'so-called priest?' What do you mean?"

"He's no more a priest than those two men that are seated next to you."

"You mean Larry and Chuck?"

"Yes. And I mean Miss Doherty and Miss Josie."

"You say they are fraudulent priests also?"

"Of course not. However, they try to give the impression that they are nuns, sisters with the Holy Order. But they are not."

"Well, just what is a priest?"

"A man ordained of God to dispense the Holy Sacraments."

"And you know that God has not ordained these people?"

"I know that they are not in good standing with the Church."

"And the same goes for the sisters?"

"It is even worse for them. They have broken their vows."

"You have proof of this?"

"Well, just look at them, sir."

I turn to Duana and Josie. Both wear mini-skirts and smile prettily.

"They look pretty good to me, Father. But I *understand* what you mean. They do look kind of sinful."

The crowd breaks up at that one. There is loud laughter.

"Order in the court! I've warned you before," the judge lashes out.

"Now, Father . . . can you tell me. . . . Why has your superior, Cardinal McIntyre, been fired by the Pope?"

"Objection! Objection, your honor! This is highly improper!" The Duck is on his feet, screaming.

"Now, calm down, Mr. Ridder. . . . Yes, Mr. Brown, that question is clearly irrelevant. The status of Cardinal McIntyre is not on trial here."

"Oh yes it is! The status of Cardinal McIntyre constitutes our evidence of self-defense!"

Pandemonium!

"Come up here at once!"

The two lawyers and the blonde reporter approach.

"Now, Brown, I hereby hold you in contempt for that remark."

"Because I disagree with you as to what the issues are in this case, you're going to throw me in jail?"

"No. Because you have a nasty way of speaking to me in front of the jury."

"Well, Judge, you haven't exactly been very nice to me, either."

"Mr. Brown, I hereby hold you in contempt once again. . . . And I hereby order you to spend the next forty-eight hours in the custody of the Sheriff. Now, go back to your seats. I will dismiss the jury for the rest of the day."

"May I be heard?"

"No."

"I wish to make a motion."

"Not now."

"I wish to enter an objection."

"Take your seat, counsel."

I stand back. I bow my head silently. The Duck and the reporter move back toward their tables. I remain at the bench. When they've stopped a few feet away, I look up at the liberal with the red hair and the pasty white skin. I say very softly, "Fuck you!" And then I quickly turn and walk back to my table.

The jury is dismissed. The judge tells the defendants of my sentence. "And if any of you want to spend the night with Mr. Brown, just say one single word."

"Don't say anything, you guys," I say to them. "Go home and work on the trial. . . . Go home and help me out with my campaign."

"I would like to be heard, your honor," says one of the defendants.

"Bailiff, take Mr. Brown into custody." He quickly steps off the bench and disappears into his chambers.

Sanchez stands by while I speak with my clients. I hand them my briefcase and give final instructions. I empty my pockets, handing my wallet to Joe. "Take this stuff with you. I'll see you guys in a couple of days. Tell the girls not to worry." I begin to turn, my hand still in my coat pocket checking to see if I have anything left. Sanchez is standing next to me. I pull out three pills. I gaze stupidly at these lumps on my palm.

"What's that, Brown?" Sanchez says.

"These?" I *look*, then quickly swallow them. "Just bennies, man."

"Goddamn, man! You really ask for it, don't you?" he says.

"Yeah, I sure do. Let's go."

"Viva Zeta!" the crowd shouts.

"Viva El Zeta!" they cheer as five guards shuttle me into the tank.

The air is foul, the food shitty. All day I sit with criminals. Then I am handcuffed and taken down a flight of stairs, into a basement where a police car is waiting for me. Four officers drive me to the New County Jail in complete silence. When we arrive at the gray complex at North Broadway and Vignes Streets, I am met at the door by a sergeant in uniform and another bald cop in a brown suit.

"Mr. Brown. My name is Lieutenant Simpson. . . . You might as well know, we're going to treat you a little bit different than our regular prisoners."

"What do you mean?"

"Well, you're a candidate for Sheriff We wouldn't want anything to happen to you while you're in here. You can understand that. So I've been specially assigned to . . .

guard you. And this is Sergeant Lovelace. We'll *both* be taking care of you."

"Listen, Simpson. I've got nothing against you people."

"The same goes for me, Brown. I wish that judge hadn't . . ."

"OK. You keep your men away from me and we'll have no problems. I want to rest anyway."

I follow Lieutenant Simpson and Sergeant Lovelace into the gray complex, my hands still handcuffed behind me. The New County Jail is a monstrous structure, a square block of granite and concrete and steel. You enter through the back, with iron at your wrists, and the door clanks shut behind you and you are in an *institution,* a world unto itself. The floors are slick cement. The bars on all doors are painted gray. The prisoners are dressed in dark or faded blue jeans and pale blue work shirts. The shirts are stenciled across the back shoulders with the words, "LA County Sheriff—Prisoner." At the entrance, men are jammed into holding cells. They stand back to back, face to face. These men are still in regular street clothes. They have just come from various courts throughout the county and are now being processed and booked, fingerprinted, scrubbed and deloused before being given their new garb and a bed. Deputies in pressed khakis and short-sleeved shirts strut around and shout orders. Prisoners are lined up, fifty at a time.

"All right, all I want to see are elbows and assholes," a short deputy barks at the prisoners. "I want you men to take off your shoes and your socks. . . . Not yet, dummy. I'll tell you when. . . . We do things by the numbers here. . . . I say, 'Go,' then I want you to turn them over like this and shake them out. . . ." He takes a pair of shoes and turns them over, soles up, and bangs them on the floor.

"All right, take them off now. . . . Let's go! All of you. Now!"

Fifty grown men. Fifty old men. Fifty young men. Fifty winos. Men in suits, in ties, in dirty pants, in clean shirts, in dirty underwear, become fifty white asses, or yellow asses, or black asses.

"OK, men. Has everybody got their shoes off? All right . . . NOW! Yes, *now*, stupid! Turn your shoes over. Bang them seven times on the floor. . . . That's it. Seven times . . . Good. Now pick up your old clothes and step into that cell and stand in line for your new clothes. . . ."

The monkeys and the mojo men crowd up to the gate. Soldiers, sailors, marines and ex-football players, sheep in a slaughterhouse, pigs in a poke, slobs in a pen; sweat and grime and dirty socks, fungus between the toes, sores on legs, hanging honky pricks and hairy black balls.

"Now, when I call out your name, you give me your last name and your last four from your wristband. Got that?"

Lieutenant Simpson and Sergeant Lovelace have wrapped a plastic band with my name and a series of eight numbers around my wrist. I have been told to stand in line with a group of fifty. We are packed so tight that our asses touch, our armpits are full of other people's noses.

"Brown, Buffalo," the deputy barks from outside the cell.

"Zeta-Brown . . . 4889," I call back.

"What? . . . I said, 'Brown.'"

"Zeta-Brown, 4889."

"What are you, a wise guy? I just want your last name."

I am standing behind fifty men. I cannot see the deputy.

"That's my name, pal."

"Oh, I see. . . . Step out here, will you?"

I push my way through the crowd, naked, my clothes in my hand. "Yeah, here I am."

"Didn't you hear me say I just wanted your *last* name?"

He is a short red-headed man with a little mustache. I have seen him a thousand times. Funny, virtually every *gabacho* I've seen in two years has had red hair.

"That's my name."

"That ain't what I got here."

"I guess somebody made a mistake."

"Well, if you want to hold up this line . . . I can wait."

He begins to shut the cell door in my face. The other naked men inside begin to grumble and stir. There is no air. Everything is under bright hot lights.

"Hey, man . . . come on."

"Yeah, we want to get to chow. . . . Come on."

"Aw, fuck you guys!" I shout.

"OK with me, Brown. You want to be a smartass and get your buddies in trouble, it's OK with me. *I* ate already."

"You're the smartass, buddy!" I shout.

"What? Hey, you step right out."

I inch closer to the door. His eyes are blazing. He reaches for my head but I step back quickly.

"You fucking grease-ball! Get out here."

He is standing outside the open door. I step back.

"Buddy, you are going to be in hot water," I say, straining to look for my VIP escorts. "I just might be your boss pretty soon."

"What? Goddamnit, step out here! That's an order!"

"Oh, fuck!"

I walk out. I am a foot taller and outweigh him by at least a hundred pounds. I stick my chin out.

"Listen, Mac, if you want to hit me, go ahead. I wish you would. Go ahead. Be my guest."

"Hey, what's going on here, Deputy?" It is Lieutenant Simpson. He rushes up and puts his hand on the deputy who is about to swing.

"This fucking Mexican is giving me trouble, sir."

"Fuck you, you goddamn Oakie pig you!" I shout into his face.

He lunges for me and I move behind the lieutenant who grabs the deputy's arm. "Hold it, partner. Hold it."

"You heard that bastard! Let me at him!"

"Damn it, Brown, step over there!" the lieutenant yells at me.

I laugh and walk away, my bare ass sneering at the deputy.

"He's, uh . . . Brown's a VIP, Deputy. Sorry."

"He is? . . . Oh, is that the *lawyer?*"

"Yeah. . . . That's him."

Sergeant Lovelace comes up and signals me into another room. "*Goddamn,* Brown! Five minutes and you're ready to start a goddamn riot. I'll have to walk you through the lines."

"Just keep those goddamn pigs out of my way."

He laughs and tells a young Chicano trusty to give me some clothes. The kid asks me my size. He takes my clothes and whistles at my sharp tie.

"Hey, ain'tchoo that lawyer, ese?"

"Yeah, man. I'm Zeta."

"Jesus, put her there, partner."

He gives me the power shake. Lovelace laughs.

When I have dressed, the sergeant takes me into a room with one wall solid plate glass. On the other side, there is a room full of clerks punching typewriters and computers. They are all black or Chicano. Twenty-five Cockroaches stand at machines and ask questions which they type into the computers. This is the check-in.

I am standing in line, waiting my turn. I notice a black girl walk over to another girl with a bushy Afro. They whisper together. The second girl looks at me. She smiles. I wink at her.

"Buffalo Zeta Brown," I tell a Chicano behind the glass. "Call me Zeta."

"Occupation?"

"Professional revolutionary."

He types it up without looking at me. I look over his head and all the clerks are gawking at me. I wave to them. I raise my fist in the air. They all smile. Some of them give me the old peace sign, two fingers stuck up like horns.

When we have finished, the kid looks at me and says, "Nice to have you here, Zeta. How's it going?"

"It ain't bad," I say.

The sergeant takes me into a huge bathroom. A row of toilets. A row of fifty clean white shower stalls. I take a hot rinse while Lovelace chats with other deputies. When I'm dry, one of these guys says, "Come on, let's have your ass out here." He holds a hose with a nasty-looking nozzle.

"No, he don't have to do that," the sergeant says.

"What's that for?" I ask.

"For bugs and stuff. We run a clean joint."

"Jesus, you want to *kill* me?"

He takes me into another room where there's a camera on a stand. He takes my fingers and dips them in black ink and takes my prints.

"So you're running for Sheriff, hey Brown?" Lovelace says.

"Yeah, I guess so."

"Listen, let me tell you something. . . ." He brings his voice down to a whisper. "I doubt you'll win . . . but just let me tell you. . . . Not all of us are happy with Peaches. . . . If by some miracle you do get the job . . . just don't forget me. I'd make a hell of an Undersheriff. The name's Lovelace. Jim Lovelace. Got that?"

"Jesus, Lovelace, what can I say?"

"Make it Jim. . . . What do they call you? 'Zayter,' is it?"

"Zeta . . . like an 'S.' "

"Yeah, I saw you on TV last night. You and that old judge are having a running battle, huh?"

"Oh, it ain't bad. I can take this shit."

"Whoee! You are something else. . . . Anyway, we got to put you in a cell now. Want some cigarettes or candy before you go up?"

"I don't have any change."

"Well, shit. . . . I'm not supposed to. . . . Give me your money."

I hand him a dollar bill and he changes it.

"Boy, Lovelace, you sure must be bucking for something," a black deputy says to him.

When I've gotten a few packs of Camels, he leads me into a corridor, up a flight of stairs, and then onto an escalator. We are gliding up when I hear someone shout at me.

"Hey, *ese*. Hey, Zeta!"

Coming down the escalator is Cobra, a CM I defended against felony assault prosecution my first year in town. He and three other friends had beaten up four cops and take their weapons away from them. Pelon brought him over to my house to sell me one of the .38 Specials. A week later his sister called me and asked if I'd defend him. She said Cobra took my money and went out to get drunk. He was on a binge when they nailed him. For some reason, I felt responsible.

"Hey, Cobra!"

"Jesus, ese. What are you doing here?"

As we pass, we touch hands.

"I'm just a criminal like you, man."

"They got you for another beef with the judges?"

"Yeah . . . Contempt of court."

"Hey, I'll tell the dudes."

"I'll just be here for a day or two."

He is out of sight below us. We turn left and climb more stairs.

"We're gonna put you on the best floor we got, Brown," Lovelace says.

"Great."

He laughs. "It's the nut ward."

"What? You serious?"

"Yeah. They're the only private cells we got. It'll be comfortable."

We turn a corner into a noiseless white corridor. It is a hospital ward. The deputies wear white uniforms. The cells are individual rooms with a small window in each door. Lovelace unlocks one and tells me that he'll get me some food.

"Just let me know if you need anything."

He shuts the door and I am alone in a white room with a mattress three inches thick on a box spring. A sink and toilet in the corner. A blue blanket and a sheet and a pillow. The floor is smooth gray cement. The ceiling is smooth and white. There is nothing to do. I sit down for a quick smoke.

Five minutes later the door opens. In pops a doctor and a nurse.

"We've come to see if you're sick."

"No, sir. Not that I know of."

"Why don't I leave you some aspirin and a sleeping pill."

"Thanks."

The next two days are the most boring in my life.

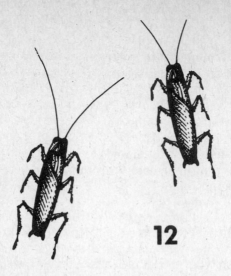

# 12

The trial of the St. Basil Twenty-One lasted one month. Nebron held me in contempt of court ten times. After the fifth time, the headlines simply said, *"Brown in Jail Again."* By the time closing arguments rolled around, the issue was no longer whether the defendants had rioted but whether or not Nebron would throw Brown in jail again. The crowds packed the courtroom and waited in the hallways for empty chairs. It was the best show in town. Standing room only.

In his closing argument, Ridder started out by denouncing the Militants. For two hours, I sat back and listened to him curse us. The jury was in the box staring down at the little Duck while he called the nuns whores and priests frauds. . . .

"We know what kind of people they are. If you want them to feel free to break up any church service for the sake of their so-called movement, you go ahead and find them innocent. . . . We've heard about the outside influences, revolutionaries, radicals, there's nothing to hide here. Brown knows this. Brown was their leader. That's been testified to by nearly everyone. Of course he's gonna get up and tell you they're innocent. But, ladies and gentlemen, there is much more at stake here than simply whether or not these people assaulted the church. . . . We know they did, we saw that on film. . . . But what is even more important is whether or not this society can afford to have them go unpunished. ... Are they simply citizens exercising their civil liberties as they would have you believe? Or are they mad dogs who would pervert all that this country stands for? ... That is what you must ask yourselves as you go in to deliberate. ... Would you want people such as these to come to your church while you were praying? ... Would you? ... I doubt it. I really doubt it."

There is absolute silence when he finishes. He sits down and I walk up to the podium before the jury and stare at them. I look into the face of each one, one at a time.

I am staring. Tears are forming. My face is warm. My eyes are glued. I close my eyes. I have my elbows on the podium. I am aware that the jury is looking at me. I am aware that the people in the audience are looking at me. I know the judge is nervous. I am tired. Rag-bone tired. Run down. Boy, I hurt in my bones. I don't care about nothing anymore. Everything is black. My mouth opens:

Ladies and Gentlemen, Friends, Enemies and Lovers,
I've got a Song to Sing for You.
It is The Song of the Cockroach People.
It is A Song of My Pain and My Pride,
A Song of My Loves and My Woes ...
And it Goes:
You Crummy Bastards, We Are Da Yout.
I Stand Here Before You With Tears On My Face,
I Cry Unashamedly Because I Am Not Afraid
To Sing of The Cockroach People ...
And it Goes:
You Crummy Bastards, WE ARE DA YOUT!

"Objection, your honor! . . . May we approach the bench?"

"Yes . . . Come to the bench, both of you."

I open my eyes and I see Mrs. Jean Fisher, juror number six, a black woman with fine legs who has eyed me from time to time. She is the one whom Duana Doherty overheard in the toilet. I have told Duana and Gloria and the whole bunch not to pester me with things that will disturb my mind. I've told them over and over, "I don't know what it means. A smile doesn't necessarily mean the person is going to vote for you. . . . Leave me alone."

"But I heard her say, 'I feel so sorry for those poor people. . . .' I'm telling you, Zeta, she didn't know I was there!"

I remember a counselor at law school named Fisher. I am looking at her legs. My mind spasms back into the past . . .

"Mr. Brown! Come to bench at once!"

It is Judge Nebron.

I go to the bench.

"Mr. Brown . . . uh, is anything the matter with you?"

"I feel tired. But nothing more."

"Well . . . are you reciting a poem to the jury? . . . I'm not saying you *can't* . . . I was just wondering."

"Heh, heh. . . . It's my sense of humor, Judge. . . . I'm coming to the point."

"Yes. . . . Well, uh, Mr. Ridder, did you wish to make argument?"

Ridder gives me a queer stare. He has fat lips. His eyes are buggy. He looks like Porky Pig. And he walks like a duck. We've been laughing at him all the way through the trial. When we pass him in the hallway we quack.

"No, your honor. I think Mr. Brown knows what he's doing. He should get down to the issues in this case."

"Well, Mr. Ridder . . . I have given *both* of you pretty wide latitude . . . This has been a very, uh, unusual trial . . . Let's get back to it."

My voice is shaky. My throat is choked. My neck is heavy. I stand before the jury box and stare into the face of each one. I repeat everything. I look them straight in the eye. One at a time, I pierce them. And when my eyes reach Mrs. Jean Fisher, I notice for the first time that she is *beautiful*. She has soft brown-bronze skin. Brilliant jet-black hair with a touch of gray. She is a teacher. From voir dire, I know that she lives in the ghetto near Watts.

I am digging the shit out of her and then I see it for one second, one split second, a mere flash of time: she's hooked before I open my mouth. . . .

"A group of law students came to me one day last fall and asked me to help them arrange a meeting with Cardinal McIntyre . . . But that's not *really* where the story begins. . . . Let me take you back to a place and time of sorrow. Permit me, if you will, this short digression.

"It is 1509 AD. . . . We are in Cuba. . . . A captain from Castile wants gold. . . . He wants land and he wants slaves. He also wants to go on a mission for his god and his king. . . . He fills three boats with soldiers, fire powder and horses, which sail west until they land on the coast of what we now know as Mexico.

"The king, the supreme ruler in the land of the Hummingbird Wizard, hears of the arrival of white men in long boats. It is a prophecy come true. For over two hundred years, the prophets of Quetzalcoatl have predicted this event. The king, Montezuma, has taken upon himself all power in his empire. He is both political ruler and chief priest. In a word, he has assumed the status of a god. Not even his family can look him in the eye. He has become the principal deity of the people of Tenochtitlan in the Valley of Mexico. The people are called, collectively, the *aztecas*.

"The captain from Castile, Hernando Cortez, burns the boats and tells his men there is no turning back. They have come to this strange land to conquer or die for the glory of God. They attack village after village, taking captives and booty. They make alliances with the natives, promising them protection from Montezuma's bloody rituals, from the human sacrifices to Huitzilopochtli, the god of war.

"Anxious to rid themselves of the burden of Montezuma, these Indians, as they are called by the Catholic Cortez, join up with the Spaniards. They march toward the capital, thirty-thousand strong . . . Through diplomacy, political chicanery and modern techniques of warfare, the white men on horses and their army of slaves enter triumphantly into the most advanced city in the world, the world's most beautiful city. In 1500 AD, Mexico City far surpasses anything that the Spaniards have seen on the European continent. There is an efficient government. It is a city with streets and canals and a sewage system, a city of gold and birds and leopards and barber shops. A land of flowers and parrots, mountains and blue beaches. They have priests and philosophers, soldiers and artists.

"And they have a king who is a god, a god who tells his million-man army to lay down their swords. . . . 'This is he of whom our prophets spoke,' Montezuma tells his people. And since he is god, they obey. And the Spaniards take Mexico by default.

"The first thing Cortez does is to take himself a woman. Malinche, to her everlasting disgrace, provides him with her brown body and her strange words.

"The second thing he does is to order the destruction of the heathen temples. He outlaws human sacrifices. He outlaws the religion that has shed the blood of thousands . . . And then he burns the books so that people will not be tempted to return to their heathen ways.

"And then he ransacks the capital and sends the gold and glitter to his king in Spain. And they rape the women. If you want to join the new nation, all you have to do is give up your slave name and your slave tongue. If you want to become a Spaniard, be baptized and take a Christian name. An attack upon the Church is an assault upon the State. And vice versa. Church and State are one.

"Three hundred years later, in 1850 AD, more white men in covered wagons come to the land of the northern deserts, the land we now call the Southwest. It is the ancient land of Aztlan, the original homeland of the *aztecas*. New invaders. New conquerors. They, too, come with fire powder and the flag of a new nation. They, too, are on a holy mission. As Cortez had done before, through modern warfare, through politics and diplomacy, the new white barbarians invade the land and subdue it. They inform the people that they now have a new government and a new religion—Christianity. They sign a treaty called Guadalupe Hidalgo. The United States pays a couple of million to an idiot in Mexico City for all Aztlan and for all the slaves living thereon. The treaty says that, if the people choose, they can remain as citizens of America or they can go south to Mexico.

"'But we are not Mexicans,' the people cry out. 'We are Chicanos from Aztlan. We have never left our land. Our fathers never engaged in bloody sacrifices. We are farmers and hunters and we live with the buffalo.'

"But they are wrong. They are now citizens of America, whether they like it or not. And we'll call them Mexican-Americans. But if they want to be Americans, they'll have to give up their slave name.

"A hundred years later, the Chicanos turn to the government and to the priests and ask for justice, for education, for food, for jobs, for freedom and the pursuit of happiness. The St. Basil Twenty-One sought an audience with the leaders of the Church and of the State. And to show that they did not worship heathen gods, they tried to attend the bloodless Mass within the sanctuary called St. Basil's. And when they entered they were told: *There Is No Room.* Leave, or we'll kill you. Or jail you. Insult you. Mace you. Kick and bite. Scream and holler. While the choir sings. '*Oh come all ye faithful . . . Oh come ye, Oh come ye . . . to* jail and court. Court and jail . . . *Come. Come! Come!'*

"Ladies and gentlemen of the jury, if we had planned to ransack the temple, if we had wanted to attack the sanctuary . . . tell me, would we have brought women and children? Would Victor have brought his grandmother? Would I have invited my three nieces? And would I, an attorney and counselor at law, would I have stood in the midst of it all with a pipe in my mouth?

"And yet, we *are* guilty of inciting to riot. We did *want* a riot. We *sought* it. And we did *accomplish* it! . . . A riot of the brain. A revolution of the spirit. . . . And the only reason the prosecution is going after us with shrieks of outrage, the only reason the State has spent such time and money, is because we did accomplish what we set out to do . . . Pope Paul did in fact fire Cardinal James Francis McIntyre because he started a riot within his own church for the grandeur and glory of *his* god—his own ego. . . ."

"Objection, your honor!" Ridder cries out.

"Overruled. Please proceed, Mr. Brown."

161

"Thank you, Judge. . . ."

I look down at the jury. They are still. Jean Fisher has tears in her almond eyes. A man from Pacific Telephone is rubbing red eyes with the back of his hand. I hear sniffles in the courtroom. I, myself, am in tears. My throat is too stuffed to go on so I remain silent for a long time. I nod my head.

"I have nothing more to say. . . . Thank you for listening to my nonsense. . . . I hope you can put it together better than I."

I return to my chair. The defendants are singularly silent. Only a cough here and there. And then:

Clapping of hands! Stomping of feet! The crowd raises its voice to the ceiling! We are in a theater. For two minutes the crowd is on its feet clapping and cheering me on. Judge Nebron says not a word.

When it dies down, Ridder gets up and goes to the jury to finish up his attack upon my character. I am a fraud, he tells them. A hypocrite with absurd theories. I am a fraud just like Duana and Larry and Chuck and Josie are frauds. But it is too late. He sounds flat and stale. He cannot match my emotion.

The judge instructs the jury. On their way out, Jean Fisher looks me straight in the eye and winks. Just a short, fast wink. Soon they are in their deliberations and we are in the hallway waiting for the verdict.

We go to a bar across the street. We feel good and drink like crazy. After three hours the waitress calls out over a microphone: "Call for Mr. Brown."

It is the clerk. The jury has a verdict.

I rush back to the booth and tell everyone to hurry. We pour out of the bar. I am walking with Gilbert and Black Eagle. Victor, the kid with the cane, is ahead of us. We are standing at the curb waiting for the light to change.

"Hey, Zeta. . . . Come here," Victor calls.

I walk up to him. He is talking to two men in suits.

"Hey, man, this is Liberace!"

I look into the man's face. Sonofabitch! It *is* the world-famous fag. The white hair and the big grin. He is wearing a pink suit, a pin-striped pink suit!

"Mr. Brown? This man tells me you're running for Sheriff."

"Yeah, I sure am."

"Well . . . I hope you win."

He reaches for my hand. I clasp his thumb. "This is the Chicano handshake," I say. He blushes and squeezes.

"Hey, Mr. Liberace, will you vote for Zeta?"

The man looks at Victor and twinkles his green eyes. "Why of course."

"Thanks, man."

The light changes and we bound up the steps to the courthouse.

When the jury comes in, I see tears on the face of Jean Fisher. They don't have a verdict after all. They want testimony read back. The court reporter reads it and we return to wait in the hallways. We sit and wait every day from nine to five, for a week. For seven days and nights we are waiting. Nobody feels good anymore. They can go to jail for a year. Ridder has told me he will seek the maximum sentence if he gets a conviction. We sit and wait in the hall. We sit and wait on the cement benches in the courtyard. We look at the waterfall and drink soda pop. The girls are at my side. Rosalie hangs her head on my shoulder. We eat burritos that Gloria and her daughters cook for us. Every day, for a week, we sit and wait and drink pop and eat sandwiches and tacos. Our lives are in abeyance.

Three times the jury asks for more instructions.

Three times I see Jean Fisher going from bad to worse.

On the seventh day the jury finally comes in with its verdict. *Six are guilty. Fifteen are innocent.* Gloria and Duana are guilty as sin, they say. Joe, Richard, Tony and Cruz must do six months. Duana and Gloria must do ninety days.

We go to my house on Sixth Street to celebrate our partial victory. The convicted ones are out on appeal bond. Their only hope is for a new trial. I doubt that Nebron will grant it. But maybe on appeal. . . . But for now, what the fuck. Now, it's time to drink beer and wine and tequila and whiskey, to smoke dope and dance to the music of Mariachis and Willie Bobo and Santana and Mongo Santamaria and El Chicano. Now is the time to forget those days and nights of fighting with the pigs. And now is the time of women.

Women, broads, wenches, witches and *viejas*. *Cholas, changas, morras y rukas*. They come in droves to the house. They come to hug and kiss the world-famous Chicano lawyer who wants to be the sheriff of seven million people. He who would make women cry with his tale of woe. We sit and laugh and drink and watch ourselves on television. We hear our voices over the radio and see our pictures in the papers. We are on the map. In the news. *Millions* have seen our faces and heard our voices.

"Viva El Zeta!" they shout me on.

"*¡Qué Viva!*"

And we drink and dance and fuck and suck and hug and kiss.

"There's a call for you, Buff," Rosalie tells me.

I go into the bedroom. "Hello?"

"Mr. Brown? . . . This is Mrs. Fisher . . . uh, juror number six?"

"Yes, Mrs. Fisher. . . ."

"I wanted to talk to you. . . . I have something that might be important . . . but not on the phone."

"I'll be right over . . . if you'll tell me where you are."

I tell the group of my call. I'll bring her over, I tell them. And I go to pick her up in Watts, the black ghetto where, in 1965, the people rose in arms against the pigs and lost thirty-five men. I remember the advice of Yorty, still puzzling over his motives.

I drive past the bar-b-ques, the liquor stores, the dark alleys. The faded buildings are covered with slogans and grafitti the same as in Tooner Flats. It is an older war zone. The debris, the burnt buildings, the vacant lots, the For Sale signs, are testimony to that early battle of the sixties.

Jean Fisher opens the door. Her black eyes are downcast. She wears street shoes and a black business suit. She leads me into her home which is soft with thick rugs. Big lamps in the corners, fish tanks and puffy couches. It is like my sister Teresa's home, my sister whose husband has forbidden her ever to call me. We sit and I wait for her story. I am alive with victory, with the tequila and the prospect of another score.

"I've been trying to get a hold of you since I got home after court."

"I'm glad you did. . . . You know, I've been watching you."

"What?"

"Well, you know."

She is silent again. Her hands are twitching. She tugs at her hair. She lights another cigarette. I see serious business ahead and wrench myself sane.

"I'm not sure if you can use this . . . but first let me say that I held out as long as I could . . . but they all ganged up on me. We finally made a . . . trade, of sorts . . . I had to give in on the two women and the four men in order to get the others off."

"Tell me what happened."

"First of all . . . that Mrs. Wells, the foreman?"

"Juror number seven?"

"Yes, she sat on my right? Well, she gave us a list . . . the second day, after I'd argued for acquittal for everyone? . . . She gave me this. . . ."

She reaches over to the coffee table and picks up a large piece of folded cardboard and several sheets of typing paper. The cardboard is a diagram listing each defendant and the direct testimony of the cops affecting each one. The sheets are outlines of the prosecution's arguments . . . beginning with the statement: "Of course we all recognize the right to demonstrate under the First Amendment . . . *but.* . . ."

She tells me that Mrs. Wells had brought these materials into the deliberating room. It is clear to me that someone had *coached* her. The methodology of enumeration, the technique of separating defendants, and the succinct outline of legal arguments can only be the work of an

165

efficient legal secretary or of an attorney. It would be impossible for a juror to construct this kind of outline during the course of the trial. And yet, every day, the judge warned jurors not to discuss, or in any way deliberate on the matter at hand, except in the jury room, *after* instructions. I am stunned, but not surprised.

"Did anything else unusual happen in there?"

"Well . . . I don't know if I should really . . . is it legal for me to talk to you?"

"Oh, sure. . . . There's nothing unethical about this. The judge has dismissed you, you are no longer a juror."

"I still feel like one."

"Well, let's get out of that mood. Why don't we go somewhere and have a drink?"

The business is over. I have a case for appeal!

"Are you sure?"

"I'm positive. Come on. Why don't you come with me to a party? Would you like to meet the defendants?"

"Oh, that would be . . . great."

She stands and goes to get her coat. She returns and we walk to the door. She is slipping the black fur coat on. I reach to help her. I lift the back of it to her smooth beautiful shoulders and she turns to me, her face to mine . . . into my mouth. *Voom*, she is in my face! Just like that. The smell of flowers, of hot flowers is on her neck, on her tiny ears, and even coming out of the dark, up out of the black coat and her tongue is firmly inside my mouth. We glide backwards into the room and we slide down without moving our faces from each other. We are down on a bed of furry animals, down and down into a bed of roses and perfume.

I am not thinking, not talking. Everything is going slowly inside the darkness of dark flesh and the clothes are sliding to the floor without a sound, without a hitch. There is no hesitation, nothing unusual. Nothing out of the ordinary. As if we'd done this all our lives, no one is nervous here and my hands glide over and over, around and around a warm belly and soft breasts of a middle-aged woman who is hungry and biting my ears and crying and sinking deeper into my stomach and down and down to my belly. Her tongue is wet, warm, sticky and slowly travels tickling, tickling down toward the beast as hard as nails. Down, down to my solid prick and around. Warm-wet-stuck-suck, down, in-out, in-out. . . . *Ayyyyyy!*

Next morning the dawn is wet with dew and fog. Jean tells me she is a widow. Her children are away at college. She has never joined any movement, just taught school and kept busy while her heart ached through the years. She will sign any affidavit, give any testimony, do whatever is necessary. Even though I have assured her she is no longer a juror, she will still feel guilty. Why? Because all during the trial, ever since the day she was selected for jury duty, she has wanted to touch me. She has wanted to hold me. And now, if only she could see me once in while? . . . She cooks breakfast for us.

"I'll be back," I say, kissing her goodbye. I feel terrific. The party is still on at my pad when I get back, the temporary end of one battle and the beginning of another.

# 13

*Who Is Buffalo?*
*Who Is Zeta?*
*Who Is Brown?*

The campaign has stepped into high gear. The publicity from the trials and my numerous contempt of court charges have brought hordes into my camp. Cockroaches from Hollywood and Venice, *vatos* from car clubs, elderly churchgoers. Cockroaches from the barrios and beaches have begun to pass out bumper stickers. Posters drawn by nuns and hippies, statements of my single-issue platform are stuck under windshield wipers. Lawyers from the National Lawyers Guild, from the ACLU and from the Legal Aid Societies have joined up to elect the radical Chicano lawyer. And I tell them I will carry the gun and clean up the town. Yes, me, Buffalo Zeta Brown!

Soon the word filters up to the movie stars. The old-timers who have hidden behind grass skirts, the ones with the mustaches, with the broken accents, the Chile Charlie types, the Sancho Panzas of America, *los tontos*, side-kicks of Zorro. And those with red hair and Jewish names: Gilbert Roland, Vicki Carr, Anthony Quinn and others whose names I have forgotten over the years.

They now wish to hold a rally on behalf of all Chicano

candidates for office. *All* Chicanos will now receive their blessings and their money. The ones who have hidden for so long, those who have not spoken up for the two years we've been at war, now they will entertain us. . . .

I have bought Rosalie new clothes. She is in a long red dress of lace and silk. Her brown hair falls over slender shoulders. She is bursting with youth and beauty. With her new glasses she looks nearly eighteen.

We enter the auditorium of the Sports Arena on the USC campus. Here, years ago, I once taught a class in the Department of Religion along with Chief Judd Davis. The huge amphitheater is packed. I have been given two seats in the VIP section and we sit directly in front of the microphones, surrounded by famous Cockroaches and politicos running for office.

A man in a gray suit walks on stage. He comes to the microphone seventeen feet from my seat. The overheads are dimmed as the spotlight blasts him, alone on the stage. It is Anthony Quinn, the most famous Chicano of them all.

"Ladies and gentlemen . . . *Señores y señoras* . . . Brothers, *hermanos* and fellow Mexican-Americans. . . . This is a historic moment. . . . We are ten-thousand strong tonight. It is the first time that we have publicly come out. . . . Many of us have been in the aisles for years. We've been backstage, or looking at the television set while so many of you have been on the firing line. . . . Tonight is just a beginning. We have formed an organization called the Mexican-American Organization. We intend to support *all* Mexican-American candidates for office. . . . Not just for this campaign, but for all of them. We have dedicated ourselves to involvement with our own people. We who have reaped the rewards of this society because we are Mexican-Americans and have hidden in our anonymity, now we come out and publicly declare that we are of Mexican-American ancestry; that we are, in truth and fact, and proudly so: Mexican-American!"

There is a smattering of applause. A shout here and there. A *grito*, a yodel of tequila breath curdles up to the rafters. . . . Viva la Raza!

"*¡Qué Viva!*" the crowd echoes feebly.

I squeeze Rosalie's arm. We sit back, listening to the music of Mariachis in cowboy outfits with shiny boots and bright buckles: *Si Adelita se fuera con otro.*

Quinn brings one movie star after another to make his or her confession. They each have the same message. They each apologize, rationalize and explain why in the past it has not been possible to come out for their *raza.* Quinn stands back, wiping the sweat from his brow. He tugs at his tie. He waits until each testimonial is over and then he slaps them on the back and tells them to sing a song, dance a jig, play your guitar, just do something for your *raza,* partner.

José Jimenez comes on stage and tells us he is going to retire his dummy slow-joe character act because it is insulting to the Mexican, he says. Mexicans, after all, are not slow slobs with tacos dripping from their hungry mouths. . . . "About time!" somebody shouts. "Big deal!" a *vato loco* yells out.

And when the entertainment and introductions finish, Quinn tells us he is going to introduce some VIPs and the candidates.

"Chicano Power!" I hear a shout.

I smile and feel surrounded with the warmth of my friends and supporters.

Quinn gives a snap look of recognition to the radical yell. He lifts his arm half-way up, beginning the power salute . . . then drops it, thinking otherwise.

"Yes, uh . . . First I'd like to introduce Congressman Edward Roybal, our first Mexican-American elected to Congress from this State . . . Señor Roybal, where are you? Stand up and take a bow."

The crowd shouts and stamps their approval while the darkness is sliced by the spotlight moving to our section, where up jumps the tall Congressman with the gray hair. He lifts an arm in acknowledgment of his office. The clapping is strong and polite for this gentleman displaying the long nose of an ancient Azteca.

"Thank you, ladies and gentlemen," Quinn tells us.

The light is back to the stage and Quinn is mopping sweat from his eyes. Dark, twisted eyes that we have seen gnarled in so many movies. I hug Rosalie. She takes a nip from my neck and scratches my palm with her trigger finger.

"And next I would like to present to you the only elected official of Mexican ances ... uh, parents ... Julian Nava is from my own neighborhood, ladies and gentlemen. . . . We're both from Tooner Flats, the toughest barrio in East LA. . . . So it gives me special pride to introduce a man who made it out of that neighborhood and went on to Harvard to get a Ph.D. in History. . . . Now he's on the school board here and we're all going to support him. . . . Julian, where are you?"

Quinn holds the mike with his right hand. He looks out into the darkness. I have only seen him once in person when, last month, he ate lunch in a Japanese restaurant near the courthouse. I was so impressed that I wrote him a letter asking for his support. Of course, he did not answer me. I expect no more help from him than from Liberace. But other than Bogart, he is still the only serious Hollywood idol I ever had.

I hear applause for Julian. The stage goes dark and I turn to see light fall ten feet behind me. Rosalie and I are also under its glare.

"Thanks, thanks. . . . *Gracias, gracias.* . . ." As usual, Julian is sharp in his snazzy suit. During the aftermath of the Blow Outs, I appeared before the school board and asked for this and that, etc., etc. . . . but Julian was smart. He nodded and smiled and showed his teeth. He did nothing. And now he blows the rafters a peace sign. He lifts the Churchill-Nixon V for Victory, which brings whistles and stamping of feet.

"Thanks, ladies and gentlemen. . . ." Quinn says. "Now I'd like to introduce ... uh. . . ." He stops. He pulls a piece of paper out of his pocket. He wipes away his sweat some more while reading the paper. Then he turns to look backstage. A man comes out and whispers in his ear. I recognize the whisperer as Guzman, the liberal director of a poverty program in East LA. A silver-tongued man who has worked with labor unions and the Kennedy campaigns and is a friend of Cesar Chavez. I remember how he tried to talk us out of picketing the Glass House. Quinn nods and Guzman leaves Quinn under the cone of white heat.

"Ladies and gentlemen. . . . I am informed that the next man to be introduced is a newcomer around here. . . . You probably haven't heard of him as much as you have of Roybal and Nava. . . . And the note says that he *prefers* to be called Zeta, uh, or, the Brown Buffalo . . . and that he's running for Sheriff under the Chicano Militant banner. . . . Señor Zeta, where are you?"

"Viva Zeta!"

"*¡Qué Viva!*"

Roars bounce off the ceiling. The light is upon me. I am seized with the flame and the roar of the crowd. Julian reaches over and shakes my hand. I lean into his ear and say, "See what I told you? You should call yourself a Chicano, *ese*. You'd get more votes." But I smile, so he smiles and pats me on the back. To him, I am just another politician to contend with. Join the club.

Roybal is standing several seats away. He waves to me through the bedlam. The stomping of feet, the clattering-clammering-deafening roar of the crowd giving up its excess of exhaltation, not to me but to the idea of a Cockroach-man sticking his thumb up the white man's ass—and getting away with it.

"Chicano Power!"

"Viva La Raza!"

"*¡Qué Viva!*"

It goes on and on. The guys in the rafters won't stop until Quinn tells them that he has a surprise.

"I've just been informed that Vicki Carr has arrived."

And the noise goes up ten-fold! The building of cement and black steel shakes like an echo chamber running amuck.

A short lady comes on stage in a swirl of colors, in a rainbow dress from the mountains of Michoacan, where the men pack guns and the women make cheese, from the land of the bloody Tarascans who never signed a peace treaty with the Spanish invaders.

She takes the mike and Quinn fades into the blackness. All eyes settle on the little broad with the fine body. Right above me, I can see her legs, her ankles under the fluffed-out lace of ribbons ready for dancing *corridos,* mariachis and *zapatios.*

She tells us she too is from East LA. . . . "And I'm gonna say it right off even though some of you might not like it. . . . *Soy chicana.* . . . I am a Chicano and *proud* of it."

"AYYYYYYYYY . . . AYYYYYYYYY . . . AYYYY!"

"¡Qué Viva La Vicki!"

"VIVA!"

Once again the rafters explode. She waves them on while I go nuts. I am in love with her. I haven't met her, I've never even seen her, I only know that she sings; and yet I am absolutely in love with her right now. I fondle her soft lashes, I stroke her red hair cascading over her shoulders.

Vicki Carr sings, then tells us she is married to a Jew. It doesn't matter, I'm *still* in love with her. She sings and coos to us in our special dialect. She tells jokes about growing up in Tooner Flats. She sings and makes us melt and tells us how she puts hot sauce on her bagels. I wish to send her a message. How can I get Quinn to tell her Zeta will take her, tell her how I can do it better than any Jew, tell her that she can eat real tortillas with *real* chile at my table.

When she finishes, the clapping is soft and slow at first. Then it builds up and up, faster and faster, harder and harder, faster-harder-faster-harder, until we are drowned in a sea of madness. Into the night ripples our hysteria. Quinn escorts her off the stage in the midst of this thunder and then returns to the mike. Looking uncomfortable, he stands with one hand at his neck, the other holding a written speech. He tugs at his black tie and says, "Ladies and gentlemen . . . uh, that was Vicki Carr. . . . And . . . You heard her yourself. . . ." He is tugging harder at his tie now, moving it back and forth, trying to get some air. He is dripping wet in the burning light.

"I guess you know, you can sense that we've been having some problems backstage. . . . You can see, you've seen . . . how some of us want to. . . . We don't know, we don't even know. . . ." He has unfastened the tie now, holding one end with the other end stuck under his coat.

"But, to hell with it! . . . "

Strip-slit, off comes the tie, cast down with one swishing hand of the Shakespearian actor on stage.

"I was going to read this speech that one of my press agents wrote for me. . . ."

He throws the paper on the floor and it vanishes into darkness.

"But instead, I'm going to read something I cut out of a magazine. . . ."

He takes still another piece of paper out of his inside pocket. Reaching for a gun or a cigarette in an old movie, Anthony Quinn. . . .

"You know, all my life, all my *professional* life, I have fought the battle of . . . I have been against nationalism from my earliest days. My father was Irish and my mother was Mexican. . . . They would both agree with those backstage who would have me call myself a Mexican-American. . . . And I have called myself that all my life. . . . I have acted every part, every race, every religion. . . . I've been Japanese, Italian, Pole, White, Black and Brown. . . . And yet, I feel like a Chicano tonight. . . . Yes, I feel like those guys up there who were just shouting for *El Zeta* . . . whoever he may be. . . . I feel like I'd like to feel like I think he must be feeling. . . . Heh, heh, I guess I'm a little confused. . . . Anyway, to hell with it, here goes a little speech which some Indian Chief gave before Congress around 1790. . . ."

But I do not hear the words. I don't need to. I become lost in a trance of my own speech to the jury, which is the same speech that Quinn is now reading while Rosalie holds my hand.

" . . . And now, my White Father, you would have us leave our homes on the range, in the mountains and near the streams where we have hunted and fished for so many moons. . . . And you whom we welcomed and fed, now you would enclose us in a land that is unknown to us, a land without the buffalos which we have learned to live upon. . . . You would put us in a corner, in a corral, surrounded by wire with iron pricks, you call it a reservation . . . as if we were criminals or animals to be caged under lock. . . ."

Quinn is carrying us along with his fine deep actor's voice, a man with blood and guts. He is crying, wiping his eyes, and as he reads his tears and emotions dig deep into our beings. And when it is over, there is a moment of silence. No one claps or shouts. Nothing is done for one full minute while Quinn stands at the mike, hands at his sides, head bent over, gray hair, at sixty, an old and wise man.

And the roar rips the top off! The singing to the ceiling, the rafters are bursting in air to the shouts and yells of the *vatos* in the balconies who have come with bottles of Ripple, a handful of reds and a toke before they entered. Tequila burns deep in the throat and we are in an orgy of nationalism, solid, tight, a rabid group in the dark looking at Antonio Quinn. *el vato número uno:*

"VIVA QUINN—VIVA QUINN!!"
"VIVA LA RAZA—VIVA ZAPATA!!"
"VIVA EL ZETA—VIVA CESAR CHAVEZ!!"
**"¡QUE VIVAN!"**

And the crowd melts into one consciousness and no man is alone in that madness any longer.


A month later, I am in the middle of another crowd, this time in the UCLA Student Union. The huge hall is packed with students, five thousand kids with shirts hanging outside their jeans. A mass of long hair, banners and buttons.

Nixon has sent the B-52s to Cambodia, code name: Looking Glass. None of the soldiers of America touched the rice paddies with their feet. Only the bombs of flaming hot goo entered the villages where the little people lived. On May 5, 1970, four young Americans were killed by the Ohio militia in that county that proclaims itself as The Rubber Capitol of the World, The Home of the Soap Box Derby, not far from Akron. And now protest meetings are being held all over the country.

Corky Gonzales is to be on the program. And so is Angela Davis, the black professor who only recently was kicked off campus by Governor Reagan's Board of Regents. I, too, have been invited to speak. The crowd rumbles with anticipation.

I am standing at the rear with Gilbert, Pelon and Black Eagle, who protect me. They all sleep at my house now. When I awake, they are stretched out on the living room floor with pistols at hand. We now have rifles in the closet. Wherever I go, they go. I have had too many letters, too many phone calls to feel safe.

We have just been to a fund-raising party at some rich liberal Jew's house in Beverly Hills. I am anxious to meet Corky, but I do not see him.

A tall kid with a bushy red beard comes to the mike. "Ladies and gentlemen. . . . Our first speaker is Angela Davis."

Roar Roar Roar. Stomp, clap, stomp, clap. Power to the People!

The lithe slow figure of the black beauty comes to the stage. She is the heroine of the day. She has told the world that she is a member of the Lamumba Club, a communist and an intellectual. The students and the professors love her. Hip-hip-hooray!

"We are here to protest the slaughter of the students at Kent State. . . . We are here to join hands to fight against the warmongers. . . . We are here to tell Richard Nixon that he can't continue to bomb and kill the poor yellow brothers and sisters in Vietnam, in Cambodia . . . or at Kent State!"

"Right on, sister! . . . Tell it like it is!"

"Now, what we've got to understand, what we've got to see, is that the war in Vietnam, just like the war at Kent State, both are products of the *system* in this country. . . . It isn't just Nixon or Reagan or Yorty or Chief Davis. It's the political system, the capitalist system, the racist institutions that are tearing this country to shreds. . . . We have got to make it clear to those men in the White House that we won't stand for it anymore!"

Cheers! Whistles!

"We have got to organize ourselves. . . . We must join together, black and white and students and old people, we must register to vote, we must get the people to the polls, we must get those pigs out of their positions of power! We must understand, we must be aware of their intentions. Nixon and Kissinger, Reagan and Agnew, these pigs have got to go! . . . "

Thunderous applause! The crowd is delirious! They *love* her. They shout and stomp their sandals on the hardwood floor. . . .

The Black Beauty is soon escorted off the stage by three black dudes with sunglasses. They look around as they walk her to the rear of the stage. The crowd continues to rock.

"Thank you, thank you, Miss Davis," redbeard says. "And now . . . if you'll hold it down . . . I'd like to introduce a man from out of state. Brother Corky Gonzales!"

There is a dribble of applause. The students don't know Corky.

The short dark Chicano comes on stage in a red shirt and black pants. His jet-black hair is cut short. He has white sharks teeth and the broad shoulders of an ex-boxer.

"Thanks. . . . And thank you, Angela. We are with you in your fight against Reagan, sister. . . ."

"Right on, brother."

"Yes. . . . Right on! . . . Now I am as angered as you over the deaths of the four students. . . . But where is Kent State? In Ohio. . . . Let me tell you something. We teach our people in The Crusade For Justice that's based in Denver, we teach our people to become involved in the *local* issues. . . . We are just as much against the war as anyone. In fact, we have greater reasons for hating this war. Our people, the Chicanos, are being killed at twice our rate in the population. Chicano, blacks and poor whites, they are the ones that die. They are the ones that are sent to the front lines. . . . Of course we are against the war. . . . But we've got to take care of business at home first. . . .

"Now I'm told that you had a mini-riot on the campus

yesterday. . . . My friends from this area have told me that the pigs busted some heads here twenty-four hours ago. . . . They tell me that the Chicano students were holding a *Cinco de Mayo* celebration at Campbell Hall and that the pigs came in and busted some heads. Young boys and girls were clubbed down to the ground right here. . . ."

"Let's hear it for the Chicanos!"

"Viva La Raza!" Thin applause.

"So I would only add that you should get involved with the struggles in your own back yard . . . not just on the campus, but in the barrios, in the ghettos, wherever you find the forces of reaction working against the people, you must join in. . . . You must not wait until an event becomes headlines, you must join with us now. . . . Which reminds me. . . . I understand the next speaker is a candidate for office in this coming election. They tell me that Zeta is running for Sheriff. . . . He is running under the banner of our new political party, La Raza Unida. . . . I would ask your support of him. Thank you." Corky steps back behind a curtain.

The students politely clap and whistle a beat. The redbeard takes the mike. "Now we will hear from brother Brown. . . . Like Corky said, he is running for office. . . . Now I know this isn't the place for partisan politics, but Mr. Brown is known for his radical defense of many political prisoners. . . . So I ask you to hear him."

I walk toward the stage. A heavy man in a black suit and white tie comes up to me. "Hey, Zeta, I'm Louie . . . Corky wants to say hello."

We shake hands and Corky emerges from behind the curtain. He throws his arms around my neck and gives me an *abrazo*.

"So you're Zeta, eh?"

"Yeah, man. About time we met."

"Go on up and give these lame gringos hell. We'll talk later."

I stand at the mike staring down on the crowd of longhairs. They are sitting on the chairs, on the floors, standing around the edges waiting to hear from me.

"Let me first say that I'm not here for votes. . . . Most of you probably don't vote, anyway. . . . And I'm about as much of a politician as Donald Duck. . . . I have come to join in protest against the war. I have come to meet with you to add my words of sorrow for the kids shot down at Kent State yesterday. . . . But more than that, I have come to ask you to join in support of the local issues. Just like Corky said . . . you know . . . death is not uncommon to us. We Chicanos have been beat up, shot up, kicked around, spat on and . . . fuck, they've taken everything we've had. . . . Death at the hands of the pigs is nothing new to us."

"Preach, brother, preach!"

"Right on, *carnal!*"

"But still I wonder . . . I must ask myself what the shouts of solidarity mean. You say to go right on, don't you?"

"Amen!"

"You say that we've got to wipe out the pig, right?"

"Right on!"

"What we need is peace and love, right?"

"Hear, hear!"

"Give 'em hell, brother!"

"Love and Peace, Peace and Love . . . with a little dope and a little rock on the side?"

"You're talking, brother. Right on!"

"Hell yes, a little dope, a little love, a cheer here and there. Let's march around the block, let's go on up to the pigs at the skirmish line and give them hell. . . . We'll kill them with our buttons and beads. . . . We'll slaughter them with our Rolling Stones albums, right?"

"Ah, come on, man." The crowd feels suckered.

"Sure, peace and love . . . Dope and rock . . . Solid, Jackson!"

"Hey, man? What you driving at?"

"Let's smother the creeps with flowers and posters, with acid and rock. . . . Right on?"

"Hey, man, cut out that divisive shit!"

"Screw you, buster. . . . I'm here to tell you that you're fucked! You don't know what you're screaming! You don't know what you're asking for! Do you realize that when it comes down to it . . . and it will come down, believe me. . . . When the fires start up, when the pigs come to take us all, what will you do? Will you hide behind your skin? Behind your school colors? Will you tell the arresting officers that you are with the rebels? Will you join up with the Chicanos and blacks? Or will you run back to the homes of your fathers in Beverly Hills, in Westwood, in Canoga Park? Will you be with us when the going gets rough?"

"Hey, man. Why don't you wrap it up?" the redbeard calls to me. The crowd is getting ugly.

"Do you realize that you'll have to shoot your mother? Do you realize that you might have to crack your uncle's head apart? Will you be willing to do that? Do you think you can slaughter your own kind? I doubt it. I seriously doubt it."

"Ah, fuck off, you creep."

"Same to you, pal. . . . And the same to all of you out there who think that revolution is a game for a spring day. . . . Viva La Raza, motherfuckers!"

I walk away from the mike. Only a handful of Chicanos cheer me off. Corky and Louie meet me at the rear while the beard introduces the next speaker. We walk into a room behind the stage.

"You are too much, Buffalo."

"Thanks, man. You ain't so bad yourself."

"Hey, Zeta, if I ever get busted I want you to defend me," Louie says.

"Who'd want to arrest you, ese?"

I hear whispering in our room. It is Angela and her bodyguards, standing in a corner. A tall thin black woman comes up to them and opens her bag. Angela and her men look at us.

"It's OK, baby," Corky says to her.

The three black men take pistols from under their coats and quickly stuff them in the woman's bag. She turns and walks out.

Angela comes up to us. Corky hugs her. She turns to me and looks at me with those big lazy eyes.

"Brother . . . you are heavy."

We touch and I give her my famous grin, the slight smirk of a *malcriado* out of his league.

"Sister, anytime you need a lawyer—or anything, you just call."

"Thank you, Brown Buffalo," the African Queen says.

We walk out into the night and hurry back to our turf. We go to *La Voz* and drink wine and later on we dance to the *corridos* of David Hippie. Corky talks with Joe, the editor. He asks about Risco and Ruth, but they have gone on to another battlefront in the San Joaquin Valley. Organizers, Risco said, should move on once the fire has been set.

Corky and Joe are talking about a massive demonstration against the war while I am drinking my wine alone. They are planning to hold the biggest demonstration in the history of the Chicano movement during the late summer. But I am getting sick of crowds, work, LA, everything. I do not join in with them. I tell Corky goodbye.

"I'll see you in August, Brown Buffalo," he says.

A week before the elections, the Court of Appeals rules on the school riot case of the East Los Angeles Thirteen. They are set free! The appeals court enjoins the trial court from proceeding with the matter. In a twenty-page opinion, "Castro vs. Superior Court, 1970," we make the law books. We have established a new precedent in the prosecution of conspiracies in a political case. So long as the Republic stands, defense lawyers will be quoting our case and I am assured of my place in legal history. We celebrate as we work that entire week.

Quinn's endorsement of my candidacy brings out the rest of the Cockroaches who have been holding back. Duana Doherty's ex-nuns ring doorbells for the glory of revolution and Zeta. Victor and the other defendants in the St. Basil Twenty-One organize the campuses and bring out the finest broads to dance with me at the Hollywood Paladium, where we hold a dance-rally on Mother's Day. Roland Zanzibar's coverage of the trials and the campaign gives me that touch of credibility which a radical buffalo needs to even *show* in the running. Everything hums along smoothly.

Meanwhile, I file a motion for a new trial with Nebron for the St. Basil's case. After several orgiastic sessions with Jean Fisher, I nail down her statement. My motion accuses the jury foreman of making an overt attempt to influence the jury. I argue that a conspiracy has taken place, that she could not have done what she did without the assistance of someone who knew law. I look straight at Ridder as I argue. Nebron denies the motion, telling me to take it up on appeal. But before the gallery breaks into rage, he says, "And I've decided to forget about those contempt citations you still owe this court, Mr. Brown. . . . It has been the most *unusual* trial I've ever witnessed. . . . I think we've all been somewhat taken with the enormity of it all. The defendants are released on the appeal bond that's been posted. . . ."

The press is waiting when we storm into the corridors. The event and the subsequent trial have given us a million dollars worth of publicity.

"Hey, Buff, what would you do if you actually got elected?" Zanzibar asks me, after the other newsmen have left. We've gotten pretty close over the months.

"I'm just glad I don't have to seriously worry about that."

"Why not, hombre? Maybe you won't win . . . but you're going to get a lot of votes. . . . And that's power."

"What can I do about it?"

"I don't know. . . . All I know is . . . I've heard a lot of talk about you, man. You must know the police are right on your tail. They're just waiting for you to make a mistake."

"So what do you suggest?"

"Just be careful, *viejo*. Be careful," Zanzibar warns. "The establishment doesn't like to give power to people like you and me."

"I guess you'd better watch out too."

"Why me? I'm just a journalist."

I laugh at him. "Are you serious? Shit, if I'm a thorn in

their side, what about you? You're doing more to diminish their power than I am. *You'd* better be careful."

When the last votes are counted, I come in second. In a field of four, in a county of seven million and with the expenditure of less than a thousand bucks, I receive some half a million votes. Zanzibar wrote in the LA *Times* in the first week of June, 1970: "Zeta's campaign was the only little ray of sunshine for the Chicanos." He calls the day after the election to tell me that an editor from *Life* magazine wants information about me. They plan to do an article on *El Zeta,* he says.

"Tell them to write to me in Acapulco, partner."

"How long you gonna be down there?"

"As long as . . . I don't know . . . My trials are all finished. The St. Basil appeals are being handled by a friend of mine, Si Herringbone. I've got no commitments for . . . I haven't had a free week . . . I have been on the run for two and a half years straight. . . . Things seem to be in pretty good shape now, I think I'll drop out again. For a while, anyway . . . maybe write an article on my own. . . . I'll send you a postcard."

Summer is upon us. I drive Rosalie and the girls to San Jose and drop them off with their grandmother.

"I have to go visit my brother, Jesus," I tell them. "I haven't seen him in ten years."

Four hours later I am in the hot muggy jungle a thousand miles from East LA. Nobody knows where I am. In my pocket I have the remnants of my entire collected campaign fund. I have sent letters to my creditors explaining that I'd *lost* and had no money; but, *after* the revolution, I would certainly pay.

I check into *La Quebrada* on the beach and call Jesus.

# 14

"*Los federales te buscan*, they're looking for you," says Anna, the tall broad-shouldered Tarascan. Jesus and I are in my room, just beginning to mix rum with pineapple juice for Planter's Punch, when Anna and La Betti come in.

Jesus is sitting, leaned back in a grass-matted chair rolling joints. He'd just come in before them with a news-paper-wrapped bundle. Two pounds of fine yellow *mota* with that smell of sin for twenty dollars. The natives laugh when you ask for Acapulco Gold. . . . There's just good *mota* and bad *mota, ese.* But we couldn't find papers to roll it in. "The foreign edition of *Time* magazine is the best paper to roll," Jesus says.

"Hey, Anna, what do you mean?" I say.

"She's just drunk," Betti says. She cuts strips of avoca-do and mixes them with pieces of lobster for the *botana.* La Betti, a french whore, lives with Jesus.

"No I'm not . . . honest. When I left here this afternoon I had to go see the doctor for my weekly check-up. Then when I took the *permiso* to the police . . . we have to do that every week . . . they called me in and started asking me a bunch of questions about you . . . and about Jesus, too. But they already know him."

"Hey, are you serious? I've just been here three days."

"Relax, man. Here, suck on this one," Jesus, my twin brother, says to me.

I haven't seen him since law school. He was arrested for possession of heroin in the early sixties and spent two years in prison. He was made an honor-trusty and placed on a farm with other dope addicts because he could get along with the devil himself. When they turned their backs on him, he ran into the night and kept moving until he crossed the border into Mexico. For five years he's earned his living off the *turistas* as guide, dope pusher or pimp. He lives on the beach eating fish and coconuts and he knows all the girls at El Club-69, where Anna and Betti work the locals and the tourists.

"The *federales* are *always* checking up on us," Betti says.

"But what do they want with *me*?"

"Hey, man, just smoke that thing," Jesus says.

I suck on the roll of *Time* magazine and zoom, zoom, zoom up to the top of the green palm tree outside my window and down to the red hibiscus, the red land crabs, the red sun sinking deep into the sea and the lights blinking now, little bits of diamonds out on the bay. Acapulco Bay, the paradise at the foot of the mountains; and coming down from the jungles of bananas, monkeys, parrots, wild birds, the burros loaded with stacks of wood, the Indians down from the hills to sell their felt paintings, their bark paintings of white lions and blue horses, strokes of fine lines from the hands of brown men and women no taller than kids. . . .

"You think it might be because of your politics?" Anna asks.

I am looking at the long legs of this brown woman who laughed at me when I told her I was a Chicano.

"¿Qué? '¿chicano?' I thought you were a Mexican just like your brother."

"What politics?" Jesus says.

"Didn't you say your brother was a politician?" Betti says.

"I ain't no . . . no soy *político*. I'm a revolutionary," I laugh.

For the past three days I've told my brother about *la*

*movida* in East LA. He has said nothing about it. He has listened and smiled and nodded his head. It is like looking in a mirror. Jesus looks like me. He is thinner, leaner, and his skin is brown from the Acapulco sun. But he looks just like me.

"What's that?" Anna wants to know.

"You know, Anna," Jesus says, "like Lopitos. *El Búfalo es como Lopitos.*"

"Oh. . . . I see."

"Who's that?" I ask.

"He used to be the mayor of Acapulco. About ten years ago he took over. . . . Hey, after we eat let's take a ride up the mountain. . . . There's a statue of him. It's really something."

"I'm game for anything. How about the girls?"

"No . . . they have to work. We'll meet them later."

"Give me some of that thing, Chouie," Betti says.

We suck up our fat joints and blow smoke into the damp humid air. The beach boys are now out looking for tourists. The Auto Lunch Cafe is down below us. Occasionally we hear a *grito*, a loud Mexican yodel from deep in the throat, and the strumming of the guitars on the sidewalk.

Later, we are standing on top of a mountain looking down on the bay. A million pin-points of colored light, like fire-flies biting the night air, jump like bouncing balls before our eyes. The tropical splendor is laid out at my feet. I suck in the cool breeze and expand my chest and I am free and cool as I stand listening to my brother speak of Lopitos. . . .

"He was a little Indian. He came out of the mountains here in the State of Guererro. He saw this mountain here that we're standing on. It was empty. Owned by an American millionaire. He decided that the land should be used by the people. As you can see, it's got the best view . . . shit, just look. Anyway, Lopitos started bringing in people from the villages. He went back to his home and started bringing in families. He traveled up into the mountains on horseback. He went into the interior where the jungle gets really thick. He went all over, telling people if they wanted to live in paradise, to follow him. . . . Twenty thousand came. The Indians and the Mexicans, the poor and the ones without land, they came and began to settle here on this mountain. They just camped out and started building homes of adobe, of grass and mud. . . . I don't know the whole story, but they say he was quite a man. A short man without education.

"Eventually the cops came, first the local fuzz and then the State troopers. . . . But Lopitos wouldn't budge. He told them that if they wanted the mountain, they'd have to kill everybody. Then they sent in the *federales* from Mexico City. . . . But the people stayed on. *Nothing* could move them. . . . Eventually the government paid off the American owner and gave Lopitos and his people the permission to stay on. . . . In the following years he built up his power and eventually became the mayor of Acapulco and he started moving out the foreign interests. He started taxing the hotels and he refused to allow any more American businesses without guarantees of protection of the coastline.

"Two years later he was assassinated. Right here on this spot. That's his grave there. Look."

We walk forward to the monument. It is simply a slab of black stone. It has an inscription on it. Jesus shines the flashlight on it:

> *La vida no es la que vivimos,*
> *La vida es el honor y el recuerdo.*
> *Por eso más vale morir*
> *Con el pueblo vivo,*
> *Y no vivir*
> *Con el pueblo muerto.*

Lopitos

"Jesus H. Christ! I've seen that before!" I shout.
"Where?"
"That inscription is on a sign in a chapel in Delano where Cesar almost died," I tell him.
"It's pretty good, huh?"

187

I shake my head and stare out into the night. Through the darkness we hear an occasional hoot in the trees. Tiny black bats flash by now and again. The moon is coming up over the islands that stand in the bay to the south.

"It's been my motto for some time now," I say.

"It has?"

"Yeah, ever since I saw it . . . I believe in it."

"How do your friends feel about it?"

"All the guys that I work with . . . we're into it heavy."

Jesus gives a chuckle. It is that laugh I've heard a million times in my youth. Just a short, biting chuckle. "Come on, man. You guys are *really* into it?"

"Well . . . we've begun to. . . ."

"How many have you killed?"

"Uh, none . . . but we've, well, you know. . . ."

Jesus laughs again. He pokes my arm and motions me to the car. We get into his chopped-up '52 Chevrolet and begin to roll down the mountainside.

"Look, man . . . I'm out of it from here, right? I'm just tired and don't care that much for America anymore . . . I'm not saying I'll never go back, but I won't until there's something to do. . . . I keep up with what's happening up there. We have to buy that goddamn *Time* anyway. I've heard about what you guys are up to. . . . It isn't much different than the blacks.

"Bullshit! The Chicano thing is different."

"Yeah, it's different . . . but from two thousand miles away it looks just the same. You stick around for a couple of months, you'll see what I mean."

"Well . . . so what?"

"Nothing . . . I was just saying that . . . the way it looks to me from where I sit. . . . Until the people, the blacks, the Chicanos, the white liberals and the white radicals, all of you, until you guys get it in your head that you're going to go *all* the way . . . I mean, like Lopitos here. When they took over the mountain there was no turning back. . . . It was life or death on the mountaintop. . . . They chose death and they beat it. You've got to accept it, look for it, stick your nose into it and fight your way out of it. You've got to find your death before you can find your life. . . . At least that's the way I see it. . . ."

"But . . . Look at what we did in the campaign. With almost nothing we got all those votes."

"But what good is that? They *gave* you those votes, man. They *knew* you weren't going to win. They were just letting you guys get your rocks off."

"Well, what the fuck are you doing? It's easy for you to sit here sucking up dope and fucking those broads."

"What? And you're not doing the same in East LA?"

"Well . . . yeah, but I'm also working."

"Bullshit! It amounts to nothing. It's just an exercise in ego-tripping."

I stare into the night. We are rounding curves and the car lights race across the jungle, striking the green trees and the red bush. I have just been wounded. Jesus is my twin, but he came out first. Our parents always called him the *older* brother. I have had to treat him with the respect that a Chicano gives to the eldest son.

"I guess you're right. . . . But at least I got in a few licks."

"Well, shit, man, I'm not trying to depress you. . . . All I'm really trying to say is . . . If you guys ever really get serious . . . I mean, if you really pick up the gun . . . let me know. I'll get in on that one. . . . And I've got lots of friends here that will join me."

"Heh, heh . . . Thanks, but . . . things are pretty cool now. The trials are over with and the campaign is over and . . . fuck it, I'm on vacation, man. I'm not planning to get into any more battles for a hell of a long time. Just show me the sinful life . . . I'm ready for it."

And with that we head into the night in search of El Club-69.

We find it stuck on the side of a hill, next to a banana orchard in *La Zona Rosa*. The road is under excavation. Massive cement pipes line the sidewalks and we have to walk in the road. Every shack is a whorehouse and bar. One joint is playing Creedence Clearwater and another is blaring out a Mexican cowboy's long lost love. It is dark, the street wet and muddy from the summer rain. Sitting on the huge cement pipes in front of the joints, I see a thousand women and little girls.

"Where you boys going?"

"Hey, mister. What's wrong with this place?"

"Come on, big boy, buy me a beer."

I am stumbling over myself. Every living thing on the street is an almost-naked broad. The make-up is slashed across ruby lips and green eyes. Here a young girl in high heels wears a bikini, a blue bikini with blonde hair. Standing next to her is a girl as young as Rosalie, in a miniskirt and a strap over her little red nipples. I step in a puddle when I turn to see a gang of fat ugly women sitting on small benches in front of the shacks. This group of grandmothers is hustling, too. They sit and sip on soda pops; they nibble on tacos from the man on the corner, ears of fresh corn from the lady with the tin tub and the fire across the street. Little kids in bare feet scatter here and there chasing after skinny dogs.

We nod at the fat guard standing at the door of El Club-69 under the blinding, blinking neon sign. We walk up the stairs and into the darkness of Acapulco's finest bistro. The waiter greets Jesus and takes us into the bar and dance floor. I am sweating and my eyes are popping off their hinges: fifty more fantastic broads! They sit talking with tourists, sailors and hillbilly Mexicans in cowboy boots and white pants. Tanned barefoot beach boys grab the girls and twirl them around to the rock and roll music of Creedence, who is number one in Mexico this summer.

Anna and La Betti come to us at our table. We order a fifth of Presidente Brandy and a quart of soda water. Anna is wearing a red negligee. Betti is wearing a toy soldier coat like in Sergeant Pepper.

"¿Quieres bailar?"

Anna, the tall Tarascan Indian, leads me onto the dance floor. It is raised higher than the tables. She has short black hair and full breasts. I can feel her heat as we move around the floor.

"Are you married?" she asks.

"Me? Hell no!"

We dance more and she pushes her belly into mine. She is running her hand down my back, tickling it with those long red nails. She lays her head on my shoulders and breathes into my ear.

"Why do you ask?"

"Oh, I just wondered. . . . You know."

"What?"

She stops dancing. She holds my hands and looks me in the face.

"I was just wondering why you've never taken me to the room."

"What do you mean? I just met you last night."

"That's what I mean. . . . I was with you all day, too."

I take her into my arms and start to kiss her but she backs off.

"We can't do that here."

"Why not?"

"It isn't allowed. . . . We have to go to the room."

We continue to dance. When it is over we return to the table.

"What's the matter with your brother?" Anna asks Jesus.

"Ah, he's got his mind back on his business. . . . He's still up north. You know how these Americanos are, they don't know how to relax. . . ."

"Maybe he needs something. . . ." La Betti says, twirling her eyelashes.

"Yeah, maybe he does," Anna says, smiling at her friend.

The two girls look at Jesus. They give each other a signal with their eyes. "Why not," Jesus says.

Betti takes a pill from the pocket of her blue soldier coat. She hands it to me and tells me to swallow it with soda water.

"What is it?"

"It'll make you relax. . . . Just drink it."

I swallow it without a thought.

"What's it called?"

"That's a Quaalude-400," Jesus says.

"What's it supposed to do?"

Jesus pours a drink for everyone and laughs.

"What do you mean, 'What's it supposed to do?'"

"Yeah, does it raise you up, get you down or what? I mean, what kind of high is it?"

Jesus looks at me and smirks. "Jesus, you sound like a hippie."

"What do you mean?"

"Why do you ask what kind of high? Isn't there just one?"

"I mean is it an upper or a downer?"

"Ah, just wait a bit. I tell you, there's only one kick. If you've been there, you know what I mean."

I wait for a few minutes and then I dance with Betti. She sticks her cunt right into me. She doesn't wait for the music. She just pastes it right up against my scrotum. And we laugh and we lean around the corners and I am soon playing with the brass buttons on her coat. She sticks her thin hands under my shirt and is playing with my chest, rubbing my tits to make them hard.

"How do you feel now?" she asks.

"I'm just fine. Relaxed as hell."

"That's because you're not moving."

She stands back and holds my hands out. I am standing still, leaning against a post at the edge of the dance floor.

"Do you want to go to the room with me?"

"I'm ready. But what will Anna say?"

"Do you like her?"

"Yeah. I've been with her all day."

"Well, let's all go to the room."

"You mean the three of us?"

"Or the four. It doesn't matter. Whatever you want you can get right here. Didn't you know that?"

My head is heavy now, my tongue is thick and the fog is beginning to roll in. I am falling and leaning and swaying back to the table and we pick up Anna and my brother Jesus tells me to stay awake and to be sure that I tell Betti what I want.

The three of us walk through the bar into a back patio where the motel rooms are lined up waiting for us. We pay the woman at the counter for the room and towels and I give the girls seven dollars each and we go into a small green room with a swirling fan above a sagging bed. I am about to sit down on the red bedspread when a man walks out of the toilet buttoning his pants. He gives us a look and almost walks out. But he turns around at the door and calls Betti. Anna is in the toilet and I am on top of the bed, my clothes still on.

"He wants to know if you mind if he watches. . . . He just wants to see us do it," Betti says.

"What is he, some kind of pervert?"

"No, he's just a dirty old man. He says he didn't get satisfied with Carmela. . . . What do you think?"

Anna is coming out of the bathroom. She is in a black baby doll, a black laced gown to her belly. Her beautiful knockers spill over the top. I reach out to her. She tumbles right on the bed.

"Tell the man . . . I don't care. Just hurry and get in."

Betti goes to the door and tells the man. He comes in and sits quietly in the corner of a low soft chair. I can hear him breathing.

Betti removes her coat and she is in pink underwear . . . pink panties. She takes them off. I am on the bed with Anna, looking at Betti in the mirror. Anna is rubbing my shoulders.

"Why don't you take your clothes off?" Anna asks.

"Why don't you?"

Both girls undress completely. They are gorgeous. Young soft bodies. Anna is brown and Betti is white. Anna is tall and Betti is short. Anna has big tits and Betti has little pears. I am on my back and one takes the left shoe and the other takes the right one. While Anna is removing my pants, Betti is taking off my shirt. I am tingling all over. The Quaalude is taking over my muscles. I am totally re-laxed, the cloud is nine and the girls are kissing me on both sides of the face. One has a tongue in my ear, the other is running her nose into my armpit and I am leaning back and sucking on a breast and Betti is touching my prick and Anna has her hand on my ass.

I hear the old man breathing in puffs in the corner. I cannot see him, I can only hear him. But I don't care anymore. I am into flesh. I grab at the legs, at the breasts, at the fine asses of these two young Cockroaches. Betti has her face in my stomach, it is going down to my navel, down to my pubic hair and further, down to my prick. She takes it in her mouth and fondles it. She is playing with me. She hardens her tongue and flicks it against my stiffening cigar. Anna is sucking my chest. She is licking me and touching Betti. I look down, I lean around Anna's shoulder and look down at them. Betti has her hand on Anna's tit. She is fondling Anna while she is sucking me. Anna has her hand on Betti's ass. I take Anna's face in my hands and gently push her toward Betti's ass which is up in the air. . . . "Go ahead," I say. "Don't be bashful."

"Oh, God," I hear Betti gasping for air.

Anna is on top of Betti now. I am in the corner of the bed watching them. Anna has her face in Betti's cunt. Betti is making animal sounds. Her breathing is getting faster and faster, louder and louder. . . . "Come on, Zeta, come on before I explode," Betti shouts. The fan is turning circles above us. We are all panting like dogs, like buffalos on the run . . . I finish Betti off while Anna licks my arms, and then I get on top of the big Indian and pump away while Betti lies back and sucks my legs. . . . We jump and we pump and we indulge ourselves until there is nothing left inside of our stomachs. . . .

When it is over, the man in the white suit and the Panama hat walks out without a word. We lie on top of the bed for a while until the heat has left. We laugh at one another. We giggle and we squirm and we promise ourselves more.

"So this is what Acapulco Gold is, hey?"

When we return, Jesus has two other women at his side.

"Well, how did it go?"

"Great. Out of sight."

"This is Stella and Margie," he says. One is a blonde in

a blue bikini with tits hanging down to her belly button; the other one is a short dark girl of thirteen. "They want to meet you," he smiles.

*Los Angeles Times columnist Roland Zanzibar killed by stray bullet during Chicano riots in East Los Angeles. Chicano leader Rodolfo Gonzales arrested.*

I am sitting at Joe's table in El Auto Lunch on the sidewalks of Acapulco. I have the paper stretched out before me on the black table. I just bought it downtown at Blum's and I have read the article twice. I am thinking of reading it a third time when Joe comes up and says, "*Ah, Señor Zeta, y ¿qué tal? ¿Qué vamos a tomar hoy?*"

What'll I have, the skinny guy asks. Here I've drunk the same *bongo* for a whole summer and still he asks me every morning, What'll you have?

"*Pues, lo mismo, hombre. Dame un Coco Loco.*"

He executes a pirouette and heads into the restaurant with the thatched palm roof. I look straight ahead at the row of little huts of palm and brown poles across the street. Blondes in white bikinis pass me by, girls with golden stomachs. I see women all around me, women with hips, swinging colored bags of grass. Little boys with hands outstretched come up and try to sell me: some gum, some postcards or a shoestring, Señor?

"*No, gracias . . . Así me gustan,*" I say and give them a nickel for their trouble. "*Aquí está tu veinte,*" I tell them.

Women in shawls, tourists with bags, broads with sunglasses over blue eyes, girls from America, girls from Brazil, broads on the streets without stockings, in high heels, whores, tourists, girls. They walk up and down the beaches; they never turn when the beach boys in bright shirts honk at them.

And I am trying to read an article about the death of my friend and the arrest of Corky Gonzales. I am trying to understand what has happened. How many hours have I spent at this restaurant? How many women have I fucked? How much money have I spent? Can it really be true

195

that the soft guy with the gray hair is dead? And are they saying that Corky killed him? The paper is a first edition with little real news. It says that Corky was arrested for Conspiracy to Incite a Riot. They have found several guns and rifles in a truck that he was using to get away.

Of course, Corky didn't kill Zanzibar or anyone else. It simply says that he crossed state lines to incite a riot. That they picked him up along with twenty-six other CMs not far from where Zanzibar was killed and they had firearms in their truck. Obviously Corky will be in need of a lawyer. I have spent a summer of girls, booze and dope. I have forgotten the battle, not even written about it. But now it is time to return to the war zone.

Minutes later, I am on the telephone in my hotel room. I am alone. I can see a fantastic view below of sharks under the belly of the dark bay. The sun is raining yellow, a golden day.

"Black Eagle, is that you?"

"Yeah, who's this?"

"Me, man. Brown."

"Zeta?"

"Yeah. . . . *Cuebole, ese.*"

"You motherfucker, where are you?"

"Acapulco. . . . I just got the news."

"You sonofabitch, where you been, *ese?*"

"No time for that now. . . . I'm coming in tonight. Get the guys together. . . . OK?"

"I don't know about that, man. . . . *You got troubles.*"

"Hey, man. . . . We'll hassle that out when I get back. . . . Just call Gilbert and Pelon."

"All right. . . . But, look, man . . . if you don't come through *this* time . . . I mean, we've been waiting all fucking summer to hear from you. . . . Where in the fuck have you been? I've got to tell them *something.*"

I hold the black beast to my mouth and I think. I am looking over the palm trees at the white sailboats cutting across the bay.

"I've been trying to set up . . . sanctuary . . . I've been talking to some . . . real heavy people . . . I've got a deal going where if . . . you know, like if you need a place to hide? OK, I can't say nothing more. . . . I've been tailed down here by . . . I know it sounds paranoid. . . ."

"What, the CIA?"

"Yeah. . . ."

"That's nothing, man. . . . Gilbert got shot by an FBI man during the riot yesterday."

"What? . . . Look, goddamnit, it's costing too fucking much. . . ."

"So what? You must be loaded. . . . Acapulco! . . . You capitalist pig!"

"That's what you guys think. . . . I'm telling you, the State of Guererro is still in revolt. . . . Shit, look, I've got to hang up, but you tell the dudes that I've been working. . . . I just haven't been fucking up. . . . All right?"

"Fuck yes, man. You don't need my permission to come back. We've been waiting for you to call all night. . . . I told Pelon that you'd be calling within a day or two."

"What'd he say?"

"Ah, you know him . . . he just said, 'I know, ese . . . I'm the dude who organized old Zeta. I should know!'"

"Yeah, yeah. . . . OK, man, look, I'll see you guys around five tonight. . . . I'm coming in on Mexicana, flight 745, leaves here around two, LA time. . . ."

"We'll be waiting, man. . . . And. . . . Glad to hear you're back with the Cockroaches, ese

Click. . . . The phone goes dead.

It is Sunday afternoon, August 30, 1970, in the year of The Cockroach. Our first martyr, Roland Zanzibar is dead.

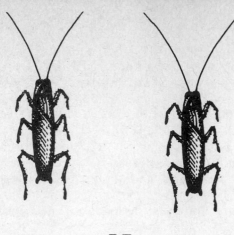

# 15

Whittier Boulevard—The Strip. Saturday morning. Mexican restaurants, Adelita's, La Iguana de Oro, The Latin Strip, dime stores, pawn shops, radio and television repair, finance companies, Woolworth's, J.C. Penney, Sears, Jack-In-The-Box, McDonald's, Department of Social Welfare, Hollenbeck Police Station. We cross Atlantic, Olympic, Indiana, Brooklyn, Soto. . . . Thousands of faces, posters colored red and green, banners of Brown Eagles, the Azteca black and white and red Thunderbird, LA HUELGA, LUCHA, MAPA, LULAC, BROWN BERETS, CON SAFOS, LA RAZA, COPA, CHICANO LIBERATION FRONT, CMO, MECHA, MALDEF, ACLU, NATIONAL LAWYERS GUILD, CHICANO LAW STUDENTS, EICC, EL TEATRO CAMPESINO, CHICANO DANCE GROUP DE UCLA, SOCO Y ZETA FOREVER, ROSE CHERNIN, DOROTHY HEALEY, NEIL HERRING, FACES OF BROWN, FACES OF LONG HAIR, BOOTS, MARCHING, FISTS SWING, VATOS LOCOS PINTOS CHICANOS HIPPIES COCKROACHES BOOT SHOE HEEL TOE TRAMP TRAMP TRAMP. . . .

We are looking at a color film of the Chicano Moratorium of August 29, 1970.

Suddenly, Laguna Park. Two square blocks. Flat green. Enclosed by wire fence and line of tall palm trees. I see a swimming pool, a gymnasium and a sandbox with swings and a merry-go-round of iron bars. Thousands of people mill around, sitting on the green grass with children, eating hot dogs, tortillas, soda pop, singing, smoking, smiling, pretty girls, young dudes a little drunk, falling, jumping, horsing around, a picnic, a Saturday afternoon in the park, groups of bearded men, strong men in brown khaki, in brown brogans. A peaceful gentle scene.

The film cuts to a ballfield in the center of the park. A wooden stage is at home plate. The camera is on the pitcher's mound.

Short dark girl of Aztlan in dress of white, ruffled in orange and red, little flowers and red-orange ribbons in her black hair: the flamenco dancer from UCLA. She dances with some kid —buck teeth, slick legs in tight cowboy pants, sombrero in hand, boots clicking at the hard floor, black hair falling over his joker face, a two-step *ranchera*.

SLASH! The film is cut to a liquor store on Whittier Boulevard, at the corner of Indiana, two blocks from the park. The camera is hand-carried and the picture bounces. It moves us toward the front of the liquor store. The sun is reflected off the lens, a streak of yellow. LAGUNA LIQUORS in black letters on plate glass; a grill of black iron bars covers it all. Inside the store, if you look close, you can see people staring through the glass into the street. These people have hands to eyes, to mouths, they are calling out to other people on the street. On the sidewalk outside the store, you see the line of helmeted pigs in leather jackets, in brown suits, in white helmets, in battle gear, with huge guns in hand, with rifles, bazookas, with tear gas equipment. You see them close up, the faces of armed men staring into the liquor store.

And now you see people suddenly coming out. Now you see a cop lunge for a kid with long black hair.

Cut to the sidewalk.

A kid is swinging at a cop. He has a red headband. The cops are pushing the people on the sidewalk. The people are being struck with the clubs.

The camera jerks. Shot to the sidewalk cement, shot up

to the body of a fat cop, camera is moving along the ground and now you see a line of uniformed cops in helmets lining the middle of the street, batons in hand at parade rest. Across the street you see a crowd of people, mostly kids, leaning back, standing staunchly, some with hands on hips, stretched out wide, feet apart, hands up in the air, yelling, shouting; but no sound on this film. You cannot hear anything but the buzz of the reel in the back of the darkened courtroom that is singularly silent now as you tense and feel strains of goose bumps in your hair because you see on film, a *real* document, not from the movies, not TV, you know it really happened, you have seen the burnt streets, you have walked them, you recognize some of the faces, some of the stores, you know exactly where the corners of Indiana and Whittier are, you have driven across that intersection a hundred times, you have eaten menudo at the restaurant on the corner, you've eaten burritos at the hot dog stand across from the park, you have been in that park yourself. . . .

I remember a winter day in 1969 when I marched with some five thousand along the same route, in the rain. We took to the streets without any fanfare. And by the time we reached Laguna Park, with rain and thunder and lightning and ice-cold wind at our faces, the crowd started to disperse. It wanted no speeches. It wanted warmth and comfort.

I remember jumping up on a park bench and grabbing a bullhorn and telling the people to return, to listen to the voices of thunder and lightning: we may be the last generation of Chicanos if we don't stop the war. If we don't stop the destruction of our culture, we may not be around for the next century. We are the Viet Cong of America. Tooner Flats is Mylai. Just because Peaches and Reddin haven't started throwing napalm doesn't mean they have stopped the war. The Poverty Program of Johnson, the Welfare of Roosevelt, Truman, Eisenhower and Kennedy, The New Deal and The Old Deal, The New Frontier as well as Nixon's American Revolution . . . these are further embellishments of the government's pacification program.

Therefore, there is only one issue: LAND. We need to get our own land. We need our own government. We must have our own flag and our own country. Nothing less will save the existence of the Chicanos.

And I let it go at that.

I did not tell them how to implement the deal.

I did not, nor did any other speaker, tell them to take up arms prior to August 29, 1970.

Again the film shows us the park, a distortion of what we saw just a few minutes ago. Then there was order and laughter. Now there is chaos: legs, arms, hair in wind, running kids, people in scrambling motions, running away from the camera, away from the cops advancing in platoon formation, a phalanx of pigs, guns, smoke, bottles in air, clubs swinging; until the formation breaks up, pigs mix with the kids in T shirts, without shirts, barefooted teenagers, mostly boys, young men, but some *cholas*, some broads with bottles in hand. They clash in the middle of the field.

SLASH!

Whittier Boulevard is burning. Tooner Flats is going up in flames. Smoke, huge columns of black smoke looming over the buildings. Telephone wires dangling loose from the poles. Everywhere the pavement is covered with broken bottles and window glass. Mannequins from Leed's Clothing lie about like war dead. Somehow a head from a wig shop is rolling eerily down the road. Here a police van overturned, its engine smoking. There a cop car, flames shooting out the windows. Cops marching forward with gas masks down the middle of the debris. An ordinary day in Saigon, Haiphong, Quang Tri and Tooner Flats.

DARKNESS.

Then the overhead lights come on, the bailiff opens the shades. Daytime in the courtroom: The State vs. The Tooner Flats Seven, charged with Arson, Riot, Conspiracy and a host of other travesties.

Torrez steps forward to the witness stand. He is a lean dark-brown Chicano, prosecuting the biggest case of his career. He has on one of his typical silk suits from Macy's. Younger, the DA, appointed him specially for this trial. Chicano defendants and defense attorney and prosecution. And there on the bench is good old Chicano lackey, Superior Court Judge Alfred Alacran. Alacran cuts a fine figure: soft gray temples, black hornrimmed glasses. An exact man who moves with deliberation. He smiles often, but not at me. *Me*, he hates. He smiles and always looks as if he just came back from Mazatlan in a Jaguar with a tall blonde. And if he were not a pig and a flunky, he would probably have been the most famous Chicano lawyer in the history of East LA.

Torrez is speaking to the witness, Peter Peaches, the man who beat me out for Sheriff.

"Now, Sheriff Peaches," Torrez says, "we have seen the film your department prepared. But could you please explain to the jury in your own words what happened after the Chicanos left Laguna Park."

Peter Peaches is smiling. Why not, when he can watch a bunch of brown pawns tear one another apart, slave against slave? He wears his khaki uniform, his military cap in his lap.

"To be blunt, all hell broke loose."

"What happened?"

He frowns, pretending to struggle with his memory. "They sent some of their men into Laguna Liquors."

I am on my feet. "Objection. . . . Vague and hearsay."

"Overruled," Alacran barks. "Proceed."

"Tell us, Sheriff," Torrez says, "where you got your information."

"We sent in our undercover man, Officer Fernando Sumaya. He has all the firsthand information you want."

"Thank you for coming down, Sheriff," Alacran says. "I believe you're excused for now." Urbanely, he consults his watch. "After noon recess, call Officer Sumaya to the stand." He rises, the courtroom heaves up. We are adjourned for lunch.

Immediately I am surrounded by my clients, asking me for the umpteenth time how it is going. Rodolfo Corky Gonzales, Gilbert Rodriguez, Jose Ramirez and Raul Raza of *La Voz*, both short tough hardnosed militants; then Waterbuffalo and Bullwinkle from the CMs, two monstrous anarchists from Aztlanvilla; and lastly my new Miss *Esa*, Elena Lowrider, a tough broad with a big hot body. We all make a lot of noise and the court reporter who is tidying up, the blonde bitch Mrs. Wilson, glares at me from behind the stand with the microphone which I use. Or which I am supposed to use, according to Alacran who had held me in contempt a dozen times since this gig began six months ago or whenever.

But I am a man with a million things on his mind and sometimes I forget to use it, forget to show proper respect and this too offends him. I have manners, but I simply forget about them when I'm with guys like Gilbert or Pelon or Sailor Boy, the little kid who came up to me a few months ago and said he was supposed to be one of my bodyguards. He'd been in prison since he was a teenager, in and out for drugs and then one death.

"I got me one *muerte, ese,*" he told me then. "So if I go back again, this time they ain't gonna cut me loose." Somebody had kicked his brother's head until the brother went blind, so Sailor Boy stuck a blade into the dude's heart. They stuck Sailor Boy into a Federal joint:

"And that's where I turned on to *acido, ese* . . . These dudes gave me some of that Blue, you know? I was just sitting in my cell alone. I hardly never went out. I just sat and read. We had all the *carga* we wanted. The guards would let us sneak it in, you know? But this one time I took some of it and, *hijola,* I got *stoned, ese.* I was reading a copy of *La Voz* my *jefita* sent me. And there was this picture of you in there. So I said, 'If I ever get out, I'm gonna go see old Zeta.' So that's why I told the dudes from PINTO I'd take care of you."

Now Sailor Boy and Pelon sit together in the first row, waiting for me. Next to them are the other ex-cons who belong to the recently-formed organization. The Pintos

wear their knife and chain scars from the old gang wars of
their youth. During those days in the housing projects, the
urban reservations set aside for Chicanos, these *vatos*
would murder one of their own at least weekly. These
children of the slums, offspring of reds and wine and welfare, had gone to jail and come out to find the new revolution just waiting for them, the original rebels. Now they
could take it out on the pigs and be called hero instead of
*loco*. Now they were former political prisoners, not ex-
cons. Now they could take up a man like Buffalo Z. Brown
and all his bullshit, and shove it in the face of those same
white men who'd been giving them a hard time from the
day they were born.

I am assuring the defendants that all goes well. "Hey,
*ese*," Gilbert says, "What's the matter? You look like shit.
Are you sick or something?" The others are looking at me
curiously.

"Forget it," I say. "I just need some spring air. See you
in an hour."

I grab my briefcase, which is empty except for a gun,
and push off. Sailor Boy joins me by the elevator. I can't
go anywhere alone. As we go down from the seventh floor
of the Hall of Justice, he talks about the film. During the
Moratorium, he was in the slam. All that he knew came
from the papers and stories from the *vatos* who were there.
This is the first time he has *seen*, *felt* the action for what it
was. He is excited.

"Did you see that?" he says. "They really *did* it, you
know? I wish I was there. . . ."

"Yeah."

"Hey, I forgot. You weren't there, either. Look, why
don't we drive over to the park right now? We can look
around and . . . you'll feel better there, I know it."

"No."

"OK, *ese*, whatever you say."

We walk out of the courthouse into the dirt and slime.
Even in spring, the smog sits on the city like moldy orange
juice. I look back. For years I have been walking in and out
of that building, into the icebox of justice and then out

into the garbage. Nobody has to tell me I'm sick. Nobody has to say, Zeta, you look like shit. I stand there, staring backward like an idiot. Sailor Boy is gaping at me. People, lawyers on their way to lunch pass us. And he wants to go to Laguna Park. The place where I once stood on a bench hollering about land and war and blood. The place where I was brought later in late August of last year, when I returned from Acapulco. . . .

August 30, 1970. Gilbert and Pelon had picked me up at the airport. On the plane I had to think it all out, what I will say to them. For years the three of us have gotten drunk together, laughed and fought together. Nobody else in the *movida* knows me like they do. Yet I am in trouble for leaving, for dropping out.

*Zanzibar is dead. Corky and Gilbert and others are up for the rap. So I am back.*

Shit, it is obvious to me that if I never went to Acapulco, everything would still be the same. Someone would be dead. Someone else among us would be framed for it and I would defend him. On that plane I got one of the biggest headaches in my life. I'm doing what must be done. Why should anybody give me trouble about what I do with the rest of my life? Is this what we've all been fighting for?

After the big hugs, I follow them out of the airline lobby to my car. Gilbert's leg drags slightly as he walks, from a fleshwound, an FBI bullet. Pelon has been driving the Mustang while I was away. From the first moment I see their eyes, I know they are with me. But Gilbert, the fat frog, is troubled; Pelon is glum. They want me to talk to them. Soon we are piled again into my blue beauty, heading east on the freeway. They tell me the events of the last few months, the day Zanzibar was killed in particular.

"Jesus Christ," I say. "Sounds like somebody masterminded the perfect crime."

"What's that, *ese*?" Gilbert says. He sits in the back. I am next to Pelon who is driving us through the afternoon. After the jungle and houses of Mexico, everything I see in LA looks dull and colorless.

"If anybody set out to destroy the Chicano movement, he couldn't do better than murdering Zanzibar and hanging it on Corky. Corky makes things happen and Zanzibar makes what's happened important."

"Corky wasn't busted for murder," Pelon says.

"So what? Roland's dead and Corky's out of action. . . . Gilbert here has to watch his step. Plus the others."

"Eh, *ese*, do you, uh, want to go home before you meet with the other defendants?" Gilbert asks. "The *vatos* are wondering about whether, uh, if they want you to. . . ." He breaks off. I have never heard him talk like that before, halting and tripping himself. Suddenly, a flash of inspiration!

"Look, you guys." I am getting mad, I still have my headache. "What the fuck do I have to apologize for? You're always telling me how you're going to shoot your arms off with junk after the revolution. Nobody is going to tell you what to do. I've been a lawyer for three years now. THREE YEARS! You know I don't want to be no fucking lawyer! So when everything's cool, I go to see my brother and relax. Nobody has a right to beef! Here I am and nothing's any different!"

"Shit, *ese*," Gilbert says, "I know that. But some of the others. . . ."

"Sure, Zeta, that's what we've been saying," Pelon says.

"All right! Where is everybody?"

"Waiting for us at the park," Gilbert says. "Except Corky. He's still in."

"Let's go."

We drive to Laguna Park, passing by the ruins of Whittier Boulevard. Not as bad as Watts, but still bad. A little reminder from the people that a war is in progress. Pelon and Gilbert carry on a running commentary. When we pass the Silver Dollar Bar where Zanzibar was killed, I see it's boarded up.

We meet Ramirez, Raza, Waterbuffalo and Bullwinkle at one of the benches. We all have known and respected each other. Aside from Corky, only Elena Lowrider isn't here. The rest of the park is pretty much deserted.

"Hey, man," Bullwinkle leads off. "What the fuck's with you?"

"Acapulco!" snorts Waterbuffalo. "*Vatos* are dying and you're off gettin' a tan."

This is it. With more energy than I have ever used at one time, I shout: **SHUT UP!**

There is a surprising silence. I calm down, just a little.

"Listen, you guys. I'm no kamikaze! Are you? Do you *want* to die? I'm a writer, yeah, and a singer of songs. I just happen to be a lawyer and a fighter. If I'm not all that, I'm dead! What the hell are we fighting for? For land and to live just like we want. Fuck it! You think I *knew* what was coming down? You think I *planned* to disappear just then? After two and a half years, just because I split for a while, just because I go around and screw who I want to, you think I'm not in this fight whole hog? You're all a bunch of goddamn idiots if you think that! No wonder you were caught. . . ."

For half an hour I rail and rant. I tell them exactly where I'm at. And when I'm finished, they ask me to defend them.

They also ask me about Corky: how does he stand? Can they trust him? Aside from Cesar Chavez, he has the biggest reputation as the toughest Chicano in America. But he is an outsider, from Denver. Can they all work together? I tell them not to worry, that Corky is a man to be trusted.

But they still want to meet him and talk with him personally. Since only Corky is not out on bail, they haven't been able to see him. After I talk with them, they *still* want to see him. They want to check out if *they* can trust him. Which means they don't trust me anymore. They just *need* me. I promise to arrange a meeting in a few days and get to work on the cases. Then we split.

The three of us drive to my house on Sixth Street. The silence in the car is heavy. The prospect of another long trial makes me sick. The togetherness of the first few years seems gone. Now that Zanzibar is dead, there is nobody to tell our story to the world. I am spinning around in emptiness, thinking of what my brother Jesus told me. Who have we killed? Just how heavy *are* we? I am confused, but by the time we reach the house I have made two decisions. When I have finished this trial, I will write my book. Without fail. And win or lose, I will destroy the courthouse where the *gabachos* have made me dance these last years with lead in my belly and tears in my heart.

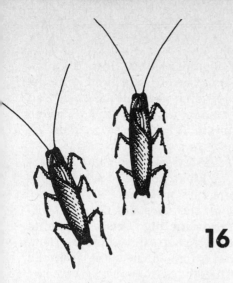

# 16

Back from the land of red crabs and hibiscus, the next six months are a roller coaster of paranoia and tedium.

It seemed that twenty-five thousand Chicanos had marched down Whittier Boulevard. But what had started as a protest against the burning of peasants in Vietnam turned into a massive public declaration by fire of their own existence. Even before the first speech, a fight broke out between the pigs and the *vatos*. An hour later, Tooner Flats was in flames. An hour later, Zanzibar and two other young Chicanos were dead, killed by agents of the SOC Squad. An hour later, Corky, Gilbert, Elena and four other CMs were behind bars, facing life sentences. The Tooner Flats Seven were indicted by the Grand Jury on felony charges of Arson, Firebombing, Inciting to Riot and Conspiracy. In addition, Corky and another man were also charged with misdemeanor gun possession.

The day I returned, after meeting the defendants, I called a press conference. The media flocks to hear again the ex-candidate for Sheriff.

"The Grand Jury which indicted my clients is a racist institution," I say to the flashing bulbs. "And I'm going after the judges that selected those jurors."

Within two weeks, I'm back into the same scene as before I left, but with a new twist. Gilbert, Pelon and I crashing in our crazy pad with a surf board for a coffee table and an enormous fish tank against the wall. In the tank we each have a mascot: fish or turtle. Sailor Boy joins the club. Rosalie and her two cousins come down from San Jose and find boyfriends among a dozen other Chicano teeny-boppers, militant groupies who move in with us. At night, everybody curls up next to a gun.

Towards the end of the first week, the night I've arranged a meeting with Corky, Elena Lowrider drives up in a purple Rolls Royce. "From a rich boyfriend," she says.

I first met Elena when I hit the streets of East LA. Gilbert and Pelon were organizing the high school dropouts and I would tag along between court appearances. Elena ran around with Cobra and some other *vatos* from La Junta. One night we all got together at Cronie's, where she and I hit it off. Finally everybody got money from some poverty program and, like the rest, she went on to college.

The last time I'd seen her was in 1969 when we bumped into each other in the Hall of Justice. She was about to be sentenced for some minor offense. She had asked me to defend her, but I was busy. She ended up doing a month or two but kept on in school. And now, once again, she has come in to see her old *amigo*, surrounded as he is with ex-cons in brown berets, bodyguards, *Soldados de Aztlán*.

She climbs out of her Rolls Royce and walks into the house as if she owns it. She hits her hard heels on the wooden floor to make them clack-clack. She chews gum, loud and brassy. She twirls it with her fingers while we talk. And then, when I reach for her left tit, she makes her green eyes go zing-zong and twitches her beak like Donald Duck.

"What are you doing?" she says. She is absolutely crazy. We hit it off again and she too decides to move into the house.

In a few hours, the leaders of the main Chicano organizations in LA will meet with the defendants and with Corky. Everybody else leaves the house for this closed meeting of all the heavies.

We sit together in the dark of the living room. Only the small bulbs in the fish tank and several candles Elena has lit give us our dim light. The men are quiet on the red rug. It has been a long tough season for tambourine men. We sip beer and talk softly while we wait for Corky to arrive.

Word of my latest speech in Laguna Park to the defendants has passed around. Some of the men look at me strangely. They know I'm no wimp, but here I am, running around the world, talking of writing and revolution and women and death. Everyone in the room is committed to death. But my commitment to death is different, larger than theirs. It is a night for interrogation and I catch them wondering in the corners of their eyes. I'm different.

Corky enters with Louie, the pockmarked ex-con. Louie is middle-aged and wears his dark suit with a white tie.

"Big Bear!" Corky throws his arms around me. He has given me this nickname because I am such a big fat lug.

Corky has on his usual red shirt and black pants. He comes in cagey like the top professional boxer he used to be. He knows the men are here to run him through some tough questions. He knows he is still considered an *outsider* to the *vatos* on the streets. Tonight, here in LA, he knows the mistrust one Chicano has for another. He understands the fear in the room toward a leader from another barrio, suspicion of a strange leader because . . . because Santa Anna sold us out to the gringos . . . because Juarez did nothing about it . . . because Montezuma was a fag and a mystic who had the fear of the Lord for Cortez or for Malinche . . . because anybody who has so little is afraid to lose what he just barely has got, saith the Lord.

"OK, you guys," I say, "here's Corky. You got some questions?"

"Hey, man . . . Don't I get a chance first?" Corky says, flashing his big white teeth.

"Yeah, come on," says Gilbert. "Sit down, *ese*, and have a joint."

"I don't smoke those little numbers," Corky says.

"He's a boozer," I say.

"The *jefe* just likes to drink Old Fitz," Louie says.

"I'm particular," Corky jokes. The men are still hard against him.

"I invited you cause the dudes want to ask you some questions. . . . I've been telling them about you. I've told them I'm going to defend you. But they keep bugging me on whether you're heavy or not. . . . So, fuck it, you answer their questions. . . OK?"

"Sure, Big Bear. Don't get excited. . . . OK, but first let me say this. . . . Whatever you guys decide tonight is OK with us. . . . We recognize we are on your turf. . . . We will support whatever you guys decide."

"Hey, *ese*," Gilbert says. "How come you guys still want to march and stuff like that?"

"Who? I don't want to march, man. I'm as tired of that shit as you. But if the people want to have a demonstration. . . . It's what they want that counts. . . . You think *I* got the twenty-five thousand out there?"

"What Gilbert wants to know. . . ." Pelon says.

"Hey, *puto*, I can talk for myself!" Gilbert shouts back.

But Pelon keeps on. "He just wants to know like we do, man. If the going gets heavy, are you guys into it?"

There is silence. We hear the buzz of the lights in the fish tank, the bubbles fizzing to the surface.

"Listen. . . . We've been at this game for almost ten years. We don't tell the kids to pick up the guns. We will not tell them to pick it up. But we do believe in self-defense . . . and if it's necessary . . . we do what is necessary. That's all."

"But you guys don't want to throw firebombs?"

"No. We don't. It doesn't serve our purposes now."

"Then why don't you tell the dudes who are doing it to stop doing it?"

"Are you kidding? . . . Man, if any Chicano comes and tells me what to do, what is the first thing I think? *Que es marrano*, right? We don't believe in telling others what to do. If you guys are throwing bombs, it must be because you feel that it's necessary to do so in order to accomplish your objectives. . . . We don't. . . . Not at this time."

"Do you support the Chicano Militants?"

He laughs. "Hey, *ese*, don't you read the papers? . . . I'm supposed to be the leader of you guys. . . . Of course I support you."

"How about the Chicano Liberation Front?"

"Who is that?" Corky says.

"Hey, ain'tchoo heard about. . . ." a kid with a beanie begins to ask.

Gilbert slaps him with a brown beret, laughing, "Don't be so *tapado, ese.* . . . This *vato* is cool."

With Gilbert's approval, Corky passes his colors. I don't tell him a word about our plans. I simply tell him that if I get caught I will not involve anyone from any of the organizations.

"I know you got something up your sleeve, Bear," he laughs at me.

"Yeah, Zeta . . . and if you need *anything* . . . just let us know," Louie gives me a big wink.

"You, too. . . . I mean, like if you need help writing your book, just call on me. . . . I'm also a writer," I say to them.

He flashes me a big grin. "Heh, heh. . . . Thanks, but I already got a publisher and an editor."

"Me, too. . . . I think. . . . I just got a letter today from some broad up in Frisco. . . . She says they would like to talk to me about doing some article or book."

"Great. . . . What are you going to write about?"

"I guess about what's happened here in Tooner Flats."

"You going to tell them *everything*?"

"Heh, heh . . . just enough to get you in trouble," I laugh.

Corky and Louie give me a queer look. But they laugh on their way out. The heavies leave and the groupies return. I get back to my serious drinking and smoking and fucking and preparing for the next day at court. Meanwhile, Gilbert and Pelon get down to work in the basement, a little room with dirt walls. The trap-door is in my bedroom. Only we three know about it. It is our secret.

About four months after the Moratorium, we manage an initial victory. I have been challenging the composition of the Grand Jury by questioning, under oath, the method of selection used by the LA County Superior Court. I have filed a brief, and the same Court of Appeals which ruled favorably for the East LA Thirteen has also granted us an order: any and all trial judges of the Superior Court are directed to take the stand and answer any and all questions I might frame.

No other lawyer has ever cross-examined a hundred judges. There is no precedent, nobody to show me how to do the job. So, as is my custom, I decide to go right for the throat of those dirty old men who sit over us in judgment. If they won't give us back our lands, at least we'll have a drop of their blood for our trouble.

I'm billed as the only revolutionary lawyer this side of the Florida Gulf. And it's true: I'm the only one who actually hates the *law*. The rest are just jiving. I'd rather spit in a judge's eye than stick a pig in the heart.

*The Revolt of the Cockroach People*

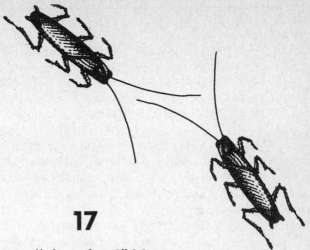

# 17

"You're going to get *all* the judges?" Mary says.

"I've subpoenaed every single sonofabitch. . . . One hundred and thirty-three of the bastards."

"Including *Older*, right?"

"*Especially* Older," I say.

"When you get *him* up on the stand, let us know," another girl says.

"I sure will. It won't be for a long time. The bastard's refused to accept the subpoena. I'll have to get another court order. . . . I'll let you know."

"We'll be right here," Mary says.

I am standing on the corner of Temple and Broadway in front of the old Hall of Justice, talking to three young pretty girls who are on their knees, in cute little miniskirts and low-cut blouses. None of them wears underclothes and all of them have bald-headed domes. A poster with red, white and blue paint announces they are protesting the political persecution of Charles Manson, the nut who allegedly masterminded the massacre of several movie stars, including one with an embryo in her fat belly. Supposedly some young kids, high on weird drugs, the Vietnam War and hard rock, under the influence of this stud who fucked minds as well as dead bodies, that *allegedly* they had, you know, decapitated, mutilated and desecrated the bodies of beautiful Jet-Setters and a fetus trying to get off the ground.

"It's political, just like your case, brother," Mary said to me when I first talked with her. . . .

"I'll know for sure sometime this month," I say again to the three girls with shaved heads and little crosses carved into their foreheads.

"Let's go," I say to Sailor Boy, the tiny quiet man who has been at my side ever since my return.

"All of Charlie's girls will show up if you let us know!" Mary yells as I walk away. Charles Older is the judge in the case of The People vs. Charles Manson. I've saved him for the last day.

"You take it now," the kid says.

He hands me my red, white and green briefcase. The guards at the entrance now search all persons entering the government buildings. Ever since the death of Zanzibar, government offices have become the favorite targets for the bombers of the underground. But the guards never search my briefcase. They have seen me on television so many times that they all call me by my first name. So when we enter government buildings, I carry my own briefcase with Sailor Boy's black .357 Magnum under the yellow pads. We are determined to go out in a blaze of glory when the time arrives.

"You're late, Mr. Brown," Alacran says.

"I'm sorry, Judge. I've been trying to subpoena Judge Older."

"Any luck?"

"No, sir. I'm going to need the court's help."

"Well, you do your best and when the time comes, we'll see what has to be done."

"Will this court make the necessary orders?"

He looks straight down at me, removes his glasses, rubs his brown smooth face with a manicured hand and says without emotion: "This court is very much aware of its powers, Mr. Brown. And you would do well to remember that when we get to our next witness. . . ."

Smugly, he leaves it hanging in air. Three weeks after I got back from Mexico, I had challenged his qualifications to sit on the matter:

"But you've already used up your *peremptory* challenge, Mr. Brown."

"I'm challenging the court *for cause*, your honor."

"You think I'm biased in the matter?"

"I'd like to have an opportunity to prove that you are, sir."

"If that is a motion. . . . I'll take that as if it were. . . . Your request is denied. Now let's proceed."

"Would the court take the stand?"

"You want *me* to testify?"

"Yes, sir."

"But I'm the judge on the matter. . . . You'll have to take that up with the Master Calendar Court. Now let's proceed."

"The defense calls the honorable Judge Alfred Alacran to the stand, your honor."

"That request is denied . . . at this time. Subject to a motion to reopen at a later time. . . . Now, let's proceed, Mr. Brown. Call your first witness."

"The defense calls Doctor Joan Moore."

I turn to see the tall woman stand. Long hefty legs in black stockings. A fleshy woman with gray hair, back in a bun. A big broad, long on words, she walks to the stand, her arm up, her fist clenched in the power salute.

"I would prefer to simply affirm my statements, if I may," the woman says. She looks at Alfred Alacran, the sharp Mexican kid who made it to the big time in Republican politics.

"Uh, yes . . . of course . . . Miss Kingsley, read the alternate form for this witness."

Once she affirms to tell the truth, she sits at the witness stand, in the little wooden box where we set them up and shoot them down, all for the price of a subpoena. Or, in her case, with the force of my winning smile and my huge shoulders. I have read one of her books on the history of the Chicanos and I was astounded to discover some *gabacha* who knew more about the beasts than I. When I found out it was a goodlooking broad, I talked to her and asked her to come to court and tell the judge who we are.

217

"But what is the *relevance* of all this, Mr. Brown?" the judge asks.

"Your honor. . . . We are claiming that this court has no jurisdiction to proceed because the indicting body was without legal power to bring these defendants to trial."

"And why is that?"

"Because the judges who selected the Grand Jury discriminated against the class of persons to whom the defendants pertain."

"And you want to define that class through this witness?"

"Yes, sir."

"Objection, your honor. . . . If I may."

"Go ahead, Mr. Torrez. . . ."

He has already embarassed me by coming up to me and deliberately shaking my hand in front of my Chicano Militant clients. "I'm doing my job, just like you, Buffalo."

"Jesus, man. You're so full of shit," I said.

He told me he was singled out to try this case. "It's no secret, man. Younger thinks the reason you win all your cases is because you're a Mexican."

"And what? The juries just tend to feel sorry for me?"

He laughed. "That's what he thinks."

"And you?"

"Shit, man. You're a good bullshitter, just like me. . . . I'm a Chicano, just like you," the prosecuting attorney said.

"Your honor," he now says in a whining voice, "Mr. Brown is just trying to tie up this court. . . . We don't need to hear from anyone. We know what a Mexican-American is. I think the court can take judicial notice that all the attorneys in this matter, including the court, are of Mexican-American extraction. . . ."

"Speak for yourself, Torrez," I say.

"Mr. Brown!" the court shouts.

"Yes, sir?"

"I want you to show more respect for all the participants in this matter."

"Yes, sir. . . . But what I meant was that just because. . . ."

"Mr. Brown! I *know* what you meant. . . . The objection is overruled. Now let's proceed with the witness."

I stand at the mike with my hands folded before me and I stare at the face of the tall Anglo schoolteacher, the professor from UCLA, from USC, from Riverside, with credentials a mile long and a yard wide.

"Doctor Moore. . . . Is there a class of persons known as Chicanos? And, if so, what are the peculiar characteristics that make up the class? If any? . . ."

"Oh, of course. Chicanos are as definable as, say an Afro-American, or black person. And Chicanos certainly have more definable characteristics than the so-called Anglo, or white Caucasian."

"What's that, Doctor?"

"Objection, your honor!" Torrez shouts.

"Overruled. Proceed."

"The WASP, or White-Anglo-Saxon-Protestant, is the common definition . . . but that also includes persons from the European countries as well as persons from Iceland and Australia."

"Who, then, are the so-called Chicanos?"

"First of all, the name is relatively new. It's been used throughout the years to refer to persons whose ancestors were native to this continent and whose last names are Spanish, or Spanish-sounding. Originally, it referred to a poor immigrant from Mexico, a *mexicano*, shortened by slang to *chicano*."

"Are you familiar with the names of the defendants?"

"Yes."

"Are you familiar with the defendants, personally?"

"Some of them."

"Do you have an opinion as to their classification?"

"If you mean racial-ethnic classification. . . Yes, I do."

"Can you describe their peer group?"

"They call themselves Chicanos rather than Mexicans or Mexican-Americans. . . . Most of them are Catholic. Most of them speak some Spanish. Most of them have had a relative in prison. Most of them have parents or grandparents who were born south of the border."

"And what do they consider themselves to be in terms of citizenship?"

"Objection."

"Overruled. Please proceed."

"Unlike the black American who *cannot* return to Africa, the mother country, the Chicano is within his *own* mother country. The international border at Juarez, at Tijuana, at Nogales, at Laredo . . . these lines are but reminders to the Chicanos of what their grandparents did to them. . . . It was their own presidents, their own generals, who sold both the land and the people thereon to the United States Government for something like sixteen million dollars."

"But Mr. Brown," Alacran butts in, "what is the *point* of all this? What if we are descendants of the prior possessors of the land? Are you saying that because the treaties between this government and the Mexican government were broken—assuming they were—are you saying that we, that is the Mexican-American, is not subject to the jurisdiction of this court?"

"No, your honor . . . I'd like to argue that position some day before the United Nations . . . but for now, we are claiming the rights to citizenship under the United States Constitution as well as the right to equal protection under its laws. . . ."

"Then why are you permitting your witness to ramble on about irrelevant matters? . . . This court takes judicial notice that the body of persons known as Mexican-Americans, or white persons of Spanish surname, are a class that can be subject to discrimination in connection with their selection to the Grand Jury. . . . So let's get to the meat of this question, Mr. Brown. . . . You've been granted the special orders by the Court of Appeals. . . . Let's get to it."

"I wish the record to show that the court is pointing its finger at me."

"The record will show no such thing. . . ."

"And that the court is hollering at me. . . ."

"Don't interrupt me when I'm talking, Mr. Brown. . . . Now let's get to the issue of discrimination. . . . Do you have any witnesses on that issue?"

"I've served subpoenas on every judge in the County of Los Angeles ordering them to appear here at nine a.m."

"Yes, I know. . . . I've told them to hold off until I call them."

"But I didn't excuse them!"

"Mr. Brown. . . . This is my court. I run the business of this court. I will not permit you to disrupt the entire proceedings of the largest superior court in the State of California. . . . I will direct the order of testimony of the judges that you've subpoened. Unless you have some special reason for wanting one before the other. . . ."

"I have no objection to the court's assistance . . . but I just don't like anyone to tell my witnesses when they can show up."

"Yes. . . . Now let's proceed."

I touch Joan's shoulder on the way out. I'll see you later, I whisper to her. She is a genius who wants to be a woman; I intend to help.

Next is Georges Sabah, the absent-minded professor with the little Chaplin mustache. He is my expert demographer from UCLA, a top man in his field.

"Based on the figures which I've extrapolated from the latest demographic surveys, I estimate that the Chicanos are approximately fifteen percent of the population of Los Angeles County."

Torrez jumps up and asks, "Where did you get those figures?"

"I called up a friend at the Department of Finance in Sacramento."

"No further questions."

Then, one at a time, the judges stumble into my lair. They trickle in through the back door in their business suits. In civilian clothes they look like ordinary men. Without their black robes and their high benches, they walk and sit and talk just as most tired older men of America do. I cannot hate them for what they look like. When I see them sitting on the slat benches outside the courtroom, when I pass and see the long thin silk socks and watch them smoke Tareyton's just like me, I don't despise them then. It is only when I think about what they *say* and *do* that the acids begin dripping into my brain. But I go on and snap for their throats with a smile, a slight twist of the eyes, the inflection of the good decent Mexican man who is simply trying to help his clients. They understand *business,* for God's sake.

When the last witness for the day has been examined, Alacran calls his bailiff, George, the big Greek, to the stand.

"Now, Mr. Christopulos, will you please advise the court what you found written on the wall outside my chambers?"

"Yeah, Judge. . . . It said, 'Kill.' And an arrow pointed to your name plate."

"Anything else unusual happen during testimony today?"

"Well. . . . This afternoon we found a fire. . . . Someone set a fire in the toilet next to the courtroom. It was just a newspaper burning in the trash can."

"And did you extinguish it?"

"I didn't . . . John, the bailiff in Judge Older's court, did."

"And did you find out what newspaper it was?"

"It was *La Voz.*"

"Do you have it?"

"Yes, sir. It's with the clerk."

"Miss Kingsley. . . . Would you please read into the record what the paper says?"

"Yes, your honor. . . . It's got a picture of, I think it's Mr. Brown and the defendants."

"Your honor . . . It's an article about this case," I say.

"Don't interrupt, Mr. Brown."

"Well, your honor. . . . If you're trying to say that one of the defendants or one of their friends did that. . . ."

"I'm not interested in your comments, Mr. Brown."

"Then why are you placing all this on the record?"

"Mr. Brown, I've asked you to stop your arguing with me."

"Well, Judge . . . I have a right to comment on anything in the case."

"If I give you permission to talk."

"We're not interested in violence, your honor."

"Well, Mr. Brown, I'm happy to hear that. . . . From certain statements you've been making in public, I wonder. . . ."

"Even Chicano lawyers have freedom of speech, Judge."

"Not when they're contemptuous of this court. . . . I don't want to hear any more of your sass, Brown. . . . Do you understand that?"

"I went to school."

"But they didn't teach you that in school, did they? . . . I want you to leave the court now and when you come in tomorrow, I want you to be dressed properly."

"What do you mean?" I shout.

"Your tie is hanging. . . . Your shirt is unbuttoned."

"It's my neck, sir. My neck is too fat."

"Just see to it that you wear something appropriate."

"It must be this shirt, Judge. It's from Acapulco."

"Mr. Brown, you're sassing me again."

"I'm sorry, Judge. I've had trouble with fat necks. . . ."

"If you don't shut up I'll throw you in the clink right now!"

"You don't have to point your finger at me, Judge. I'm not a little kid. And you're not my father."

"For that remark, I hereby order you to spend the next two days and nights in the county jail. . . . Mr. Christopulos, take Mr. Brown into custody."

"Your intimidations aren't going to work, Judge. I'm going to keep talking so long as I think it's going to help my clients."

"And that's where you're confused. . . . You're not helping your clients with all this smart talk. Now take him away."

"Viva La Raza!" the spectators roar.

Alacran jumps from his bench and hurries into his chambers behind it. I lift my arm to my clients who stand quietly and watch George take me into the holding tank behind the judge's chambers.

"Viva El Zeta!"

Soon I am alone in the dungeon. Again. I lay stretched out on the hard wooden bench until the court business for the day is over. And then I am transferred back to the LA New County Jail where my friend, Sergeant Lovelace, has prepared my old cell in the nut ward. I sleep and exercise for two days and nights and on Monday morning I am ready for action again.

The battle continues. One judge after another. The same shit from out of the mouths of tired old men. Day in, day out. For months I bring them up to the stand and wait for their lies. Six hours a day I question the bums. Three hours in the morning, three in the afternoon. Words, words, words!

It is five o'clock, Friday afternoon. I am down to my last judge, Charles Older. I am waiting for the old bastard to come into the courtroom. The court is filled with young girls. Charlie's Girls with shaved heads: young Americans without brassieres, kids in sandals, groupies of the Acid Jesus, they wait quietly as they have for the past year since the arrest of their guru. Across the aisle, to their right, sit the friends of the defendants. And the Zeta girls, the little levi's and brown berets. Rosalie and her cousins are sitting with their boyfriends. They treat me as their uncle; during the recesses, they hit me up for a dime for the coke machine. All of us are waiting for the bad-mouth judge who resisted the subpoena for a month. . . . Until I finally sent Sailor Boy and his buddy, Papoose, from PINTO.

"I told his clerk I wanted to give the judge a subpoena, ese."

"But the old bitch said to come back later, man," Papoose, the mean ex-con growled.

They waited out in the corridor until the judge came out with his two deputy-sheriff bodyguards. He's been in fear of his life ever since he started the Manson trial, the papers say.

"I walked up to the dude, *ese*, and guess what?"

"The *pinche chota* pulled out their guns, man."

"So I just threw it at his feet and said, 'Hey, Judge, this is a subpoena. You got to come to court.'"

"He'll be here," I said. . . .

Now, with the room packed with partisans, I stand and walk in front of the crowd. I look into their innocent faces. I lift my hands to the air, a conductor of the choir in the courtroom. . . .

"All right, children. If you'll all turn to page seventeen we'll sing one stanza of "What A Friend We Have In Jesus."

*What a friend we have in Jesus,*
*All our sins and grief to bear.*
*What a privilege to carry*
*All our griefs to Him in prayer.*

The gallery joins in with me. The thin voices of the girls of the sixties join with the garbled grunts of the ex-cons, ex-junkies and present revolutionaries to sing President Eisenhower's favorite hymn.

"Hey, Buffalo, hey, man!"

It is George, the bailiff. He is rushing up to me with his hands in the air.

"Jesus, man. You want me to get fired? . . . Come on, Older's here."

Both judges come out of Alacran's chambers. Older is in a gray suit. Alacran takes the bench in his robes.

Older sits at the witness box. My clients lean forward to see the toughest judge of them all. This is the one that doesn't take shit from anyone. He's no pussy-assed liberal. Not even a conservative with a conscience. He's just like me, a fanatic who believes he's always right. And if you don't like it, motherfucker, do something about it. He stares me straight in the face.

"Is your name Charles Older?"

"Mr. Brown," Alacran interrupts, "This court may take judicial notice that the witness is Judge Older. Proceed."

"Will the court please order the witness to answer the question?"

"No. Proceed."

"Are you a judge?"

"Mr. Brown," Alacran interrupts. "Let's proceed to the main issue. . . . The record will note that it is now five-fifteen p.m. and we have granted Judge Older's request that his appearance be postponed until now because of his crowded calendar. . . . Proceed."

"I object to the court's interruption of my examination of this witness."

"Proceed."

"Isn't it a fact that you are a white Caucasian?"

"That's none of your business."

"Will the court please instruct the witness to answer the question?"

Alacran looks at me. He folds his hands in front of him and then slightly turns, with a half-bent shoulder, toward the witness stand.

"Uh, Judge Older . . . Justice Krause has issued an order that states, in effect, that the racial background of the jury selector is one possible area of inquiry."

"I haven't read it," Older growls.

"Uh, Mr. Brown, let's proceed to another area."

"Will the court please instruct this witness to answer the question?"

"Proceed."

"Isn't it a fact that all your nominees to the Grand Jury are white Caucasians?"

"I don't see what that has to do with their qualifications."

I say nothing. I look at Judge Alacran.

"Objection, your honor."

It is Torrez. He hasn't spoken one word in court for the past three weeks. It finally got to him, too. He has heard the same lies as I have heard. So what now?

"Mr. Brown is cross-examining his own witness."

"I agree, Mr. Torrez. I was wondering if you were going to object. . . . The court on its own motion rules that the witness belongs to Mr. Brown. . . . Please limit yourself to direct examination. Proceed."

"But this man is obviously hostile to the defense."

"Objection, your honor. . . . There's been no showing that Judge Older is hostile to anything."

"I most certainly am not hostile to this case, Fred," Older butts in from the witness stand. They both belong to the same tennis club.

"Objection, your honor!" I shout. "Will the court instruct the witness to limit his comments to answering my questions?"

"Mr. Brown!" Alacran shouts. "You will treat this witness, and every witness before my court, with respect."

"I was entering a proper objection. . . ."

"And you will not interrupt me. . . . Now, let's proceed."

In the twinkling of an eye, the court is black. We are in total darkness.

"Uh . . . heh, heh. . . . The record will note that the lights have gone off. . . ." Alacran begins.

Older says in the darkness, "Judge, you should know that I've received certain threats. . . ."

"Yes, Judge. . . . Bailiff? George? Where are you?"

"Over here, Judge. I'm looking for a flashlight."

"Does anybody have a match?"

"I refuse to answer that question. . . ." a voice in the back calls out. Giggles. Squirms. Light nervous laughter.

"Sergeant Hamilton? Are you there?" Older calls out.

"Yes, sir. We're here. We have matters under control, sir."

It is, I assume, the voice of his bodyguards. The voice comes from before me. He must be in the reporter's room, next to the judge's chambers. I wonder how many of those bastards are stashed around here.

Blink. We are in light. Laughter from the courtroom.

"Now please proceed."

"Are you a Protestant?"

"I'm certainly not going to answer that question."

"Your honor?" I say meekly.

"Judge Older . . . Justice Krause also said that the religion of the nominators, that's us . . . We are obligated to give that information in this motion."

"But it is an invasion of my privacy . . . And under the Constitution, I don't think Krause can do that."

"Your honor . . . Will you please tell this witness not to give legal argument?"

"Listen, Mr. Brown, you can ask all you want, but I'm not going. . . ."

"Uh, Judge Older?" Alacran says. "Please, let's not argue with counsel. . . . Now proceed to another question."

"Do you know what a hippie is?"

"Objection, your honor!" Torrez shouts. He seems to be coming back to life.

"What can that have to do with this motion, Mr. Brown?"

"Under the ruling, we have a right to inquire into the types of persons excluded . . . if there is such a type."

"And can you tell me what a hippie is?" Alacran says to me.

"Well . . . I'd say this court is filled with them."

"Where?"

"A hippie is like a cockroach. So are the Beatniks. So are the Chicanos. We're all around, Judge. And judges do not pick us to serve on Grand Juries."

"Mr. Brown . . . You will please confine yourself to *legal* arguments in my courtroom. . . . Continue."

"Have you ever nominated a person under thirty to serve on the Grand Jury?"

"I don't know any that are qualified."

"How about blacks?"

"If you mean Negro-Americans . . . no. I don't know any."

"You don't know any that are qualified? Or you don't know any people of that race?"

"I've already answered the question."

"What a joke!"

"Who said that?" Alacran growls. He is flashing green eyes over my head toward the rear. It sounded like a girl's voice.

"George, did you see who said that?"

"No, sir."

"I did it."

I turn to see the girl with the shaved head and the fine little body, a cross on her forehead and a gold ring through her left nostril. It's Mary.

"What's that in your hand?" the judge asks.

"A paper sack."

"Stand up when you speak to this court."

Mary stands up.

"Bailiff, take that bag away from . . . What's your name?"

"Mary Brunner."

"She's a witness in the case in my court, Judge," Older whispers from the witness box.

"George, did you find anything in the bag?"

"Yes, Judge. . . . A banana and some yogurt."

"*Yami* yogurt, your honor," Mary says with a straight face.

"All right, that's enough. . . . I hereby order this courtroom cleared of everybody except persons from the media and relatives of the defendants. . . ."

"Objection, your honor."

"I don't want to hear any argument from you, Brown."

"But we have a right to an open trial. . . ."

"Bailiff, please call more men if you need help clearing this courtroom. . . ."

"Up yours, *puto!*" I hear a shout from the rear.

"Your honor. . . . Can the witness be excused?" Torrez says.

"Will you have more questions, Mr. Brown?"

"Not that you'll permit me to ask. . . . And it's no use anyway, he's not going to answer anything."

"The witness is excused, the court is adjourned for the day.

And he hurries off the bench and follows Older into his chambers. We are all in fits of laughter. The girls and the cons are hugging one another. George throws his hands over his head and says to me, "You bastards are something else."

A young girl from Charlie's crew is about to throw her

arms around me when, wham!

Elena sticks her butt in front of the broad and gives her the old heave-ho.

"No more, Zeta. . . . You got your honey, remember?"

"Besides, ese, she's a gabacha," Sailor Boy throws in.

It burns me up; I, who could have taken up Charlie's crew of acid groupies, am to be denied their pleasures. Not that I want them, but shit! Whose life is it? Cockroach is a big word.

People are talking, looking, watching me out of the corners of their eyes. Nobody tells me what to do, but it's easy to tell what pisses them off. Sure, I'm the hottest thing in court, straight-shooting from the hip with a kill every time. But look at those faces: too many women, Zeta. And your writing.

The book offer has made me enemies. That I would think to make money off the struggle for freedom of the Cockroaches has made some people whisper traitor, vendido, tío taco, uncle tom and a capitalist pig to boot. Some of the dudes from PINTO are angry in private.

I have explained it a thousand times. I have no desire to make a martyr out of Zanzibar. I know he has been murdered. Only Gilbert and Pelon know how we intend to avenge him. But now there is no Zanzibar to tell our story, no way for us to use the media to get us back our land. I shouted it to the rooftops: we need writers, just like we need lawyers. Why not me? I want to write. The vatos listen to me carry on, but who knows what they think? Gilbert, Pelon and Elena stand by me. But after the trial, when nobody needs me anymore, what then?

And I get it from the gabacho end, too. One day I went to speak to Jim Bellows, a gray-haired handsome executive, then in charge of West Magazine, the Sunday supplement of the gargantuan LA Times. He was very interested in the story of the Chicano Militants. He said he'd been thinking about running something on the subject for some time but he knew of no one who was qualified, who had a grasp of the situation.

"Do you know anyone?" he asked.

"Well . . . I'm certain that there are many men. . . ."

"Name one."

"Well . . . *I* write. And I'm familiar with the story."

He looked down on me and smiled. "But you're a lawyer, aren't you? I mean, aren't you the lawyer for the people arrested during the riots?"

"So? There were murders. The people should know that."

We were silent, an impasse.

"Mr. Brown. . . . If you can suggest the name of any other person, I'd be happy to speak with him."

"You don't have *any* reporters here in the building that you think could handle it?"

He smiled at me. "Oh, of course. But you said you wanted a man who could tell, what was it, the *Chicano* point of view?"

I swallowed my throat and gave him a list of five names of various professors from UCLA and USC whom I knew to be on familiar terms, if not with the events, at least with the Militants. I thanked him and got up to leave.

"Mr. Brown . . . I'm sure you understand why we can't have you, an attorney, writing the article."

"No, sir. Why don't you tell me?"

He breathed deeply, stretched his shoulders and said, "Well . . . It's a question of ethics, I guess."

"'*Ethics?'*"

"You would be giving yourself . . . publicity. You'd be writing about the defense point of view. We would then be obligated to give equal time to the District Attorney's Office."

"You think I'm doing this for *publicity*?"

"Well? . . . Isn't that what newspapers are all about?"

I nodded, shrugged my shoulders and walked out without another word. . . .

All this paranoia and work make me tired. As Pelon drives me, Gilbert, Elena and Sailor Boy home, I feel like if the Chicanos could get back only the Golden Gate Bridge, I'd be happy. It even crosses my mind that Sam Yorty had foreseen this all long ago, when he advised me to riot.

Somehow, he knew it would start to destroy us because he knew I would be in Acapulco at the time because . . . I pull myself together. Tomorrow will be the finale, the decision on the whole show for the last six months. I tell Elena to feed the fish and then go to sleep.

"I'm ready for you now, Judge," I say to Alacran.

"What? What do you mean by that remark?"

"I mean, the defense would like you to take the stand and testify. You were one of the judges who selected the Grand Jury that indicted my clients. I'm ready."

"Oh. . . . Well, I'm not. Your request is denied. We will commence with the actual trial on Monday morning."

"Now wait a minute, your honor! Aren't you even going to listen to argument on this motion?" I can't believe my ears.

"I've been listening to you and reading your briefs since last fall, Mr. Brown."

"But you have six months of testimony to digest. You have six months of rulings to reconsider. If you decide after hearing that the Grand Jury is defective, you won't have to go through another long trial. . . ."

"I know all that . . . But Justice Krause did not order this court to stop the proceedings of the trial. . . . After all, that's what we're here for, aren't we. The order just said to give you a fair hearing, not a final ruling. . . . So be prepared to start selecting a jury this Monday. Good-day."

"Goddammit, Alacran. . . ." I begin, but all he does is throw me into jail again. While I am cooling off in my bare white room, I realize that the issue isn't dead. So, all right, we have a trial. Even if one of the defendants is found guilty on the felony charges, we can still appeal for a final ruling. This makes me feel slightly better, but when I am released the next morning, I show Elena and Sailor Boy our basement workshop. Somebody is going to pay.

And two weeks later, staring over my shoulder with

Sailor Boy still wanting to go to Laguna Park, I see that I too am paying. Yeah, the star is paying for his own movie . . .

"Hey, Sailor Boy, did you ever see the movie, *Viva Zapata?*"

"Yeah, *ese*, he was a great man. Too bad they had Brando in it, you know?" He is surprised at the direction of my thoughts. After all, why would looking at a building make me think of that?

"Do you think you would have done what he did?"

"What's that, *ese?* He did a lot."

"On your wedding night, with the woman you loved, would you learn to read?"

"Well, I don't . . ." He breaks off.

"I can fight like hell . . . but *that* far, to forget everything else, my life . . . I don't know either."

We go to lunch.

# 18

After the recess, Fernando Sumaya takes the stand. He is a young light-brown Chicano in a black police uniform. His badge is very prominently displayed. A clean-cut type, he looks like a friendly traffic cop.

Sumaya tells his story sincerely. He never once raises his voice or gets mad at anyone. Not even when the bully, Buffalo Bullshit Brown, el Zeta, the hot-shot lawyer prances in front of him, up and down, smiling in a bright tie, lashing out, arguing, always in a sweat, in a hurry, in my pain. Sumaya's first assignment after police academy was to infiltrate the Chicano Militants. He drove them around in his car for six months before the day of the riot. Finally, Torrez' examination takes the testimony to the night before the shit hit the fan.

"That Friday night, I went to a meeting at a house on Sixth Street."

"Whose house was that?" Torrez asks. I have been waiting six months for this bombshell.

"At the home of Mr. Brown."

"Mr. Buffalo Z. Brown? The attorney for the defendants?"

"Yes, sir . . . But he wasn't there."

"Who was at the meeting?"

"All the defendants and about ten other people whose names I don't know."

*The Revolt of the Cockroach People*

"And what was said?"

"They were talking about the march and demonstration for the next day."

"Was there any talk of violence?"

"The defendant they call Waterbuffalo, his real name is Ralph Gomez, he wanted to know if Corky carried a gun."

"What did Mr. Gonzales say?"

"He said that he, personally, didn't carry one; but he had friends who did."

"Did you see any weapons in the house that night?"

"Yes, sir. The place was loaded. There were all kinds of guns and rifles. Dynamite . . . flares . . . Gasoline, everything."

"Now, on the day in question, did you see any acts of violence committed by any defendant?"

"After the police started shooting the tear gas, I ran with Ralph and Richard, they call him Bullwinkle, and we went and threw some firebombs."

"You saw both defendants throwing firebombs?"

"Yes, sir."

"Where?"

"First at the Safeway Store on Fourth Street . . . then later at the Bank of America on Broadway Avenue. . . . They threw three at each place."

"No further questions."

I get up. At this moment I am very conscious of the jury, of the four young Chicano chicks that for some reason Torrez has allowed to be seated. Sumaya's testimony is bad, but has Torrez forgotten that young people usually vote for the underdog? And why did he let in the social worker, Miss Betty Irish, is it? He said he wanted a balanced jury, but does he know something I don't? I begin with a few warm-ups:

"Officer Sumaya, did you find any communists in the organization you were sent to infiltrate?"

"At their meetings they read stuff by Che and some other communists. But no, I don't think *they* were."

"Didn't you hang around with them like a *carnal*? Wasn't your name Frisco at the time?"

"Heh, heh. . . . Well, that's what the guy's called me."

"And you'd worked with Sergeant Abel Armas of the SOC Squad, right?"

"Yes, sir. He is my superior."

"And you told him of the plans of the CMs the night before the march?"

"Yes, sir. I called and told him that the guys planned to start a riot."

"And were you given any special instructions for that day?"

"I was just told to stay with them, report in once in a while . . . and not to break my cover."

"Even if you saw felonies being committed, you were not to interfere, is that it?"

"Yes, sir."

"Even if it meant death?"

"I guess I would have stopped it if someone was going to get killed."

"Didn't you in fact see someone killed?"

"Not when I was with the defendants."

"Didn't you in fact see Roland Zanzibar have his head blown open with a tear gas projectile?"

"*Objection*, your honor!"

"Yes, please come to the bench, counsel."

We walk up to the bench to talk to Alacran.

"Mr. Brown, do you want to open up that line?"

Torrez says, "I hope he does."

"The murder of Zanzibar is crucial to our defense."

"Proceed, please."

"Now, Officer. . . . You did, in fact, see the killing of a person on that day, didn't you?"

"No. I was close, but I didn't see it."

"You were at the Silver Dollar Bar on the afternoon that tear gas was fired into the place, is that correct?"

"Yes. I'd gone in there to get something to drink."

"Were you familiar with any of the persons who were in there?"

"I had seen Mr. Zanzibar before. And I knew that the three men with him were employees of KMEX."

"Were they already inside when you arrived?"

"Yes. They were at the bar."

"Didn't you talk to them?"

"I, uh . . . I think I said hello."

"And then what did you do?"

"I . . . went to the toilet."

"And then you made a phone call, didn't you?"

"I don't remember. It's been a long time."

"Didn't you, in fact, call your superior, Sergeant Armas?"

"Well, I called him several times that afternoon. . . . There was such commotion . . . I don't know if I called him from in there."

"All right . . . What happened after the visit to the bathroom."

"I went back in the bar and had a drink. . . ."

"Yes. . . . Then what happened?"

"I saw Mr. Restrepo, one of the television reporters with Mr. Zanzibar . . . I saw him talking to Roland and then I saw a . . . a can of tear gas on the floor."

"Next to the jukebox?"

"Yes. . . . And then I heard a shot."

"Did you see where it came from?"

"From the door . . . the curtain was partly open. . . ."

"Did you see anyone at the door?"

"Yes."

"Who?"

"I think his name is Wilson."

"Don't you know him?"

"I didn't at the time . . . I'd been working undercover since I'd become a policeman. I only talked to Armas. He was the only one who knew that I was a police officer."

"What did you do after you saw Wilson fire into the bar?"

"I hit the deck."

"You did not, by any chance, notice the bleeding body of Zanzibar on the floor a yard away?"

"No."

"Then what?"

"I got up and ran out."

"Which way did you go?"

"The back door was open. I just ran out into the alley."

"Then what did you do?"

"I went back to the CM office."

"Didn't you make any calls before getting back?"

"Oh, yes. I think I called Armas."

"What did you tell him?"

"What I'd seen in the bar."

"Did he give you any special instructions?"

"No. He just said to go look for the CMs."

"Now, during the time you were in the bar . . . did you see anyone with a gun or a weapon of any kind?"

"No."

"And you are certain that you did not report a person with a gun? You didn't call the police or Sheriff to report an incident at the bar prior to your exiting?"

"Not that I remember."

"In other words, you *might* have done it?"

"I don't know. I just don't remember."

"But you do remember throwing bombs with Water-buffalo and Bullwinkle?"

"Yes, sir."

"You threw some, too?"

"No, sir. I just watched them do it."

"And did you see where they prepared them?"

"They said they got them from your house, sir."

"This is the house on Sixth Street? Where you saw all the arms and ammunition?"

"Yes, sir. And the dynamite, too."

"Did you report *that* to your superiors?"

"Yes, sir."

"What time did you tell them what you'd seen?"

"Early in the morning, before the march."

"And you had reason to believe that some of the persons present were going to use these weapons during the demonstration?"

"That's what they said."

"And did you make any attempt to stop them?"

"I was told not to break my cover."

"Did any police officer make an attempt to stop them?"

"I guess it was too late by the time they got there."

"Oh, did they go to my house?"

"I'm not sure."

"I have no more questions of this lying spy."

"Objection!"

"Contempt, Mr. Brown!"

"Ah, just put it on my tab!"

"Step down, Officer. You are excused. Call the next witness."

The bailiff goes out the door and comes back with the big crew-cut blonde deputy in khaki clothes. He is sworn in and sits in the witness box.

Tom Wilson is a professional cop. Twenty years on the force, beginning with traffic tie-ups, then on to narcotics investigations, jumping to juvenile investigations of gang wars in Tooner Flats and finally settling down as the hit man with the SOC Squad. He carries the little bazooka which shoots out the ten-inch projectiles.

"We received a call from an unidentified source at approximately sixteen-thirty hours on 29 August. We were instructed to proceed to the area of the Silver Dollar Bar on Whittier Boulevard. Upon our arrival we were confronted with a mob of rioters. Fire engines blocked the streets. The buildings next door and across the street were in flames, smoke was shooting up and there was general commotion."

"How many of you were there?" Torrez asks.

"I don't remember."

"What did you do?"

"We got out of our cars and called out to the persons inside the bar. We told them to come out with their hands in the air. When they refused to come out, I fired into the bar."

"Did anyone give you specific instructions when to fire?"

"We had general orders to fire when we thought it necessary to protect life and property."

"Could you see inside the bar?"

"No, sir. A curtain hung across the door."

"Did you know who was in there?"

"No, sir."

"Did you know how many persons were inside?"

"No, sir."

"Did you know that certain personnel with television station KMEX were inside?"

"No, sir."

"Why, then, did you fire?"

"Because we had information that a man with a gun was inside."

"And is it common to fire a bazooka into a building with people inside?"

"It seemed reasonable to me."

"You were the head of your squad at the time?"

"I was the senior officer at the time, yes, sir."

"Thank you, Sergeant Wilson," Torrez says. He starts to walk back to his table, but suddenly turns around. "One last question." He looks at me with his sneaky eyes. "If you would have wanted to murder anyone, would you be likely to do it by shooting a tear gas projectile through a curtain which made it impossible for you to see your victim?" Both he and Alacran wait for me to come up screaming. But all the idiot has done is to open the subject for my cross-examination. I smile delightedly.

"No, sir," lies Wilson.

It is now my turn at bat: "Sergeant Wilson, isn't the weapon you fired supposed to be used only in a situation where a suspect has barricaded himself behind walls?"

"Yes, sir. That's what the instructions read."

"Do you consider a curtain a barricade?"

"No, sir."

"Then why did you fire into an open door?"

"I didn't know the door was open."

"You didn't see the curtain swinging, how should I put it . . . swinging *breezily* in an *open* doorway?"

"I didn't see it like that, no."

"And the back door? Didn't you know *it* was open?"

"No, sir. I didn't know. I wasn't familiar with the building."

"Not familiar? Isn't it true that in twenty years of police work you had been in that bar many times?"

"Well . . . now and again."

"And you have sworn that you had no knowledge that Roland Zanzibar was inside the bar?"

"Yes, sir."

"I take it this means you did not receive a phone call from Officer Sumaya which pinpointed Roland Zanzibar at a table which your police training would allow you to hit regardless of any curtain. . . ."

"Objection!" shouts Torrez, almost upsetting his table.

"Sustained!" shouts Alacran, but I am looking at the jury smugly. "Mr. Brown, you will not badger the witness!"

"All right, Sergeant Wilson, returning again to your testimony. You received information that a person inside had a gun. You did not receive any firing instructions about. . . ."

"Objection!"

"Contempt!"

I still plough on.

"You were told it was a man?"

"I assumed it was a man."

"You saw a woman coming out of the bar when you first got there, didn't you?"

"I told some people coming out to move out of the way."

"How did you know *they* weren't the ones with the gun?"

"I had no way of telling either way."

"So you just decided to blow the place up, didn't matter who got hit, right?"

"I evaluated the situation, sir. We were in the middle of the bloodiest riot I've ever seen in my twenty years on the force. There had been lots of shooting all around that day. They went wild, beating up police officers, breaking and entering, looting and burning. . . . If I misjudged the situation . . . I guess you can blame it on the circumstances."

"Did you ever find a man with a gun inside?"

"One of the men who owned the bar had a rifle ... And a man who owns a bakery next door, he had a gun."

"Did you arrest either of them?"

"No, sir."

"Why not?"

"They're business men. They keep those weapons to protect their property. There's a lot of strong arms around that neighborhood."

"Did you check to see if they had licenses to carry those weapons?"

"I was of the opinion that those men needed those weapons to protect themselves and their property. You don't need a license in a situation like that."

"Who told you that?"

"That's just common sense, Mr. Brown."

"Not only I, but the defendants agree, Sergeant. Thank you. No more questions."

"Call your next witness."

"Officer Valencia."

George goes out and brings in the sleek suave mustachioed Chicano cop that arrested Corky. He smiles at us as he passes on the way to the witness stand.

Valencia looks like Corky. He was born and raised in Tooner Flats, he tells the jury. He was working out of Ramparts Police Station on the day of the riot. He and a partner were assigned to cover the general East LA area.

"We were driving down Whittier Boulevard when we saw this big flat-bed truck. The defendants Gonzales and Miss Elena Lowrider were in the cab sitting next to the driver. There were approximately twenty-five suspects in the back of the truck. I pulled them over."

"Did you know any of the persons on that truck prior to stopping them?" Torrez asks.

"No, sir."

"Did you know the names of any of the suspects before you pulled them over?"

"No, sir."

"Why did you stop them?"

"To warn the driver. The people in the back were standing up and waving their arms over the sides."

"You were aware of the riot going on at the time, weren't you?"

"Yes. We'd heard reports over the radio."

"Do you recall any specific reports?"

"I heard an officer say that the rioters had killed some police officers. Or shot at them."

"And did you have any suspicions about the persons in the truck?"

"No, sir. I just stopped them for their own safety."

"Then what happened?"

"I checked out the driver's license. . . . Then when I came back to the truck, I saw Mr. Gonzales make a move for something under the seat and I ordered him out."

"He was seated between the driver and Miss Lowrider?"

"Yes, sir. I drew my service revolver and ordered them both out. . . . And then I saw a gun fall to the floor of the cab."

"Where did it fall from?"

"From out of Mr. Gonzales' hand."

"*Mentiroso*, you liar!" Elena shouts.

"Now Miss Lowrider . . . if you make another outburst like that I'll revoke your bail and hold you in contempt."

"But he's lying, Judge!"

"I've warned you. Now proceed, please."

"No more questions," Torrez says.

I calm Elena down and then launch into him.

"Didn't you in fact know that you were arresting the alleged leader of the Chicano Militants?" I yell in his face.

"Not until later on that night."

"Didn't you find some pamphlets and newspapers in the truck?"

"Yes, sir. But I didn't read them until we got back to the station. . . . That's when I saw a picture of you, Mr. Brown, and Mr. Gonzales. . . . I didn't know until then who the suspect was."

"And that's when you decided to book *all twenty-six people in that truck for burglary?*"

"No, sir. That decision was made by my superiors. I

just wrote the police report and they booked the suspects."

"But you arrested all twenty-six, didn't you?"

"Yes, sir."

"Why did you do that?"

"Because . . . I found a gun in the cab and we found another gun in the back of the truck."

"*And* because you found three hundred dollars in the pockets of Mr. Gonzales' pants, right?"

"Under the circumstances . . . Yes, we thought it reasonable to arrest these people."

"Why is that?"

"There were shootings, burnings, lootings. . . . Everything was happening at once. We were in a battle situation. I used my best judgment."

"Is it normal for your superiors to tell you what charges to book suspects on?"

"Well . . . normally, we do our own booking. But in this situation, I asked them what I should do."

"Who made the decision?"

"I don't know."

"Aren't you the investigating officer on this case?"

"Yes, sir."

"Then whose name did you put on the police report?"

"I listed Armas, Sergeant Abel Armas, as the booking officer. . . ."

"And also Chief Judd Davis?"

"That was just a formality. I don't think he had anything to do with it."

"No more questions."


It's another two months, when we are summoning witnesses for the defense, before I have a chance to prove that Judd Davis *did*, in fact, have everything to do with it.

"I hope he's out there," I tell Corky. I have subpoenaed him, but I haven't seen him in the courtroom area.

And then smiling Judd walks in. He nods to me. I smile back, and recall our days together at USC my first year in LA. Both of us taught a seminar in the Department of Religion. "Conflict In Urban Society" was the topic of the year-long seminar. The first day of class, two hundred straight WASPs from the high-class university cheered Davis and booed me off the stage. Throughout the year I told them all about my cases and my clients. The last day of school they laughed *him* off the stage. When he got appointed to his present position by Mayor Yorty, I wrote him a note saying, "I hope you remember that classroom discussion is protected by the First Amendment . . . from one chief to another . . . Zeta."

He replied, "Dear Buff, I know that deep down inside you are a good man. I know that someday you and I will both be on the same side . . . Chief Davis."

"Hi, Judd," I say to this big Irish cop who teaches Sunday School. Our smiles and good humor are the professional touch of deadly enemies.

"Mr. Brown! You'll address the witness with the proper respect."

"He's an old friend of mine, your honor."

Alacran looks down at Davis.

"*I* don't mind, Judge. Mr. Brown and I taught school together."

"Let's proceed."

"Now, Chief. . . . You're aware of the incident which surrounds this prosecution, are you not?"

"I've kept up. . . . It's very important."

"And when did you first hear of the defendant Gonzales in connection with the arrest of August 29?"

"That was the day of the Chicano riots, correct?"

"Yes, sir. The day the police murdered. . . ."

"Mr. Brown!" the judge shouts at me.

"I'm sorry, your honor, I couldn't resist."

"Proceed."

I look at the jury. I happen to look into the face of Betty Irish. She is looking directly into my eyes. Jesus. Back to work.

"I heard about *you* first, Brown."

"In connection with *his* arrest?"

"Yes . . . My men told me about the incident at the jail. . . . You should be more careful."

"Mr. Brown . . . uh, come up to the bench."

We march up to the judge's bench. She may be a bitch but Mrs. Wilson has a fine ass. I look down her blouse while she types on her little black box. I once asked her to have a drink with me. She said *after* the trial.

"Mr. Brown . . . *Where* are you going with this witness?"

"The chief is referring to an incident at the jail after the arrest of Mr. Gonzales. I went over to visit him . . ."

"Just a minute, your honor. . . ." Torrez butts in. "What happened after the arrest is irrelevant."

"Well, let's hear what it is first. . . . Then I'll decide if the jury should hear it. Mr. Brown?"

"I went to the East LA Sheriff's Substation to visit my client. I'd just gotten off the plane a few hours before. At the station, three men with rifles stopped me from entering. We had a few words. They ordered me at gun point to leave the area. They said a curfew had been ordered. I showed them my bar card and they pointed their rifles in my face. So I left."

"And what does that prove?"

"That Davis knew I was hooked up with Gonzales as well as Zanzibar."

"So what? It's a matter of public record that you and your client belong to similar organizations. And, in fact, Mr. Zanzibar had interviewed you many times. . . . Isn't that so?"

"Yes, sir. . . . And that's exactly why they first ordered the death of Zanzibar. . . . He talked too much. And specifically because they knew he had photographs of what really happened that day back at the park. He had those films with him at the moment he was killed. They were never recovered."

"Wait a minute. You're losing me."

"Me, too, your honor," Torrez says.

"I'm saying . . . that the motive for the death of Zanzibar was the fear that he'd expose the true facts of that day. . . . He could show *who* started the riot and document some of the specific acts of brutality. . . . And . . ."

"But his death is not in issue here. . . . It may be slightly circumstantial evidence of the *fact* of a riot . . . but we can't go into the causes of his death. . . . Besides, the Coroner's Jury already disposed of that issue, didn't it?"

"Their verdict of justifiable homicide is mere opinion as well as hearsay," I say.

"Well, I could argue. . . . Anyway, Mr. Brown, I am not going to allow another public airing of the causes of the riots or the causes of the death of Zanzibar. . . . Let's proceed."

"But we cannot establish our defense without it."

"Let's proceed. I've ruled."

"I'd like to make an offer of proof."

"Go ahead."

"I'd offer to prove . . . that if Davis were permitted to testify, he'd say that the decision to book Gonzales on felony conspiracy charges was motivated by the fact that the cops had murdered Zanzibar."

"The question," says Torrez, "is so absurd, I have no objection to Brown making a monkey out of himself."

We march back to our tables.

"Chief . . . what motivated you to book Gonzales on a felony charge?"

"I didn't make that decision. I left it up to the men out in the field."

"But you were asked about it?"

"There's discussion about a lot of things, Mr. Brown. We even talk about you."

"I'll bet . . . What was said, and by whom?"

Judd Davis looks at Judge Alacran. Fred looks at me. Am I nuts? I smile and wait for the answer.

"Well . . .we had information that your house was being used to store weapons and dynamite. . . ."

"Go ahead, Chief."

"We knew that you were the reputed mastermind. . . . Our information had led us to believe that you were the person primarily responsible for all the bombings, the burnings . . . That is, that you were the brains behind the operation."

"And who told you that?"

"Officer Sumaya, for one. We have other informants."

"And what did they tell you?"

"They told us quite a story. . . . Do you want to hear all of it?"

"I'd only like to hear the parts that are relevant to this case, Chief Davis," Alacran says.

The jury is getting jittery. My clients are on edge. I am about to be exposed as the biggest scoundrel of all time and still I stand at the mike, my face cool, my eyes sharp. . . .

"Well . . . our information is that you directed the bombings during the riots."

"From Acapulco?"

"No, not the riot of the twenty-ninth."

"Which one?"

"Well . . . they say that you've been the leader ever since you got kicked out of the inquest."

"You mean the inquest into the death of Zanzibar?"

"They say that ever since then, you have been directing the activities of the Chicano Liberation Front."

I laugh. Down deep in my gut I laugh. I can hear Gilbert laughing with me. I can hear the dudes who presently live in my own pad on Sixth Street. . . . Right now the bastards are probably brewing up some molotov for tonight's action and here I'm being called the *mastermind*. . . . Those guys wouldn't do what I told them to do if their lives depended on it. They are *vatos locos! Nobody* tells crazy guys what to do. . . . It is *they* who have converted me and driven me to this brink of madness. It is they who are watching and wondering and complaining about me. *I* am the sheep. *I* am the one being used. But, why not take the title on my way out? Sure, I'm the mastermind. Why not?

So I laugh. I smile. "Now, Chief . . . Tell me . . . Do you believe those stories your undercover spies tell you? I mean, do you really believe that I am the leader of those persons who are throwing firebombs every other day at banks and schools and government offices?"

Judd Davis looks at me and purses his wet fat lips. "You know, Brown . . . I told them you and I both taught in the

Department of Religion at USC. . . . I told them you used to be a Baptist preacher. I told them . . . I listened to you myself for almost a year. I heard you drive those innocent kids up the wall with all your talk of revolution. . . . And, you know, that's the problem. You people say things that sound, well, like radical. But it's really those swimming-pool communists that do the most harm. . . . Those people who tell the poor people to take up arms from out of their comfortable homes in Beverly Hills. . . ."

"Do you think I'm telling the people to pick up the gun? Come on, Davis!"

"No . . . I told them that you probably just let them use your house. . . . I can't say that I have any hard information that you actually *direct* people to commit acts of violence."

"Do you think that Corky did?"

"Well . . . Officer Sumaya says not."

"Objection, your honor!" Torrez shouts.

"Yes, we've already heard from that witness."

"Do you know who the man was that called in reporting that there was a man with a gun inside the Silver Dollar?"

"No, sir."

*"Isn't it a fact that Wilson killed Zanzibar because you felt he knew too much?"* The jury is leaning forward.

Judd Davis looks me straight in the eye. "That's no more true than the allegation that you're personally ordering the bombing of our government buildings. . . . You're getting paranoid, Brown."

"I have good reason for it, Chief."

"If you two are finished," Alacran says.

"Yes, your honor . . . No more questions."

"You're excused, Chief Davis. . . . We'll be in recess until nine a.m. tomorrow morning. . . . I'd admonish the jury once again that you are not to discuss this case amongst yourselves or with any other person. . . ."

I stand in the middle between Corky and Cesar Chavez while the crowd roars. I have asked Cesar to be a character witness for his protégé. They are number one and two in the Nation of Aztlan. And I have brought them together during this period of crisis for the entire Chicano movement.

I have not seen Cesar since I first began in LA. He is still my leader, but I no longer worship him. I am pushing for Corky because when things go political, I will push for the more militant of the two. Corky laughs at me. He tells me that Cesar's work is more important than both of us combined. Speak for yourself, I tell him.

Cesar walks into court with a limp. He is still dark and solid. He wears brown brogans and worn faded levi's with a checkered shirt. His kidneys are permanently in pain since his fast of '68. He refuses to take pills for the pain, he tells me. But he uses a rocking chair that the Kennedys gave him.

"Mr. Chavez, will you please tell the jury of your acquaintance with the defendant Gonzales."

"Yes . . . I've known Corky for eight years. I've met him at various places throughout the country during demonstrations against the war, in the struggle for justice of the black, the Chicano."

"And do you know persons that have stated an opinion of him?"

"Yes."

"And what is that opinion? What kind of reputation does he have?"

"They say he has a good one. He is an honest man."

"Thank you. No further questions."

I look toward Torrez. I know he will go for Cesar's blood. And I've not prepared him as I do other witnesses. I just told him to name drop once in a while. The jury is staring at Cesar up on the stand. The court is hushed. His testimony, although it has nothing to do with the guilt or innocence of any defendant, has become crucial in our struggle for credibility.

Corky has already testified. He merely said that he had authorized his bodyguards to carry weapons to protect the women and children that he brought with him from Denver. Louie testified that he carried the .22 blue-steel Beretta found in the cab of the truck but that he'd given it to Elena to carry in her purse. Elena has testified that she had it in her purse and that when she moved out of the cab, the purse fell open and the gun dropped out. She said that Corky knew nothing about it. And both Waterbuffalo and Bullwinkle have testified that they only drove around in Sumaya's car during the riot. They said that he, the cop, wanted them to stop and throw firebombs along the way.

*All of them . . . every single witness, both prosecution and defense . . . is lying.* Or not telling the whole truth. The bastards know exactly what we have done and what we have not done. They *know* for a fact that Corky was not involved in any conspiracy, in any arson, in anything. And they know how and why Zanzibar was killed. But they have all told their own version of things as they would like them to be.

"Mr. Chavez . . . You know of Mr. Gonzales' reputation in Denver?" Torrez asks.

"Yes, sir. I know many people in Denver."

"And you say that he has a good reputation up there?"

"Yes, sir."

"Now, if I were to tell you that the Denver Police Department has a *different* opinion of him . . . would that affect your opinion?"

"Well . . . it could . . . But I don't know any policemen in Denver, so I can't say."

"I see . . . Now if you heard that the Los Angeles Police Department had a poor opinion of Mr. Gonzales' reputation for truth-telling . . . How would you feel about that?"

"I guess they do now, since the death of Zanzibar . . . but I don't know any policemen around here. I'm from Delano."

"And what if I were to tell you that the Delano police thought Mr. Gonzales had a bad reputation?"

"Oh, well that's different. . . ."

"Yes? How so?"

"It would affect my opinion quite a bit. . . . You see, I know the Delano policemen. . . . They're a bunch of liars."

Laughter in the court! Alacran yells and pounds for order.

"Any more questions, Mr. Torrez?"

"No."

"The witness is excused. . . . Is this your last witness?"

"The defense rests."

"We'll hear closing arguments now. Mr. Torrez?"

"I'll waive my opening and respond to Mr. Brown."

"Mr. Brown?"

I look down at my clients. They look up at me.

"May I have a moment to confer?"

"Yes. The court will recess for five minutes."

We get up and go to a room in the rear of the court.

"If I don't argue, then Torrez can't respond. . . . It's up to you guys. What do you think?"

"Shit, man, the jury's heard it all. . . . They're bored."

"But old Zeta can make them cry . . . I've seen him do it."

"Yeah . . . but old Zeta is not the best man to do it anymore. . . . Don't forget, the jury has heard about *me* as much as it's heard about *you*. . . . Maybe they won't believe me, either."

We talk and we argue and we finally decide.

"Your honor, in the interest of justice. . . ."

"I don't want to hear any speeches, Mr. Brown."

"Yes, sir. . . . The defense will offer no argument."

"Fine . . . In that event . . . I'll instruct the jury now and then they'll go to deliberate. . . . Ladies and gentlemen of the jury, it now becomes my duty to instruct you as to the law on each of the counts presented to you in this matter. . . . Now in order to find the defendants guilty, and each of them, you must find that each and every element of the offense listed. . . ."

*The Revolt of the Cockroach People*

# 19

We've waited for fifteen days. Or is it fifteen years? We've been coming to this courthouse for nearly a year on this case. A year ago they killed Zanzibar and only now have we come to the end of the trial. Only after we spent our last dime, wore ourselves to the bone and marched a thousand miles on the sidewalks of LA, only after I have really broken down with paranoia and suspicion, only now has the jury come back and told us what we knew all along: the Tooner Flats Seven are innocent of all the felonies.

But they did find Corky guilty of misdemeanor possession of a weapon. The jury didn't buy my argument that he had a right to carry a gun to protect himself. I told them in my opening statement that we would show that Corky had received numerous threats upon his life and had a right to carry a gun for self-defense, if not for the defense of others. Just like the bakery owner next to the Silver Dollar Bar. But that idea was too far out for them.

So now Alacran has sentenced Corky to forty days and nights in the New County Jail. I told him to look up Sergeant Lovelace when they took him away. He just laughed and said he'd probably see me in the clink before he got out.

"What do you mean?" I asked.

"I'm not stupid, Big Bear. I *know* things."

Minutes later, I am in a toilet on the sixth floor of the

Hall of Justice. The crowd is still up on the seventh floor. The whole building is storming with cops, but mainly up on the seventh floor and down in the first-floor lobbies. While the people cheered as the pigs led Corky out, I slipped around the corner and ran down the steps to this john in one corner of the building. Alacran's chambers are directly above me and he is in them. He usually takes his time about coming out.

The others are there already. They'd been coming in, one at a time, all during the day. Little by little, they've brought in all the materials they need for the time bomb. We've got seven big ones to blow a hole in this cement-concrete-steel building, right under that motherfucking greaser. The sonofabitch refused to even listen to my motion for a new trial. He just laughed when I told him that he'd not yet made a final ruling on the Grand Jury issue. He said, "Your motions are denied. Take it up on appeal."

"But you know that the precedents say that a disparity of such proportion is, prima facie, discriminatory."

"Yes, Mr. Brown. . . . But I believe those cases were politically motivated. . . . I believe that by the time this case gets up on appeal, if it does . . . I believe that the new judges on the Supreme Court will rule my way."

"But that isn't the law of the land now. . . . You are bound to rule according to present law . . . not anticipated future decisions by the Nixon court."

"Ah, Mr. Brown, now you're talking politics. . . . You seem to confuse politics with law quite a bit. . . . Is that what they taught you in law school? What kind of place did you learn to practice in as you do?"

And then he laughed. And then he sent Corky to jail for forty days and nights. In the usual gun possession case, the defendant is given perhaps a day or two in jail. I even got Gilbert off one time on a simple gun possession case—they'd found it in the glove box of the car—with a fifty-dollar fine. But because Corky is who he is and my client, the bastard gave him forty days.

"Hurry up, you guys," I hiss at the men working like katzenjammer thugs at my command. Gilbert, the fat frog, Pelon in his blue beanie, and little Sailor Boy with the shiv down his boot in case we get caught. . . .

"Let's go, ese. It's done."

"Did you set it for half an hour?"

"Yeah. It'll go off around five-thirty."

We hurry out into the corridor where Elena is waiting. She touches the elevator button as soon as she spots us. By the time we reach her the elevator is waiting. We go back up to the seventh floor and join in with the crowd.

"You're all invited to a party at my house!" I shout to them.

"Viva Zeta!" they call to me.

We hurry quickly down the steps and go out the building to the car that Elena has parked in the judges' parking lot next to the courthouse. Alacran's car is still there. We are into traffic at Sunset and Temple before we take a breath. . . .

Soon we are at the pad on Sixth. The party has already begun. The teeny-boppers, the groupies, the *vatos*, the *locos*, the ex-cons, the militants, the nuns, the hippies, the Cockroaches, everybody is there to celebrate our great victory. The music and the wine are flowing tonight, baby! The radio is *loud!* This is the end to all the work, suspicion and grind. This is *it*.

*"We interrupt this program to bring you a special news bulletin. . . . The LA Hall of Justice at Temple and Broadway has just been rocked by an explosive blast. . . . We have no details at this moment. . . . We repeat, the Hall of Justice has just been shaken with a massive explosion and we'll bring you up to date as we receive further information. . . . And now back to our Soul Brother . . . and the new Smiling Faces. . . ."*

"Viva La Raza!" Gilbert shouts.

"Hey, did you hear that?"

"That's the place where you guys were just at!"

"Hey, man. . . . Do you think Corky is OK?"

"Sure, man. . . . He probably set the bomb off himself," I laugh.

"Hey, Zeta, let's go for some more beer," Gilbert says.

"Yeah. . . . Elena, you and Pelon and Sailor Boy. . . . Why don't you come with us?"

We are outside. The party is still going on. The kids are whooping it up. I hear them cheering and shouting and lifting their fists to the skies, to the heavens, wherever Huitzilopotchtli is hiding.

We are driving in the black station wagon we got from Papoose. During the trial he got busted. He knifed another ex-con right in the gut, in front of a dozen members of PINTO. He ran, but the cops caught him outside the county limits. He told me the dude had called him a *rata*. If you call a Pinto a traitor, you have a fight on your hands. I couldn't defend him. I told him it was personal. We only did political cases, I said. . . . He understood, he said. He just wanted to tell me what happened. . . . Now he is doing life.

"Look . . . We've got to finish it off," I say.

"Well, let's go," Elena says.

We drive to the corner of Soto and Brooklyn. In the parking lot of La Copa, I take Elena to the phone booth. I hand her the note to read. I dial the number of the police department where a recorder will take down your voice with your complaints.

"Attention . . . The bomb that just exploded today in the Hall of Justice was done in memory of Roland Zanzibar and The Day of the Chicanos. . . . This is the Chicano Liberation Front. . . ."

She reads it twice into the phone. She hangs up and we get back in the car. We drive silently onto the freeway, the radio tuned to the all-news station. And then it comes:

*"The bomb that exploded in the toilet of the men's room on the sixth floor has now been determined to have been made of dynamite and black pipe. . . . One person has been found dead in the rubble. We repeat, one young man of presumably Latin descent has been found dead in the wreckage of the toilet in the Hall of Justice. . . . Damage to the property was limited to the toilet itself. . . . In further developments, the judge in the trial of Rodolfo Corky Gon-*

*zales today sentenced the forty-four-year-old militant from Denver to a term of forty days in the county jail. . . ."*

I'm back on the road now. I am driving my blue Mustang down 101 at a fast clip. I have the top down and the breeze is cooling off my fat brown face.

As Elena watched, I packed my meager belongings into the trunk of the car. This crazy *chola* who could fuck like a hurricane, chewing her gum, zing-zang with her eyes. Who maybe because she's so crazy, understood me better than the rest. Accepting me, but still getting her licks in. I have kissed her goodbye. She just laughed and said I'd be back. Maybe she's right, though I feel through with the bit. I'm on my way to Frisco Bay.

No, they didn't catch me for any of the shit I've pulled. But the fact of the matter is, they *know* exactly what I've done. That is the frightening thing. Those bastards know every single act of violence I ever pulled off with the lunatics from Tooner Flats.

But why don't they arrest me? Why don't they haul me in? That's the nut. That's the old apple. If you can figure that one out, you'll be as smart as me. And just as paranoid.

All I know is, the whole game is down to me again. Just me. If you'll remember, I did come in second in a race against a pig like Peaches. Against all odds, I sprung loose the East LA Thirteen, the St. Basil Twenty-One and the Tooner Flats Seven. What would ever happen if I met a *carnal* with a soul like mine, going in all directions, half-assed but free? Or if I could take it, what would happen if I ever got serious?

I am serious.

No, I don't feel guilty about the kid that got killed. I feel terrible. But not guilty. Lots more will die before this fight is over. The truce we've signed for the moment doesn't mean anything. Just because the Viet Cong or the Chicanos temp rarily lay down their arms doesn't prove shit. For me, personally, this is a kind of end. And a beginning. But who cares about that? I was just one of a

257

bunch of Cockroaches that helped start a revolution to burn down a stinking world. And no matter what kind of end this is, I'll still play with matches.

It's in the blood now. And not only my blood. Somebody still has to answer for Robert Fernandez and Roland Zanzibar. Somebody still has to answer for all the smothered lives of all the fighters who have been forced to carry on, chained to a war for Freedom just like a slave is chained to his master. Somebody still has to pay for the fact that I've got to leave friends to stay whole and human, to survive intact, to carry on the species and my own Buffalo run as long as I can.

Zeta, goodbye.

When the Brown Buffalo left LA and headed for Frisco Bay in the Spring of '72, he had no way of knowing that the Feds from the Treasury would be waiting for him to cross the border. He didn't know that he'd meet up with Jesus again, either. Or that he'd go on to Ziquitaro and marry a Tarascan princess. He knew his name, yeah, and just a little more.

Hell, when I split the Chicanos, like I told Gilbert: "I'm going to write my memoirs before I go totally crazy. Or totally underground."

"Hey, ese. If you get back into it, look me up."

"Sure, man. You can be my dynamite man when I go after the real big ones."

And with a Chicano handshake for Pelon, Sailor Boy and Gilbert, I took off and headed for the bright lights and white women of San Francisco to write my swan song about all my friends and our many problems. And the rest of that story we shall shortly come to tell, but for now, this is enough. . . . Adios!

*The Revolt of the Cockroach People*

# AFTERWORD

When my editor suggested that I write an afterword to this re-
printing of my father's books, I was at first somewhat surprised.
I had never considered the idea and was not quite sure what
I would say, but then it occurred to me that I do have some
thoughts about my dad that I would like to express. I hope that
what I discuss here will give readers an understanding of what
it was that prompted me to try to get back into print these two
very important works of Mexican-American literature and of
1960s counterculture.

I have the good fortune to have parents who have always
been a source of strength and inspiration to me. And the older
I get, the more I appreciate, respect and understand them.
My mother is alive and well and happily remarried, and I
continue to enjoy a very special relationship with her. As for
my father: I was fourteen when he disappeared from Mazatlán,
Mexico, via a friend's sailing boat, in June of 1974. I was the last
person, as far as I know, to speak with him. Literally moments
before he got on the boat that he was planning to ride back to
the States, I told him I hoped he knew what he was doing by
going back on such a small boat. He said he hoped I knew what
I was doing with my life. In the following years there were rumors
that he was shot by one of the "thugs" he was hanging around
with in Mexico, or that he was spotted somewhere off the coast
of Hawaii or Florida. The bottom line, however, is that no one, to
my knowledge, knows for sure what happened, including the

FBI and the U.S. Coast Guard—or so they say.

The fifteen years since my father's death have been a time of soul-searching, sadness and seemingly endless philosophizing about my own mortality. One result, perhaps inevitably, of all this has been a desire to "resurrect" Zeta, as it were, and to somehow increase the public's awareness and understanding of his life, work and what he stood for. My first project was to reprint his books, *The Autobiography of a Brown Buffalo* and *The Revolt of the Cockroach People*, which have been out of print since the early 1970s. I have been told, incidentally, that those first editions are now collector's items. The current Vintage edition is the culmination of a five-year effort, and I hope it reaches all who remember my father, especially the East L.A. Chicanos and all the other close friends and relatives who were part of that turbulent period in the late 1960s and early 1970s. Even for those who did not know him at all, reading the *Autobiography* will, I think, provide humor and instruction in the struggle for self-definition, something we all deal with at some point. Both books, taken together, will be helpful for those seeking a history and understanding of the events during the sixties and seventies concerning the fight against racism, poverty and oppression, particularly as it pertained to the Chicano community.

There are two additional projects that I hope will shed light on my father's work as well as preserve it for future generations. One is the establishment of the Oscar Zeta Acosta Collection in the Chicano studies collection of the University of California at Santa Barbara. This will include papers, letters, files and videos and will be accessible to the public. In view of the recent development of scholarly interest in Zeta and his books, this will be a significant additional resource. The other project is a motion picture based on one or both of the books, which is currently being negotiated. I am taking extra care to ensure that the film will be an accurate and genuine portrayal of his life and times.

My father used to ask me rhetorically, especially when we were on top of a beautiful mountain in Colorado or by the sea in Mexico, "Today would be a great day to die, wouldn't it?" As a child, this dying business seemed a bit scary, something I didn't want to think about. But now I know what he was trying to tell me: "You've got to live one day at a time, and you must live each day as if it would be your last." And this is exactly how he lived his life. Sure, he planned some things, such as preparing his trial briefs for an accused Mexican youth who also happened to be suffering deep down from the effects of so-called Manifest Destiny. But, basically, my dad was one of those rare people who could become totally absorbed in the present.

Every century a few individuals are born who are destined to lead the weak, to hold unpopular beliefs and, most important, who are willing to die for their cause. My father's whole life was given to the fight for "the people," as he used to say. Unfortunately, we don't have the benefit of whatever wonderful things he might have done with the rest of his life (barring the fantastic possibility that he's alive on some island planning the next revolution). But in the years that he did give to the struggle against racism and oppression in America he was a fearless and committed fighter. He was often followed by the law during these violent times in Los Angeles in the early seventies; friends of unpopular ideas are always held in suspicion. He used to warn me, knowing that such violence surrounded his life, to be prepared for the possibility that he might be gunned down by his adversaries. Even his own people betrayed him on occasion. Of course, all this was deeply disturbing to me. But the riots, the violence, the arguing, never seemed to bother him. He knew it was the price you had to pay for waging an unpopular war.

The search for truth and justice consumed my father's life and is an important part of both his books. Zeta was never more angry and savage than when he felt he was being lied to. The unfortunate fact is that this search is probably what, oddly enough, led to his ruin. Things just seemed to have become too intense for him in those "final days," with riots of escalating ferocity, enemies constantly following him, the drugs, the confusion over his destiny. Despite the madness in his books, is it possible to garner some sense of hope and redemption from reading them, to see that women and men can elevate their humanity by overcoming all that resists them? I think it is; that is my father's ultimate legacy to me.

I'd like to thank my editor, Robin Desser, for her encouragement and advice in getting the books back into print. My mom, Betty Acosta Dowd, deserves acknowledgment not only for being a wonderful mother but for putting up with my dad and giving him inspiration in those early years. Thanks to Ann Henry and family and to the late "Owl" (my dad's best friends) for all those late-night talks about the Buffalo and the universe; to Irwin for giving my dad medicine when he was sick and for preserving the Buffalo on video; to Susan Warshauer for her endless enthusiasm, advice, encouragement and love in helping to make my dad's "resurrection" a reality; to Hunter Thompson for immortalizing Zeta into the legendary Samoan attorney and, of course, for the intro herein; to my grandparents, Ed and Ruth Daves and Juana and Manuel Acosta, for teaching me and my dad faith, hope and charity; to my dad's sisters, Anita, Marta and Sally, and his brothers, Roberto and Al, who had to live with the Buffalo; to my aunt Gina who always spoke to my dad face-to-face and consequently was someone he respected. Finally, I must acknowledge the impressive writings of the professors of Chicano literature and other scholars who have contributed greatly to an increased understanding of Zeta and his work. To all others too numerous to name, I give my sincere thanks.

Marco Federico Manuel Acosta
*January 1989*
*San Francisco, California*

*Afterword*